I0564262

THE OLD GODS
AWAKEN

THE OLD GODS AWAKEN

Donald Tyson

WEIRD HOUSE PRESS TRADE PAPERBACK EDITION © 2024

Editor & Publisher, Joe Morey
Book design by F. J. Bergmann

ISBN: 978-1-957121-84-0

Weird House Press
Central Point, OR 97502
www.weirdhousepress.com
Join the Weird House mailing list at our website!

List of Illustrations

Table of Contents

AZATHOTH

SONG OF AZATHOTH

1.

Two men sat on a long porch in the early evening, sipping beers and listening to the chirp of insects in the tall grass of the back lawn. The grass was tall because the owner of the house on the slope of Palomar Mountain, astronomer Daniel Foy, seldom bothered to cut it. Every so often, the bug zapper suspended above their heads announced the death of another mosquito or hapless moth. The night sky was clear, the temperature mild. The valley floor far below sparkled with the lights of San Diego County. From somewhere in the distance came the drawn-out howl of a coyote.

"What we're looking at hasn't been seen with the naked eye for over four centuries," Foy said.

"What's that?" Alberto Vincenzo murmured. He had been half-dreaming, listening to the melody that played inside his head.

"The supernova." Foy pointed upward at a bright red spark high in the southern heavens. "The last visible supernova in our galaxy was the Kepler Nova in 1604."

"It's certainly impressive," Vincenzo agreed. He sipped his beer, and realized it had gone flat in the open bottle. Idly, he thought about getting a fresh bottle from the fridge, but decided standing up to go into his friend's kitchen was too much trouble.

"It's the brightest object in the night sky, apart from the Moon." Foy said it like a proud parent.

"It puts all the other stars to shame."

"Doesn't it, though. It's got us up at the observatory puzzled."

"How's that?"

"Well, for one thing, its increase in brightness is sustaining itself longer than is usual with supernovas. For another thing, it's a strange color."

"You mean the crimson?"

"Actually it's more of a scarlet. Supernovas are usually blue-white. To get such a big one near the center of our galaxy of this color is unheard of."

"What do you think is causing it?"

"I'm just a technician, remember? I don't do theory."

"Maybe it's an evil omen," Vincenzo said with a smile. "I heard some religious nut on the television the other day, saying it was the harbinger of the apocalypse."

"Don't be so quick to mock. Supernovas have always been regarded as dire portents sent to humanity from the gods. They share that in common with comets. There is no denying that they have corresponded to times of mass destruction due to earthquakes, volcanoes and other disasters."

"Coincidence."

"So you would say. For a composer of classical music you are the most materialistic son of a bitch I've ever known."

"Well, you're the most romantic astronomer I've ever known."

"I'm the only astronomer you know."

Vincenzo pointed at a star that was not nearly as bright as the supernova. "I bet that star is jealous."

"That's Sirius, the Dog Star, faithful follower of Orion the Hunter."

"Are you sure he's so faithful?"

"What do you mean?"

"Maybe he's stalking Orion, waiting for his chance to bring

him down by the heels and rip his throat out."

"You are in a pleasant mood tonight."

"I'm sorry, Dan. It's the damn melody I've got playing in my head. It won't stop. As entertaining as it may be, I don't want to listen to it day and night."

"Tell me about it," Foy said, sympathy in his voice.

Vincenzo sipped his flat beer and made a wry face the other could not see in the darkness.

"It's strange. I mean, I've often had melodies stuck in my head, but they usually go away after a day or two."

"How long have you had this one?"

"Weeks. Come to think of it, the melody started around the same time the supernova appeared."

"Can't you just ignore it?"

"No. I've tried, but it won't let up. Don't get me wrong, it's pleasant enough to listen to. It's like clear notes from a Pan flute, or maybe a medieval recorder. But the funny thing is, it never repeats."

"I don't follow you."

"All music is made up of repetitions of sequences of notes. It is one of the invariable rules of music. This melody never repeats. It's like the numerical sequence Pi—no repetition, but even so the music is beautiful. Unearthly."

"You probably just need a good night's sleep," the astronomer said.

"I haven't slept in three days, not for more than an hour or two at a time," Vincenzo admitted.

They sat in silence.

"The entire sky is thrown out of balance with that supernova," Foy mused. "It's as if a stone of chaos was cast into the still, dark pool of the night sky. Who knows what ripples it is stirring up?"

"That's uncommonly poetic, even for you."

"I've been doing some research on the mythology of supernovas," Foy said. "Some of it must have stayed with me. Anyway, you're the materialist, not me."

"I may have to take sleeping pills," Vincenzo said. "I don't know what else to do."

"Why don't you turn your lemons into lemonade?" Foy said.

"How do you mean?"

"Turn the melody playing in your head into a composition."

Vincenzo sat up straight in his chair. For some reason, this thought had never occurred to him. "That's not a bad idea. I could write down a section of the melody and orchestrate it. The L.A. Philharmonic has been looking for something new. They might even let me conduct."

He stood up, unable to contain his excitement. "I have to get back to Los Angeles and get started on this. Who knows how long the melody will continue to play?"

"You're welcome to spend the night here, as always," Foy said.

"Thanks, Dan, but I need the software on my computer."

He heard the other man stretch and stand. "The next time you come, I'm going to show you the big telescope."

"Do I get to look through it?"

Foy chuckled. "Afraid not. It's set up for instrument observation only. But when I come to L.A. we can go up to Griffith Observatory and have a peek at the supernova. It's got a ring around it, you know. You can't see it yet with the human eye, but it seems to be getting bigger."

"Let's do that the next time you're in the city. Maybe I'll discover a new comet, and they'll name it after me."

"Unlikely but not impossible. The twelve-inch Zeiss refractor at Griffith is a good old scope."

2.

Vincenzo drove his pearl-white Jaguar sedan recklessly down the winding mountain road. The melody in his head taunted him with its impermanence. Each sequence of notes was heard once, then gone. So much of it had been lost to the past already. He felt a knot of paralyzing anxiety in his chest that it would stop before he could transcribe it. When he rolled through the gates of his house in Pacific Palisades two and a half hours later, he almost ran inside to his studio. He didn't even bother to fix a meal. He sat down at his desk computer and began to type.

The computer had a specialized composition program that allowed him to type notes and chords of music onto a musical stave. He transcribed the melody as it piped in his head for just over forty minutes. Only then did he stand up, stretch his back, and pour himself a shot of Haig & Haig from its crystal decanter on the sideboard. The music continued to play unbroken in his mind as he sipped it, maddening but also beautiful.

Returning to the computer, he pursed his lips and thought about orchestration. This was going to be a completely original composition, but that did not preclude him from using some of the standard devices of classical composition to relieve the monotony of the single melodic line. He decided to introduce a kind of repetition by having different sections of the orchestra reappear at regular intervals. The horns, the strings, the woodwinds. Underneath it all he laid down a majestic percussion line. He also found that he could slow down the notes or speed them up in different sections of the composition, which created its own unique effect. But underneath it was the same unique melody that had played one time in his head, and never would again.

When at last he sat back, he had sketched in the entire composition. It still needed a lot of work, but the bones were there. He went to the piano and played through the opening minutes. It sounded good in his professional ears, and had the added appeal of being totally unlike anything else in the world. Glancing at the wall clock, he saw that it was almost sunrise. He still had not eaten anything.

He went into the kitchen and threw a frozen chicken dinner into the microwave, then ate it while the gravy was still hot enough to burn his mouth. He needed sleep. The melody had receded somewhat in his mind, perhaps because he had concentrated so hard and so long on the section he had extracted for his composition. He decided not to take a sleeping pill.

As he got nearer, he realized the enormity of the bloated thing.

Exhaustion brought sleep more quickly than he expected. He found himself in the nightmare that had become all too familiar over the past few weeks. He was floating in the black of outer space. Before him the supernova hung against the stars, looking bloated and evil, like the bloodshot eye of an angry god. A red ring of fire surrounded it. He knew that inside the ring was a kind of stinking, poisonous effulgence. Then he saw the supernova transform into a series of musical tones that sounded on some kind of flute, and realized he himself was also made of a series of notes. In the back of his mind the melody continued to play, coiling itself slowly around the egg of his consciousness like some great cosmic serpent.

He felt himself fall backward through space, away from the supernova. It diminished in his sight until it was just a red star. He found himself lying on rocky ground and climbed to his feet. He was in a small valley bounded by low black hills. Something was wrong with the perspective. It felt confining, as if the hills were painted backdrops in a theater. He looked up. In the starry night sky above his head a circle of monstrous forms wheeled and danced in slow motion to the shrill piping of a flute. At the exact center of their ring burned the supernova. As he squinted up at them, for a moment they changed into constellations of stars, then changed back to became the bloated dancers.

Some distance away, at the base of one of the hills, a large black slab of stone lay on the middle of an elevated rock ledge. The crudeness of the slab made it difficult to judge if it was artificial or natural, but it resembled some kind of platform or altar. On top of it lolled something that looked a little bit like a naked man, but even more like a gigantic, bloated leech.

Vincenzo felt physically sick as he gazed upon it. Ropes of matted, greasy black hair hung down from its head. Filth covered its pinkish skin. The sockets where its eyes should have been were puckered pits of darkness that wept whitish pus. Its fat, stubby fingers held something pressed to its blubbery lips. With a shock of recognition he saw that it was a small white flute carved from ivory, or perhaps from bone. This was the source of the melody that was driving him insane.

Dizziness gripped Vincenzo and made him stagger. The scene before him changed into geometric lines and curves. The fat thing became a series of equations that meant nothing to the composer. Math had never been his strong suit—he had barely been able to complete pre-calculus during high school. The musical curves changed into a string of binary numbers that uncoiled in an endless ribbon across the stars. He looked up and tried to follow it with his eyes, then bent over with hands on knees, taking shallow breaths. The vertigo passed, and the monster on the throne reappeared, along with its stench of unwashed flesh.

As it continued to pipe forth the strange, unending song on its flute, every so often it would produce a sour note. So unstructured was the music that he had failed to notice this before, but in his dream it was obvious. He realized that the little flute was defective in some way. Now and then it sent forth a note that was sharp or flat.

He knew that he must be dreaming and expected to awaken from moment to moment, but the scene before him never wavered. Summoning his courage, he walked toward the creature, which was elevated above his head on the ledge. As he got nearer, he realized the enormity of the bloated thing. It was gigantic, easily ten times the size of a man. It gave no sign of being aware of his presence. Yellow liquid trickled from between its fat thighs and down the front of the stone slab. Wrinkling his nose in disgust at the smell, Vincenzo realized it was urine. All the while the melody continued. He wondered how long this monstrous obscenity against nature had been playing on its flute.

Some impulse he could not resist made him approach and extend his hand upward toward the creature's fat, naked thigh. He did not know what he intended to do. From behind the slab a black shadow came rushing forward and loomed over him. It was tall and slender, vaguely humanoid, but threatening in a way that terrified him. Its blazing eyes were the same bright scarlet of the supernova. Vincenzo received a strong intuition that it would be a bad idea to touch the monster, a very bad idea for him. He jerked back his hand before his fingers made contact with the filth-covered pinkish skin, and then found himself tumbling upward through space, the stars whirling around him. He woke in his own bed, his body slick with sweat and the top half of his black silk pajamas stained with white salt and sticking to his skin.

He lay back on his damp pillow and drew ragged breaths, his heart hammering inside his chest. The dream was already fading, but he held onto the images of the dancing giants, the bloated monster on the altar, or throne, or whatever it was, and the looming shadow with eyes of fire. They seemed to possess a significance far beyond that of any ordinary nightmare. There was something else in the dream, some other detail that felt important, but try as he would he could not recall it.

Half-remembered fragments of the dream stayed with him all morning. He found it impossible to work on his new composition, so he decided to go for a run along the beach to clear his head. The fresh sea breeze and the heat of the sand radiating upward alternately cooled and warmed him. He forgot everything beyond the rhythm of his running body, the panting of his breath, the beats of his heart. Even the endless melody faded into the background. When at last he stopped, drenched in sweat and gasping for air, at one of the elongated parking lots that ran along the shore between the beach and the highway, he found himself re-energized, more alive than he had felt in weeks.

The parking lot was more than half empty. Near a cluster of tall palm trees was an elderly black man, sprawled across the pavement. He had on a ragged and dirty undershirt, canvas shorts, and worn sneakers. The brim of the red baseball cap on his head was pulled low over a pair of dark sunglasses. At first Vincenzo thought the old man had fallen. Then he realized he was drawing on the pavement with colored chalks. Beside his chalk picture rested a red paper cup for donations.

None of the tanned young people coming and going on the beach gave him so much as a glance. Vincenzo would have passed him like the rest, except the old man was humming as he drew. The composer stopped, listening to the melody that came from the artist's throat. It was an echo of the melody that played in his own head.

The old man finally noticed his shadow and peered up.

"Donations be much appreciated," he said in a scratchy voice.

Vincenzo dug in his pocket and pulled out a handful of change, then dropped the coins one by one into the cup so that they clinked together. "That song you were just humming, where did you hear it?"

"They sent it to me. I'm supposed to prepare the way, to let folks know."

"Know what?"

"That they be comin' back. Yessa, they all be comin' back that's been gone for so, so long."

Vincenzo looked at the drawing on the pavement and felt a shock of recognition. It was the midnight valley of his nightmares. There was the same bloated blind thing lounging on its rocky throne, its flute clutched between its fat paws, and there behind it reared a menacing shadow that had no details. Above their heads blazed, not the red supernova, but a great red eye that glared down like the vengeful eye of God.

"Where did you see this?" Vincenzo demanded, surprised by the harshness in his tone. Why he felt so afraid, he could not have explained.

The old man gave no indication that he heard. "The ones that be here already be startin' to wake up and move around, and the ones that be somewhere else be startin' to come here from far places. But they move quick, quick, like ghosts, see?

It won't be long afore they gets themselves here with the others. Nosah, we ain't got long to wait."

He tittered, coughed up phlegm and spat it to the side, before continuing to work on his drawing.

"Does the song have something to do with the big red star in the sky?"

The other did not respond.

Vincenzo hummed a portion of the notes that played in the back of his mind. The old man began to hum along with him, note for note.

"The picture you're making, did you dream it?"

When there was still no response, Vincenzo reached down and shook him hard by the shoulder. It felt thin and frail under his fingers. The sunglasses fell off the old man's face. He stared up, and Vincenzo saw that his eyes were covered with bluish-white cataracts. He was blind.

"You be one of us now," the old man said. "I know you, brother." He pointed at his blind eyes with two fingers of his right hand, and then pointed them at Vincenzo. "I see you. You bear your testimony and I'll bear mine. These here be end times, yessir, the end of all and everything, 'cept there ain't no savior on a white horse with a sword this time around."

He chuckled, and Vincenzo realized he must be insane. He started to back away.

"Don't go yet, brother. Stay and talk. I'll tell you 'bout the Old Ones."

The composer began to walk more quickly. He glanced over his shoulder and realized the old man had pushed himself to his feet and was shuffling after him. Vincenzo reached the highway and paused, waiting for a break in the traffic, then jogged across the busy road. Heat washed up from the black surface and enveloped him.

Behind he heard the shriek of tires, followed by a dull thud. The old man had walked in front of a red pickup truck and been thrown a dozen yards farther down the highway. He lay unmoving, face twisted backward on a broken neck. His cloudy dead eyes stared at Vincenzo, and his mouth gaped in mute accusation. Vincenzo turned away in horror and jogged from the gathering crowd, the voice of the street artist still echoing in his head: "You be one of us now. I know you, brother."

4.

Vincenzo located Lena Gault in one of the anthropology labs on the University of California at Berkeley campus. He stood in the open doorway of the lab, watching her. She was wearing a white coat that hung open in front. Her gray hair was cut shorter since the last time he had seen her, a year or so ago. It hung straight down to just below her ears, exposing her deeply tanned neck with all its wrinkles of age. No woman with a shred of vanity would have even considered wearing her hair in such a style, but Lena was oblivious to both fashion and personal appearance.

The thick black-frame eyeglasses on the end of her nose were secured by a chain around the back of her neck. She let them drop to her flat chest and applied a set of calipers to an oddly shaped skull on the work table. He rapped on the open door, and when she took no notice, rapped a second time, but louder. She raised her head with a frown. She recognized him and her sun-browned face broke into a broad grin.

"Maestro. Come in, come in, don't stand in the doorway. What do you make of this?"

Vincenzo entered and walked around the work table. She held the skull up for him to examine. It was hideously distorted, its cranium elongated and enormous. Its eye sockets seemed unnaturally large.

"Is it human?"

"That is the general consensus of my colleagues. As for myself, I am not so certain."

She spoke with precision and just the faintest trace of a German accent. As a girl she had grown up in East Berlin under the Stasi, before the fall of the Berlin Wall. The rigor she had learned as a child was still with her.

"If it isn't human, what is it?"

"That is the question, isn't it? If it is not human it must be something else. But what? It can't be an animal—who ever saw an animal with a brain case of this size? If not an animal, and not a man, then something other, shall we say. Something from outside, perhaps."

"Outside what?"

She shrugged her narrow shoulders. "Who knows. Maybe outside everything."

"Is it unique?"

"No; we are finding them all around the world. This one came from South America. There are also human skulls distorted in a similar way, but in those cases it is obvious that the distortion was caused by pressure applied to the soft skull of an infant as it was growing."

"Maybe that was done to imitate the appearance of whatever wore this skull," Vincenzo suggested.

"Bravo, Al. Your mind is far too good to be wasted in the arts. You should have taken up anthropology."

Vincenzo scratched the top of his head, which had begun to itch as he stared at the dome of the skull. "I wonder if you could spare me half an hour or so? I'd like to ask you about something."

"Of course." She set the skull down with care. "Walk back with me to my office. We'll talk there."

Her office was uncommonly large for a professor of anthropology. The windows faced north, and the sun that lit the green lawn beyond the shadow of the building did not reach into it. As a consequence the office was cool and somewhat dark. Through the windows Vincenzo could see the university campus stretch into the distance, dotted here and there with students sitting under the trees. She shut the door, closing out the sounds from the corridor, and indicated a chair at the side of her desk.

He looked around the office. Little had changed. It was still lined with old books and odd bric-a-brac she had picked up on various expeditions around the world.

"How long has it been?"

"We last saw each other when I came to the premiere of your Fourth Symphony, remember?"

"Of course. That was quite a night," he said.

"You deserved it. You gave the world a masterwork."

Vincenzo hesitated. "This is going to sound silly, Lena. I'm almost afraid to ask it."

"Whatever it is, ask."

"I need your impression of a dream I've been having. Of its imagery, I mean. I need to know if it has any symbolic meaning or connection with reality."

"How often have you had this dream?"

"Every night for weeks. It's reached the point where I know it's a dream the instant it starts, but I have to let it play itself out in my mind. It's probably a trivial waste of your time, but I can't shake the feeling that it has some meaning I should understand."

"Let me be your analyst," she said with a smile. "I work cheap."

She studied Vincenzo's face as he described the images in his nightmare. She did not interrupt, but let him talk until he ran out of words.

"What I want to know is whether my dream has any significance from an anthropological point of view."

"All our dreams have anthropological significance, Alberto. Read some Jung. Dreams tap into our racial memories."

"How far back do those memories go? Because what I see in my dream seems really, really old."

"Opinions differ. Most psychologists would tell you that the whole concept of racial memory is nothing more than a fantasy. Some would say the memories go back to the dawn of the human species. A few might even say that they go back to before our species existed, because after all, we didn't spring out of nothing, we evolved from earlier species."

"But what does the dream mean? It's driving me crazy, along with the music playing in my head."

"The music you spoke about, you can hear it now, as you are talking to me?"

Vincenzo nodded.

"And the music started at the same time the supernova appeared?"

"That's about right. Or shortly after."

She tapped her fingers on her wrinkled lower lip, smiling slightly, then got up from her chair and went to a bookshelf. Pulling down a large leather-bound volume, she set it on her desk and thumbed through its pages, then tilted the book up so that Vincenzo could see it. One page was occupied by a woodcut that showed twelve bloated shapes in a circle. In the center was a reclining humanoid figure that held something small to its mouth between its fat hands.

"That's it," Vincenzo said. "That's my dream."

"It's an obscure myth cycle," Lena said. "Not many know of it. Even so, it is oddly persistent in the backwaters of the world. The Inuit of Greenland preserve a form of it in their verbal history. When you know where to look, you find bits and pieces of it in many odd localities that are separated by thousands of miles. The Outback of Australia. The Congo. Tibet."

"Tell it to me."

She leaned back in her chair and stretched, looking at the ceiling, then began. "It is said that before humanity was created from the clay of the earth, this world was ruled by mighty gods that came from Outside. What Outside may be is never specified, but in general it means beyond everything we know. These gods go by many names in different languages, but most translate into English as the Old Gods or Ancient Ones. These Old Gods are not like the gods worshipped by most of mankind. They have no interest in humanity. To them, we are like insects, a nuisance to be disposed of.

"In ages past beyond reckoning, so the legend goes, they fought each other for dominion over our world, and in the process laid waste to it. Eventually they established a peace of sorts, each of their races ruling over its own portion of this planet. Then, for some reason that is never explained, the situation changed, and the gods withdrew themselves into places of hiding, where they are still. One form of the myth says that something happened to the stars, and that when the stars changed, their light—or, more properly translated, their color—became poisonous to these elder gods, who were really space aliens, from our modern scientific perspective."

"I don't see what this has to do with my dream."

"Of all the Old Gods, only one has never appeared in our world. He reclines on his throne in the center of the vortex of chaos, which is said to lie at the root of creation, and plays ceaselessly on his bone flute. Around him dance the gods of the zodiac. As his music flows out, it brings into being all things that exist in the universe, and at the same time, it dissolves into nothingness all things that have reached the end of their being."

Vincenzo felt his heart rate quicken. "Does this god have a name?"

"He has many names in different cultures, but the ancient Egyptians called him Azathoth. He is described by them as blind, and is said to be an idiot who knows nothing about what he creates or destroys with his music. The notion that creation is caused by the breath of a god is common enough in world mythologies. In this instance, the breath is articulated, not by words as is usually the case—read the first chapter of Genesis, and consider it with the first sentence in the Gospel of John—but by the notes of a melody that has neither beginning nor end. The Azathoth myth teaches that should the song of this blind idiot god ever stop, even for a single instant, all of creation would cease to exist so utterly, that it would be as though it had never been created."

"Azathoth," Vincenzo said softly. For some reason it pleased him to have a name to attach to the bizarre images in his nightmare. It felt like a kind of control. Suddenly he realized what he must title his new orchestration.

"In my dream there is a shadow standing behind Azathoth. Do you know anything about that?"

"What does it look like?"

"Like a shadow. I mean, it's tall and slender, but I can't make out any details except its eyes, which are red—the same color as the supernova, actually."

"That's interesting. It may be an obscure ancient Egyptian god called Nyarlathotep, who in some forms of the legend is supposed to be charged with the safekeeping of Azathoth. He prevents anything from disrupting the flow of notes from Azathoth's flute."

"What can you tell me about him?"

"Well, for one thing, he is malicious. Of all the Old Gods, only Nyarlathotep involves himself with humanity. He seems to derive a kind of amusement in tormenting our race, in the same way a naughty boy likes to torment flies by pulling off their wings. He is said to have a capricious sense of humor. It's probably best if you stay as far away from him as possible, even in your dreams."

He thought about the shadow, and remembered feeling a kind of awareness emanate from it. The memory made him shiver. "Is there anything else?"

"That's about all I can tell you that might have any bearing on your dream. The myth cycle of the Old Gods varies from region to region, of course. Azathoth is only a small part of it. He doesn't play an active role. In this sense he is somewhat similar to the god Damballa in Haitian Voudoun, who never speaks—an immensely powerful serpent god, but not a god concerned with the things that occupy humanity."

Vincenzo stood up. "Thanks for doing this, Lena. The dream has been driving me crazy."

She stood and patted him on the shoulder. "Don't worry about it. This damned supernova is disturbing the sleep of more people than just you. Half my students are complaining about nightmares."

This reminded him of the elderly black man in the parking lot. In the days since the incident had occurred he had done his best to forget it. He described his encounter and the accident.

"Fascinating. And you're sure the melody he hummed was exactly the same as the melody you hear in your dreams?"

"Note for note."

"And he called you brother?"

"Yes. But he must have been crazy. I'd never seen him before in my life. He was just one of those old homeless men you run into everywhere these days."

"Well, the music is over for him now, isn't it?" she murmured as she searched for a pen and paper to jot down a note. She passed the paper to him. "This is the number of an acupuncturist I know. He's very good. He may be able to help you sleep."

Vincenzo accepted the paper and pocketed it.

"Maybe when the supernova finally fades, the dreams you and others are getting will end, and the melody will stop playing in your head."

"At least I was able to put the music to good use," he said.

"How is that, Al?"

"I recorded a portion of it and orchestrated it. The Los Angeles Philharmonic has been rehearsing it for the past week. Thanks to you, I now have a title for the piece—*Azathoth*."

"You recorded the melody you hear in your dreams?"

"I'm hearing it right now. It's like a radio I can't turn off."

"What does it sound like?"

Vincenzo hummed the clear flute-like tones of the ceaselessly varying melody.

"You are hearing the music of Azathoth's cracked flute," she said in wonder.

"Why do you call it cracked?"

"Didn't I mention that? The universe is an imperfect creation, so anything that exists in it must also be imperfect. Azathoth's flute is cracked to make his music imperfect."

"That's it!" Vincenzo said, clapping his hands so loudly she flinched. "That's the part of my dream I could never remember. Some of the notes are wrong."

"I would hope so," she said dryly. "If the music of Azathoth were perfected, the myth says it would destroy the world."

He was so excited he barely heard her. "Lena, you are hereby invited—no, commanded—to attend the premiere performance of my latest composition tomorrow night, at the Walt Disney

Concert Hall, eight o'clock. Please don't say you can't make it."

He hurried from the office before she could think of a tactful evasion.

5.

The first violin squinted at the music sheets in his hand with disbelief, then stared at Vincenzo. "Are you joking, Maestro?"

The use of the term "maestro" was not lost on Vincenzo. It was a mark of respect from the elderly violinist that was usually reserved for the regular conductor of the symphony, and Vincenzo appreciated it.

"Don't get your catgut in a knot, Louis," he joked. "It's only a few notes."

"But we rehearsed a different sheet. You can't expect us to change on the fly the night of the premiere performance. It's preposterous."

"I've marked the notes that have been changed in red. The changes are not technically difficult. I'll be here to lead you through them. I'm sure your people can handle it."

"Well, I am not so sure."

"The woodwinds are not complaining. Neither are the horns."

"This is unprofessional, Alberto, that's all I'm saying. We should have had at least one rehearsal with the changed score."

"It just wasn't possible, Louis. No time. These changes were absolutely at the last minute."

Louis shook his head, making the cloud of white hair that surrounded it jiggle, but Vincenzo managed to placate him and get him to go back to his chair. More than a few of the musicians were scowling at him when they thought his eyes were averted. He heard them grumbling among themselves. Well, no matter. It could not be helped. The changes were too important to omit from the premiere performance of the piece. If the play was a little ragged, he would take responsibility onto himself.

Anxiously, he watched the hall fill up. It was not going to be a full house, but that was hardly to be expected at the premiere of a completely original piece, especially with him conducting. The stars of the orchestra were not present tonight. If the piece received good reviews, maybe they would be there on the next occasion it was performed.

Assuming there ever was a next time. He was keenly aware of the huge gamble he was taking with his career, which until now had moved along at a respectable if uninspiring pace. The audience and the critics were looking forward to his fifth symphony, a work that had been in progress for more than a year. Instead, he was giving them something out of left field, something for which they had no benchmarks. It was an enormous risk to his reputation. He felt excited and reckless, and he was forced to admit to himself that he liked the feeling.

He peered at the audience around a doorframe, trying to spot his friends. It was hopeless, of course. There was too much movement, too many people. The floor plan of the hall was open, with the orchestra seated in the middle and tiers of seats on all four sides. This made for great acoustics, but there was nothing to hide behind. Nervousness increased inside him as he watched the rest of the orchestra take their places, all of them dressed in formal attire. Then it was his turn. Conscious that every eye was upon him, he carried his ivory baton to the podium and waited for the mutter of the crowd to die into silence.

Somewhat theatrically, he tapped the podium with the baton, raised both his arms, and caught Louis's red-rimmed eyes with his own. The violinist nodded. Vincenzo brought his hands down, and the hall filled with the melody. It started quietly, than built up in power as it progressed until it crested and fell back to the thunder of the kettle drums, rising and falling away again and again, like waves of the sea rolling in and breaking on a beach.

As he conducted, Vincenzo became conscious of a curious sense that he was under observation. It was not the usual attention of the audience, but something larger and more distant that watched him. There was almost no emotion in the observer, merely attentiveness with just a trace of amusement. It was stranger than any feeling he had ever experienced. Somehow he never doubted it was real. A higher intelligence was looking down upon him from an elevated vantage and listening to what was taking place in the hall. He did not have the luxury to pay full attention to the feeling, but pressed on with the music to its final conclusion. It trailed away, becoming the same simple melody line that it had been at the opening of the piece, bringing the audience around full circle. Cymbals brushed together softly, and the notes of the melody, grown slower and slower, at last ceased.

The silence that followed terrified Vincenzo. For a moment he wondered if he had gone deaf. Then thunderous applause crashed around his ears. He turned and regarded the audience behind him, which stood from their seats and cheered loudly. He bowed from the waist, and stood waiting while the orchestra took its successive series of bows. It was a heady moment, in some ways even more satisfying than the night his Fourth Symphony had premiered. On that night he had held some expectation of how the audience might react, but tonight had been a blank slate. It appeared that they liked it—not only liked it, but liked it a great deal. He caught Louis's eye as the old man filed off the stage with the other violinists trailing behind him. Louis grinned and gave him a thumbs-up.

Vincenzo made his way back to his dressing room and set his conducting baton carefully back into its box. He loosened his white tie and collar, than removed his formal evening jacket. No matter how many times he wore a jacket with tails, he could never get used to them flapping at the backs of his thighs. He noticed that someone had sent him a bottle of white wine on ice. There was no note, but whoever had sent it must have been aware of his dislike for champagne. He uncorked the bottle and filled a long-stemmed glass with pale-golden liquid. He was drinking it when Lena Gault entered.

"Congratulations, Alberto. It was a triumph. This is truly your night."

"The world didn't come to an end," he said, pouring her a glass of wine.

"No, nothing changed. I confess I was a little apprehensive."

"Don't tell me you actually believed that old myth?"

"Believed it, no, but I've been doing archaeology for many years, and I've learned not to casually discount the racial wisdom of ancient peoples."

She took the proffered glass and sipped from it with pleasure. Vincenzo turned back to the mirror and took off his tie.

"Do you hear something?" she said.

"Hear what?"

"Listen. It sounds like it's coming from outside the hall, on the street."

He cocked his head and found that he did hear something. It was almost like distant screams. Then he noticed rapid footsteps pounding in the corridor outside the dressing room, and excited voices. The door burst inward, and David Foy stood there in a tuxedo, breathing heavily. There was an expression of absolute horror on his face. They stared at him with incomprehension.

"The world has gone crazy," he said at last. "It's the most horrific thing I've ever seen. I think I'm going to be sick."

"What are you talking about?" Vincenzo said.

"Everybody outside the hall, they've all . . . they're all . . ."

He threw up across the flowered red carpet of the dressing room, than lifted his sweating face to stare at the musician with tortured eyes.

"Tell us," Lena said. There was dread in her precise Germanic voice.

"Everyone out on the street, their faces . . ."

"What about their faces?"

The astronomer's eyes widened. "They're covered with some kind of smooth, white film. It's like a Halloween mask."

"Maybe they were masks," Vincenzo suggested. "Maybe it's a practical joke of some kind."

Foy shook his head. "It was real. When they saw us coming out of the auditorium, they screamed and ran around like crazy people. One of them, a woman, got hysterical and ran right into me. I saw her close up. Her face was like wax. It stuck out from the middle and it wrapped over her eyes and teeth. Her hands were covered with the same waxy film. There was some kind of growth coming out of the top of her head that hung down to her shoulders. They were all monsters, Al."

They left the auditorium together. The scene outside was bedlam. Audience members in evening wear were running for their cars, falling down, and screaming at hideously disfigured people with white faces and strange mats of fiber on their heads, even though these monsters were not threatening anyone. They seemed to be making just as strenuous an effort to get away from the concert goers as the concert goers were making to get away from them.

"Dear God, what happened to their faces?" Lena said, clinging to his arm.

"I don't know. Acid, maybe, or fire. They look like they've been bleached. And they're so smooth."

"Look over there," Foy said, pointing across the street.

Vincenzo looked and felt sick. It was a dog on a leash. The entire outer surface of the poor animal's body was covered with shaggy fibers.

"We have to get out of here," he told the others. "We'll take my car, go back to my place."

He picked his way with care through the screaming, terrified pedestrians on the street and led them into the parking garage under the concert hall. The madness was just as great in the garage. They almost got run over as a black Mercedes blasted past them with its horn blaring. Police cars had begun to arrive when he drove out of the garage entrance, but he managed to get away before the area was cordoned off. The insanity was localized. Away from the hall, the streets were deserted of pedestrians, as was usual for this part of Los Angeles. Even so, he did not allow himself to relax until he pulled the Jag up his driveway and the iron gate closed behind it.

They went into the house in silence, too shocked by their recent experience to speak. He poured Lena and Foy shots of Scotch at the bar, then one for himself. They drank theirs like water.

"It has to be some natural disaster," Foy said. "A gas leak at some chemical refinery, or a fire."

"Perhaps they were only masks," Lena said.

"No, remember the dog," Vincenzo told her.

She shuddered at the memory.

"Turn on the television, Al," Foy said. "Maybe there's something on the news."

Vincenzo found the remote and clicked on the wall screen. He scanned through several channels until he found a breaking news report that showed a television journalist with a microphone standing in front of the Walt Disney Concert Hall. Her smooth, waxen face made him feel sick. The sidewalk behind her was blocked off with yellow police tape that fluttered in the evening breeze. Blue and red lights flickered on the tops of squad cars and ambulances.

"Listen," he said, turning up the sound.

". . . a while ago was a scene of total chaos as the audience attending a concert performance of a new piece by composer Alberto Vincenzo left the building, all of them seemingly unaware of their horrifying injuries, the cause of which is still unknown. Ambulances are conveying the victims of what is conjectured to have been an act of terrorism using an unknown chemical or biological agent. We cannot show you the injuries, but in some way these poor people have been stripped of their skins, not only over the surface of their face and hands, but over their entire bodies. One doctor who did not wish to give his name told me that none of them should be alive. Yet in spite of their obvious fear and confusion, none of them complained of pain. This has led one chemical weapons expert to speculate that the agent used to remove their skins destroyed the pain receptors. . . ."

Vincenzo muted the sound, and they sat watching normal-looking people in evening dress being loaded into the backs of ambulances on stretchers by hideously deformed medical attendants.

"I don't understand," Foy said. "What the hell's going on?"

"I don't know Daniel. It doesn't make any sense."

Lena Gault said nothing. She stared at the pictures that flickered over the television, tears streaming down her red cheeks.

"What the hell," Foy said, looking down. "There's blood on your sofa, Al. How did that get there?"

He squirmed around to look at different parts of the white leather seat cushion, then stood up.

"I think it's coming from me."

"Take off your jacket and your shirt, Daniel," Vincenzo said with concern. "You're bleeding."

Foy set down his glass and stripped off his suit jacket and white shirt, which was soaked with patches of blood. As he pulled the shirt open, his intestines spilled out with a wet sound across the carpet.

"You're bleeding, too," Foy said in a numb voice to the composer.

"We all are," Lena said. Both her eyeballs fell from their sockets, first the left, then the right. They hung over the raw, blood-red muscles of her cheeks. She stood up and began to pull off her evening dress.

"What are you doing?" Foy said.

"Don't you understand, Albert? I feared something like this but I never thought it could really happen."

As her dress came over her head, Foy watched her intestines drop from the cavity of her abdomen to the floor. Her kidneys and liver hung down to her thighs on strings of connective tissue. Through her naked ribs he could see her beating heart begin to droop lower. Everything inside her body was coming loose. He lost the sight in his left eye. Feeling with his hand, he discovered it hanging down over his cheek.

"Did those monsters do this to us?" Vincenzo asked in bewilderment. Inside his pants, he felt his testicles dangling down inside his left pant leg. The muscles of his thighs slipped sideways across his femurs and made him stagger.

Foy began to make a low moaning noise. With his one good eye Vincenzo saw his friend's body slowly collapse in upon itself into a pile of loose organs and bones that somehow was still alive.

"They aren't the monsters," Lena said, her voice changing in pitch as her lungs began to slide down from their places in her rib cage. "We are the monsters, Alberto."

"I don't understand."

"It was your music. You should never have fixed the bad notes. The song of Azathoth was not meant to be perfected. It changed the nature of reality for those who listened to it. But don't you see? We didn't notice the change, because it was *still our reality.* Our changed reality can't persist in the greater reality of the world around us. It's breaking down, and us along with it."

Vincenzo tried to speak, but his tongue fell out and his jaw bone dropped to the floor. Still contained to some degree in his tuxedo, his body settled slowly downward like a melting candle into a puddle of bloody organs and bones in which floated his evening jacket, pants and red shirt that had once been snowy white. His remaining eye settled on top of this mass of protoplasm. It twitched left and right frantically, but all he could see was the ceiling.

He began to scream, and could not stop screaming. There was no sound, only a series of bubbles that rose from the bloody mass and broke on its surface with soft pops.

SHUB-NIGGURATH

The Black Goat

1.

The fire road came to an abrupt end on a ledge of rock with a six-foot drop. The driver of the Jeep Cherokee turned it around with difficulty in the dense brush, so that it pointed back the way it had come, and killed the engine. Two men got out.

"Welcome to Louisiana, Harding," the driver said. "My dear home state, which I hoped never to see again as long as I was living, but here I am."

The other man looked around at the thick woods choked with undergrowth and frowned.

"Looks like the ass end of nowhere."

"We ain't reached nowhere yet," the driver said with a crooked grin. "We got to hike for miles before we get to nowhere."

The two were completely different in appearance, yet in a strange way very much alike. The native of Louisiana was thin and wiry, with that tough thinness that is so much stronger than it looks. His lean body was nothing but ropes of muscle with deeply tanned skin pulled over them. The man named Harding was a little older, a little plumper, but only by comparison. In a city fitness center he would have been said to be in good shape. His hair was buzz-cut, military fashion. A blurred tattoo of a lightning bolt was visible on his shoulder where it stuck through his denim cut-offs. The way he moved was precise, with no wasted energy.

They pulled back packs out of the Jeep and slung them over their shoulders.

"Which way, Boggs?"

"There ain't but one way to go, Sergeant. Unless you think we can walk through that." He pointed casually at the wall of undergrowth on either side.

Snorting in disgust, Harding let himself drop off the end of the rock ledge and began to follow the path on the other side. Boggs fell into step behind him, whistling through his teeth.

"You're sure this is the only way in?" Harding said.

"I was born not thirty miles from here. I know these swamps."

"I just don't like involving outsiders. It's trouble."

"I told you, we can't get to the crash site on our own. We need a couple of good ol' boys to take us there."

"How do we know we can trust them?"

"You can trust 'em if you want. I ain't trusting nobody, not even you."

Instinctively, Harding felt the checkered butt of the army Colt tucked into his belt. He felt a little itch between his shoulder blades and ignored it. Boggs wasn't going to try anything until they got to the money. That was when the fun would start. He slapped the back of his sweating neck and cursed. They had walked no more than a mile and already he'd been bitten at least a dozen times. Where the sun shown between the trees above their heads, it felt hot on his scalp. He paused to dig a cap out of his pack and fitted it to his head.

"I still don't see why we couldn't just drop down on lines from a chopper right on the spot. We've got the GPS coordinates. We know exactly where the fucking thing crashed."

"We could maybe get in that way," Boggs said. "But there's no way we could ever get out, not on our own, and not with the money. Do you know how big a pile seven million dollars in cash makes? We couldn't carry it."

Harding stopped suddenly. "What the fuck."

Hanging from a tree limb that projected over the path was a kind of crude collage composed of woven twigs tied together with red yarn. It hung down like a ribbon just above their heads. There was a primitiveness to it, a savage quality that was emphasized by a naked skull tied to its end. The eye sockets of the skull stared directly into Harding's eyes.

"What is this, some kind of warning?"

"Them things is all over the place hereabouts. Don't you pay it no mind. Someone's just trying to scare people away."

"What kind of skull is that?"

"That'd be a goat skull, I reckon."

"Goat. What the fuck?" He started to tear the thing down.

"Best to just leave it be," Boggs said quietly.

"Why is that?"

"Bad luck to touch them things, that's all. Best just leave it."

Harding grunted, but let go of the totem, and the two men edged around it.

As they continued onward, the ground began to get softer and wetter. Spanish moss hung down in grey-green streamers from the trees. In places they had to wade through pools of stagnant water.

"Best watch where you step," Boggs said. "We're getting into the swamp."

"Is there quicksand?"

"No such thing as quicksand. You need to watch out for snakes. They get you on the ankle, you won't be able to walk."

Around noon they reached a cabin on the edge of the bayou. It was built on stilts and had a rusted roof of galvanized steel sheets. A dock projected into the water with several boats tied to it.

"Comin' in," Boggs said loudly as they approached the shack. "We're expected."

There was no movement from the structure. The two men approached cautiously, their military training taking over. Boggs banged on the door with his fist, standing to one side, while Harding scanned the dense trees behind them.

"You in there, Dupree?"

"What you want?" The voice inside the shack was not welcoming.

"That you, Leroy? I sent word yesterday. We need a guide."

The click of a trigger sent Harding into a crouch with both hands on his extended Colt.

The man who stood at the edge of the trees didn't flinch. He continued to point his rifle at Harding's stomach. He spat tobacco juice to one side and grinned toothlessly. "Best put that thing away," he said with a trace of French accent.

Harding slowly uncoiled his body and slid the .45 into his belt, then spread his empty hands.

"What you playing at, Tull?" Boggs said. "We're here to do business."

The man with the rifle tilted it up and set its stock on the ground. "That you, Homer Boggs? Shit, I thought you was dead over in 'ganistan or one of them places."

The door of the shack creaked open on its leather hinges and another man came out. He was naked to the waist and had a gut that hung over his belt. His skin was so dark, it looked like old leather. He cradled a shotgun in the crook of his arm. "Reckon these be the two men Floury came to tell us about," he said to Tull.

"Don't you recognize Homer? This here is Homer Boggs, Jake Boggs' boy."

"Well, you're all grown up," the shirtless man said.

"Tull, Leroy." Bogg nodded to each man in turn. "We need you boys to take us into the swamp."

"Is that so?" Leroy Dupree eyed them skeptically. He nodded at Harding. "This one know what he's signing on for?"

"He knows it ain't no little girl's birthday party."

"You know where we're going?"

"I got a GPS unit, and I got the coordinates."

Tull Dupree spat on the boards of the step and smirked.

"But do you know where we're going?" Leroy repeated.

"Up near Devil's Pot."

"Shit," Tull said.

"That's not a good place this time of year."

"I know that, Leroy. Everyone knows you stay away from the Devil's Pot when it's wet, but we got no choice in the matter. We'll pay you five hundred dollars to take us there and back, cash up front."

"Each," Leroy said.

Boggs hesitated. "Sure, each. Cash on the barrel. Can you get us in there?"

Leroy looked at his brother, who spat tobacco juice past the step and into the algae-covered water. Tull shrugged his narrow shoulders inside the dirty long-sleeved undershirt he wore.

"I reckon we'll get you there all right. What you going to do there?"

"That's our business," Harding said.

"It ain't just the swamp, Homer," Leroy said. "There's other things. You're from here, you know what I mean."

"I know," Boggs said. "But there's no help for it, we got to go in."

2.

"Why aren't we taking the swamp boat?" Harding asked as they loaded supplies into a fiberglass canoe.

Boggs glanced at the large, flat-bottomed boat with a propeller in the back to push it through the air. "You need a road to drive that thing on," he said. "There ain't no roads where we're going, Harding. Hell, we'll be lucky to get the canoe through."

Leroy looked at Harding with a doubtful expression. "You ever been in a canoe?"

"No."

"Step in the center. Just sit on the floor. Don't rock around or you'll tip us."

The bottom of the canoe was wet. Harding laid down his backpack and sat on it, being careful not to rock the narrow craft from side to side. Boggs climbed in front of him, Tull took the bow and his big brother sat on the stern seat. The brothers pushed off with paddles and soon they were skimming through impenetrable green water that could easily conceal alligators and water moccasins a few inches below the surface.

After a while, Tull began to sing in French, and his brother joined in on the chorus. Boggs looked back at Harding and grinned. Harding just shook his head. The two deep male voices were strangely harmonic as they echoed from the passing cypress trees with their hanging veils of moss and trailing vines. The mosquitoes whined in Harding's ears, eliciting a periodic slap and a curse from the city man.

"You army man?" Leroy asked close behind him.

"SEAL."

"Navy man, then. I guess you can swim."

"Like a fish."

"Best not try swimming in these waters. Gators get you real quick. Pull you down and take you for a ride. You know the kind of ride I mean?"

"No."

"They grab hold of you, and then they spin you under the water until you don't know what's up and what's down. In that murky water you can't see nothing. They keep you down until the bubbles come up."

"How do you break free?"

Leroy laughed. "No such thing as breakin' free, boy. Not once a gator gets you down there."

"Keep your knife handy," Boggs told him.

Harding touched the sheath knife at his belt. "Can you fight off an alligator with a knife?"

"Probably not," Boggs said.

The trees closed in and the waterway narrowed. They followed a bewildering series of twists and turns. The sounds of the swamp were eerie and strange to Harding. He recognized the croak of a bullfrog, and the cries of some kind of bird in the trees above his head. For a while a snake undulated lazily through the water, keeping pace with the canoe. The Dupree brothers ignored it. The afternoon lengthened. Harding wondered if he was going to reach the crash site before dark.

The bottom of the canoe rubbed against weeds and mud. Tull jumped out and grabbed the bow to steady it.

"Everybody out," Leroy said.

Harding looked around. They were still in the middle of the water, but the way was choked with weeds. He climbed out carefully. They started to drag the canoe forward, wading up to their knees in places, the soft water-plants crushing under their boots. The brothers kept their guns cradled in their arms, and ceaselessly scanned the surface of the water around them. The mud released clouds of stinking swamp gas at every step. Harding wondered what had happened to the snake that was following them.

"This is the most miserable, godforsaken, hellish place on the entire fucking planet," he muttered.

"Welcome to Louisiana," Boggs said. The brothers didn't even laugh.

They pulled the canoe over grassy, reed-covered hillocks that were almost high and firm enough to be above water, but not quite. At other times they waded up to their chests. The light began to fail.

"We're not going to make it before dark," Harding told Boggs.

"There's a moon," Boggs said.

Periodically Boggs checked his GPS unit. The brothers knew where they were going—he didn't have to correct their course. Between the tree branches above their heads the stars came out. Tull set a lantern in the bow of the canoe on the end of a stick he propped up. Opening the shade, he lit its wick with a match. The lantern cast a yellow circle of light around them.

"Look at that thing up there," Boggs said, pointing up at a bright red star that glared down on them.

"That's the supernova," Harding said. "It's been all over the television news."

"What's a supernova?" Tull asked.

"Some kind of star that blew up. They say it's going to fade away to nothing in a few weeks."

"You shouldn't talk about it," Leroy said.

"What do you mean?" Boggs said.

"Bad luck. The old conjure woman down at Papp's Creek says it's an omen. Says it's the eye of Her."

"Eye of her? What eye of her?"

"Her, Her. Don't you city people know nothin'? The Black Goat. She lives in this here swamp."

"You shouldn't talk about Her, Leroy," Tull said.

"What is this Black Goat? Some kind of local monster?" Harding asked.

"Call it what you like," Boggs said. "Devil. Monster. God. People in this swamp been worshipping the Black Goat for as long as anybody can remember. They say the Indians worshipped her before the white man came to America."

Harding got a creeping feeling between his shoulder blades that he didn't like. He recognized it from his tours in Afghanistan. It was a feeling of being watched and listened to. The shadows had gradually closed in around them until it was impossible to see more than a dozen feet in any direction by the patches of moonlight that found their way down to the surface of the water. For the first time he started to worry about something other than alligators and snakes.

"They say She be one of the Old Ones," Leroy murmured.

"Who are the Old Ones?" Harding asked.

"Indians say they be the gods who ruled the earth in the Before Times, before there was any human beings. But they all gone now, except for Her. They say She still here, in the swamp."

"Has she got a name?"

"Don't say it," Tull told his brother.

"I ain't going to say it."

"I heard it from my grandmother, when I was about six

year old," Boggs said. "She made me promise never to repeat it to nobody, and I kept my word."

"You're not six any more, Boggs. What's the fucking name?" Harding demanded in irritation. The whispering was starting to get on his nerves.

Boggs hesitated. "Shub-Niggurath," he said in a low tone. Harding heard Tull spit tobacco juice into the water.

For a few moments the night sounds of the swamp stopped. There was dead silence. It was so quiet, Harding could hear his own heart beating. Then, gradually, the piping of the frogs and the chirping of insects resumed.

"You shouldn't have said Her name," Leroy told Boggs.

"Hell, Leroy, it's just an old Indian superstition, you know that."

"I know, but even so, you shouldn't have said it."

They came to deeper water and climbed awkwardly back into the canoe from the top of a rotting stump. For a time the brothers paddled, dipping their blades silently into the water. The canoe glided through the darkness like a ghost. Leroy suddenly backed water.

"Listen," he said. "Hear that?"

They sat listening. Harding realized it was the sound of distant drums.

"Put out the lantern," Leroy told Tull. The shade clinked, and the circle of yellow light around the canoe disappeared.

They continued forward more cautiously. The beat of the drums grew louder. Mingled with it Harding began to hear shouts and screams of human voices.

"Must be quite a party," he murmured.

"I told you it was a bad time of year to come to the Devil's Pot."

They emerged onto an open expanse of water that was like a lake in the midst of the swamp. In the middle of this lake there was an island of trees. Lantern lights glowed between the ancient trunks.

"This must be one of Her nights," Leroy said.

"The plane has to be somewhere on that island," Boggs said, staring at the glowing dial of his GPS.

"Maybe they found it," Harding said. "Maybe that's why they're so happy."

"Maybe. Or maybe it's still up in the trees."

"We can't wait all night," Harding pointed out.

"We'll land on the far end of the island. With luck we can find the cargo and be gone before they know we were even there."

"Do you know what they'll do to us if they catch us?" Leroy asked him.

"I got a pretty good notion," Boggs said.

"Just so long as you know," Leroy said. Tull spat tobacco juice into the water.

3.

It was a relief to be out of the swamp. The island was marshy in places but at least they could walk on it without sinking to their knees in mud. The drums and the chanting were loud in their ears, but the glimmer of the bonfire and the lanterns through the trees reassured them that they were some distance away from the cult of worshippers. Every now and then a blood-freezing scream went up into the night air.

Boggs wandered around, staring at his GPS unit, while Harding and the Duprees sat on the side of the beached canoe and watched. Finally Harding got frustrated and went over to him. "Can you find it or not?"

"I found it," Boggs said with a gleam of white teeth that was barely visible in the moonlight.

"Well, where is it?"

Boggs pointed up above their heads. Harding looked up into the trees above but could see nothing.

"Are you sure? Maybe you should check again."

"It's up there."

"Shit."

Harding broke out his climbing gear from his pact. He had hoped he would not need to use it, but things in life were never easy. He attached spikes to his boots and looped his climbing belt around the trunk of the tree nearest to where Boggs was getting his signal. The brothers watched in silence.

"Here goes nothing," Harding said, and began to loop his way up the trunk of the tree. He was soon lost among the leaves to those watching from below. He had to unhook and re-hook his belt several times to get around projecting limbs. Then the branches got so thick, he dispensed with it completely and climbed the tree like a monkey. The drums were louder up there. He could see the redness of the bonfire shining up against the canopy of leaves at the other end of the island.

He felt the plane before he saw it. Running his hand along its wing, he tried to make sense of it, then realized it was upside down. With care he crawled out on the underside of the wing until he reached the door. He got a lucky break in that the door was not blocked by branches. With difficulty he worked the closing mechanism and it dropped open.

"I'm in," he called down softly. There was no answer.

He didn't bother to repeat the words, but climbed into the cabin of the single-engine craft and peered around in the dim moonlight. He was fairly sure the light of the pencil flash he carried would not be seen by the cultists at the far end of the island through the masses of intervening foliage, but even so he left it in his pocket.

The pilot was still strapped into his seat. There was something strange about his silhouette in the silver light that filtered through the plane's windscreen. At first Harding thought that his head was lolling down against his chest. Then a thrill of fear ran through him when he saw that there was no head, just a raggedly torn stump of a neck. It must have been torn off in the crash, he reasoned. He looked around the cabin but the head was not there.

What he found were four canvas duffle bags. Each of them, he knew without looking into them, was filled with cash in the form of mostly tens and twenties. Drug money came in small bills. He went to the door and leaned out.

"I found it," he said in a low voice.

Ducking back inside, he felt the plane shift with a groan of tortured aluminum. He froze in place listening for more sounds, but none came. He realized that he was gripping the door frame hard with both hands and deliberately relaxed his fingers. Crawling toward the rear of the plane, he grabbed one of the duffle bags and dragged it toward the door. It was heavy, as he had expected it to be—each bag held almost two million dollars. He slid the duffel bag out onto the inverted wing.

"One coming down," he said.

The bag crashed through the branches. He heard it hit the ground with a thud. Boggs cursed.

"You almost hit me."

"Next time, look up."

In quick succession he dragged out the three remaining duffle bags and let them drop through the leaves. He half-expected the plane to slide out along with them but it gave no additional indication of shifting. With a feeling of relief he left through the door and lowered himself down the tree on a line.

Boggs and the brothers had the bags already loaded in the canoe by the time his feet touched the mossy ground.

"Let's get the fuck out of here before those cultists—"

He stopped talking. Boggs was standing to one side with an awkward body posture. The Duprees were next to the canoe. Both had guns in their hands. Leroy's shotgun was directed at Boggs. Tull pointed his rifle at Harding.

"Take it out and drop it," he said.

Harding made no argument. He used his finger and thumb to pull his .45 from his belt and dropped it into the tall grass.

"I guess five hundred apiece wasn't enough," Boggs said.

"This here a four-man canoe," Leroy said. "Each one of these sacks weighs the same as a man. There's just no room for you boys. You understand how it is."

"Sure," Harding said.

He threw his knife. The point caught Leroy in the left eye socket. The Cajun pulled the trigger of the shotgun as he fell back, but the shot went high into the trees. Harding was diving forward after his Colt when he heard Tull's rifle. He got hold of the gun and pumped three bullets into Tull before the toothless man could fire a second time. From the corner of his eye he saw Boggs drive his own knife into Leroy's heart.

There was sudden silence. Harding realized the drums and cries had stopped on the other end of the island. He heard a mounting murmur of male voices and several shouts of outrage.

"We have to leave now," he told Boggs, who made no argument.

Together they pushed the canoe into the water and climbed in over the bags of money. The canoe sank dangerously low, so that the silvered surface was only an inch or so below the top edges on either side. They found the paddles and used them to push off from the clinging mud. Then they were gliding over the Devil's Pot away from the island.

"They'll be coming after us," Boggs said from the bow.

"Maybe. But they won't find us in the dark."

The canoe wobbled unsteadily and water slopped in over its side.

"Be careful," Harding hissed. "You'll tip us."

Boggs didn't answer. He dug at the water with his paddle, sending splashes back into Harding's face. Without warning, the canoe rode up on a submerged log and the two went into the water. It was not deep, only about four feet or so, but the duffel bags soaked up the water like sponges. Whereas dry they had weighed around one hundred fifty pounds each, wet they were closer to three hundred pounds. With great effort the two men managed to load them back into the canoe, which sank dangerously low. It was obvious it would never carry both the money and the two of them.

"We'll have to wade on either side of it to keep it from tipping," Boggs said.

Harding heard a shout from somewhere behind them. Turning, he saw a lantern, and realized it was moving across the water.

"We need to get out of here," Harding said.

"Which way do we go?"

"How should I know?"

"Use your GPS."

"It's at the bottom of the swamp, along with our packs."

They wasted no more words, but pushed the canoe along between them into a narrow body of water that progressed between hillocks of weeds and overhanging cypress trees. In the night sky above them, the red eye of the supernova glared down.

"I think this is the way we came," Boggs said from in front.

"Are you sure?"

"No."

The voices and the lanterns fell behind and were lost amid the enclosing trees. They came to a place where the water became more shallow. Eventually they were forced to drag the heavy canoe through the clinging mud. As they pushed against it, their legs sank up to their knees.

"I don't remember this part," Harding said.

"It don't matter; we're here now."

Harding couldn't argue with this bit of Cajun philosophy, so he said nothing. He had retained his paddle and had tucked it into the stern of the canoe. Boggs had lost his. Harding wondered if the canoe was riding high enough in the water to bear his weight alone. But how could he climb into it without tipping it over?

Boggs abruptly stopped. "Do you hear that?"

"Hear what?" Harding asked in annoyance.

"Listen."

Harding listened to the stillness. From some distance away he heard a soft splash, and then another, and another.

"What does that sound like to you?" Boggs whispered.

"It sounds like something walking through the swamp. Something big."

"It sounds like that to me, too."

"That's impossible, though. Nobody can walk through this swamp."

Boggs grunted and pushed the canoe over a ridge of mud.

The water deepened on the other side, and Harding found himself floating. He hung onto the stern of the canoe and began to tread water, feeling for the muddy bottom with his boots. One boot hit something that moved under it. Fear took over. He began to flail the water with his legs.

"What are you doing?" Boggs hissed. "You'll tip over the canoe."

Before Harding could answer, Boggs let out a scream of agony. Harding felt the canoe wrench to the side. Frantically he fought to keep it upright while probing the depths for something firm to stand on. He realized that Boggs was no longer at the bow. Some distance away, the water thrashed and boiled violently. Harding caught a glimpse of a flailing white hand in the moonlight. The thrashing ceased, and ripples spread out from the place.

He continued to kick the water, moving the heavy canoe slowly forward, until his feet made contact with something hard. At first he thought it was an alligator, then realized that it was a sunken log. The ground continued to slope up until he was walking in water no deeper than his knees. He looked behind him. Of Boggs there was no trace. The swamp had swallowed him up. In the stillness he heard again the regular splash of footsteps that were impossibly large. The thing that made them must be gigantic. It was still following him.

Harding straddled the stern of the canoe and tried to sit down on it, but almost dumped out the bags of money. There was no way to get into the canoe without something firm to steady it against. He looked around for a log or a snag that he could rest it against while he climbed into it. The footsteps came closer. They sounded like they were no more than a dozen yards behind him. He pushed forward with frantic urgency, not daring to take a moment to look behind. To the side he saw a lantern light gleam between the trees, and from the opposite side he heard a shout. The cultists from the island had managed to close around him.

With a curse, he upended the canoe and dumped its cargo into the water, then started to wade away with

. . . he found himself looking into the face of an enormous creature . . .

frantic motions. His boots sank into the mud at each step and defied him when he tried to pull them out. It was exhausting work. The faster he tried to flounder through the water, the slower he progressed. The water deepened and he swam, grateful to be free of the clinging mud if only for a few minutes.

Something struck his cheek. He pulled it off. It writhed around his wrist and tightened. Realizing what it was, he crushed the life from it with his fist and let it float behind him. He knew he was finished. The poison would go to his brain. He struggled onward, forcing his way between the trees of this endless nightmare swamp. His head began to spin and a redness came into his eyes that stained the moonlight with blood. He didn't know if he was swimming or crawling. The cool mud squished between his fingers.

A giant hand closed around his chest and lifted him high into the air. It turned him, and he found himself looking into the face of an enormous creature with long, spindly legs and arms, and a narrow dog-like head that had ears squared off at their tops. The head tilted to the side on its elongated neck as it studied him. This gave Harding time to study it.

The hunched posture of the thing and its grotesquely long limbs reminded him of a praying mantis. It must have stood at least thirty feet above the swamp. Shaggy black hair, like the hair on a goat, covered its body. A long tail with some kind of barbed hook on its end lashed the night air behind it. On its narrow chest he saw three pairs of swollen breasts that dripped milk from their nipples. Between the rows of these tits gaped a vertical slit that looked like a vaginal opening. The enflamed moist lips on either side of the slit pulsed open in a rhythmic way. Lower down on the thing's shaggy belly, an erect penis that was more than a yard long bobbed up and down as it shifted its footing in the mud.

The hermaphroditic monster pulled Harding closer and sniffed the air loudly. Harding found himself laughing weakly when he realized it was smelling him. This couldn't be real, he thought. He must be delirious from the snake venom.

"The devil on stilts," he said, giggling to himself.

The creature reached up with its gigantic clawed hand and stroked Harding's hair as though gently stroking the hair of a doll. Without warning, it tore his head off. The crunch of his skull between its powerful jaws was loud in the night. From out of the darkness on either side came exultant cries in a language neither English nor French.

"Iä! Shub-Niggurath! Nah-fagz xaloth 'k-ri loh, akai 'k-ri loh, 'k-ri loh."

CTHULHU

What the Sea Keeps

1.

Captain Kane Phillips walked the length of the *Courser*'s dining hall, surveying the faces of the three young men and two young woman who stood there, waiting for him to speak. Their eyes were bright, their expressions eager. He liked that. They should show keenness, he thought, given the importance of the job they were about to undertake.

"Sit down. You must be tired. It's a hell of a long flight from the mainland."

The helicopter that had carried them across the South Pacific from Chile had departed the ship's landing pad, and night lay against the glass of the portholes, turning them into black mirrors. An intimate golden glow emanated from the overhead lights. The five took chairs at one end of the long table that dominated the room, by unspoken consent leaving the chair at its head vacant. Phillips slid into it.

"What we are about to do will be the most important thing any of you do in your entire lives," he said at last. "This is the greatest scientific discovery of the century, and you have been chosen to investigate it. You are all top divers, the best in your field. But the kind of diving you will be doing on this expedition is unlike any you have done in the past. The ruins of the city are seven miles down. Seven miles." He let the number sink in. "Do any of you have any conception of what that means?"

One of the men, who had the sun-bleached hair and tan of an Australian surfer, grinned. "A whole lot of cold and dark, mate."

"If cold and dark were all we had to worry about, Rogers, it would be a cake walk," Sue Kowalski told him. She was an athletic blonde with short-cut hair and crystal-blue eyes.

"It means you will be encased in hard suits the whole time," Phillips said. "The ADEUs will become your world. You will learn to respect them and rely on them for your very lives."

"What's an ADEU?" a black man asked. His shining bald head had a distinctive white scar running across its left side.

"Autonomous Deep Exploration Unit," Kowalski told him. "But what it really means, Digger, is kiss your ass goodbye when you climb into it."

"Some of you have had experience in similar suits, others have not," Phillips said. "These are the latest design. They will go deeper for longer than anything else ever built, and they'll keep you alive."

"You hope," Kowalski said.

"No, you hope. You'll be the ones inside them. I'm too old for such silliness." Phillips started to cough and had to bend over while he held onto the table until the fit passed. The younger men and women regarded him with concern.

"It's nothing," he said at last, straightening up. "I took some lung damage on a dive a few years ago. I got over it but the doctors tell me I can't do any more diving."

A slightly built Chinese woman raised her hand. "Captain, perhaps you could tell us more about our mission. Specifics, I mean."

"You signed up without knowing what you were signing up for?" Kowalski said.

"Yes. When I saw who I would be working with I knew I had to be a part of it, but all I was told was that we would be exploring a lost city."

"The imperative was to get you all here as quickly as possible," Phillips told them. "We're in international waters. The news of this discovery is bound to leak out. We don't want the Russians or the Chinese showing up and stealing our finds out from under us."

"International waters is an understatement," Jake Rogers said. "We're next door to Point Nemo, the furthest away from human habitation it is possible to get on this planet. There are no nearby islands, no fish in these waters. It's like a marine desert down there."

"I don't see how we can be going seven miles down," said a diver with black hair slicked back close to his skull, and matching black eyes. "We're on the East Pacific Ridge, right? There's no trench under us."

"The city is in a kind of subsidence zone between two mountain ranges," Phillips explained. "That's how it was missed for so long by hydrographers."

"We're diving into a hole, Scarpelli," Kowalski told him with a grin. "We know how much you love that."

"Shit," the Sicilian diver said.

Ling Wu raised her eyebrows. "Did I miss something?"

"A few years ago Scarpelli went down into a hole and got stuck in an underwater cave. He almost ran out of air."

"I hate caves," Scarpelli muttered.

"Captain, it doesn't make any sense that a city would be way out in the middle of the South Pacific, so deep under water," Rogers said.

Phillips smiled. "What if I were to tell you that it isn't a human city?"

"Oh no, not ancient aliens," Scarpelli said with a groan. "Please tell me I didn't get lured all this way to look for aliens."

"Did you ever hear of R'lyeh?"

Scarpelli looked at Phillips blankly.

"I'm not surprised; it's not a common mythology. The Pacific Islanders say it's a fabulous city of gold that sank under the sea long before there were human beings, and trapped all its inhabitants underwater. But somehow they didn't die, and they are still there in their tombs, sleeping and dreaming. Any of you ever hear of it?"

All the divers shook their heads.

"It's better this way. You'll be coming on it with fresh eyes."

"City of gold, did you say?" Digger Jones murmured.

"So the myth goes, but the mythologies of the world are littered with El Dorados."

"Is there any real chance of treasure down there?" Scarpelli asked.

"We won't know until we look, will we?" Phillips clapped his hands together. "That's it for tonight. It's late. You've all had a long flight from Chile. Get some sleep. We'll show you the ADEU units in the morning."

They broke up and wandered toward their cabins. Sue Kowalski found herself on the *Courser*'s deck with Jake Rogers. They went to the rail and stood looking up at the night sky, which was thick with stars. The Milky Way was so bright it almost looked like a road across the heavens. A brilliant red star, much larger than any other, blazed in the west.

"They say the supernova is starting to fade," he murmured. "I don't see it myself. If anything, it looks brighter."

"I've gotten used to it," she said. "I'll miss it when it's gone."

They looked at the red star in silence.

"How long has it been?"

"Two years," she said.

"Seems longer. Where have you been keeping yourself?"

"You know how it is—you follow the work."

"I heard you were in Bali, diving some wreck."

"For a while. I've been taking time off."

"What do you make of this one?"

She shrugged. "It's good money, and a chance to work with good people."

"But what do you think of the story Phillips gave us? Do you think there's really a city seven miles down? It sounds crazy."

"Why would he lie?"

"I don't know, but an alien city? I've chased myths before and never found anything to show for it."

"Like I said. Good money, people I can rely on to have my back. It's enough."

"There was a time when you wanted more."

She looked at him. In the dim glow from portholes of the cabins his face was shadowed, unreadable.

"Yeah, well, things change."

He covered her hand on the rail with his. "Not everything changes."

She gently pulled her hand away. "I'm going to bed. You should get some sleep, too. Big day tomorrow."

The first mate of the *Courser* was Jackie Moon, a middle-aged Korean man with a potbelly. He opened the access port in the front of an ADEU that hung over the deck from two steel cables on the end of a crane. The heavy steel plate clanged reassuringly as it folded back on itself.

The large transparent dome in the front of the head made it look a little like Robby the Robot from the old movie *Forbidden Planet*, Rogers thought. There were lighting units attached to the shoulders. The left hand had delicate extensions that were like slender fingers, but the claw-like right hand was more massive, and clearly designed for heavy work such as moving large objects.

"Each of these units costs twenty-seven million dollars. It's imperative that we don't lose any," Moon said.

Ling Wu looked at Digger Jones, who let out a short bark of laughter.

The Korean frowned. "As you can see, you don't wear an ADEU like a suit of armor; you sit inside it. That's why it was unnecessary to custom-tailor the units to your body size. Your hands fit inside these control sleeves. We call them waldos. They operate the grappling arms of the suit and most of its other controls."

"How does it walk?" Rogers asked.

"It's gyro-stabilized, of course. You can't tip over. You move your feet inside these boots, just as if you were walking across a floor, and the suit will imitate your motions. It's designed to be completely intuitive. There's really no learning curve."

"What if the little bubble-window breaks?" Scarpelli said.

"It's a new layered nanocomposite form of polycarbonite. It's stronger than the steel of the suit."

"Good to know, since we're going to be trusting our lives to it," the Sicilian said dryly.

"The systems have been fully tested under the most rigorous conditions." Moon pointed at a red lever. "Now this is your emergency surfacing lever. Do not pull this lever. If you do, the unit will automatically return to the surface and there's nothing you can do to stop it."

"We're going to be under one atmosphere, right?" Digger Jones said.

"One atmosphere pressure, sea-level normal oxygen-nitrogen balance. As far as your body will know, you might as well be walking in Central Park."

"How long do the batteries last?" Sue Kowalski asked.

"Six hours. But there's an emergency reserve in case you get into some trouble."

"How much of a reserve?"

"About an hour. But don't worry about that, if you run into a problem, all you need to do is pull that red lever. But remember what I told you—never pull the red lever."

"Because that would be bad," Ling Wu said.

"I'm glad you all have a sense of humor," Moon said. "You're going to need it down there." He pointed at a small control panel. "These are your thrusters. When you come to a place you can't walk, these will lift you over the obstacle. Use them sparingly, there's a limited charge of compressed air. The gyros will keep you upright."

He shut the front of the suit with a clang. "Any questions?"

"These suits have been tested at seven miles, right?"

Moon looked at Kowalski without saying anything.

"They've been tested at the depth we're going to use them, right?" she repeated.

"Not exactly."

"What do you mean, not exactly?" Rogers demanded.

"They've been pressurized to that depth, of course, but this is the first time they will be used in the field under such a high pressure."

"Great," Scarpelli said. "We're lab rats."

"There was no opportunity to test everything," Moon explained. "We are under a time constraint. We need to get results before this site is overrun."

"I guess we'll be doing a field test today," Rogers told the other divers.

Kowalski rolled her eyes. Scarpelli laughed.

"We'll go down in teams of three units," Moon said. "That way, if there's a problem we can send down the other team to solve it. We should be able to keep working continuously in shifts."

"Who is the sixth diver?" Rogers asked.

"I'll be leading one of the teams," Moon said.

"Excuse me? How much diving experience have you had?"

"I'm proficient on the operation of the ADEU, and I've logged hundreds of hours in simulations."

Kowalski looked at Rogers, who shook his head.

"I don't like it," he said. "You haven't had enough real-world experience."

"Don't worry about me, I can handle myself."

"I'm not worried about you, I'm worried that one of us could get killed trying to save your sorry ass."

"We'll just have to see about that, won't we?" Moon said, meeting his glare. "I'll be leading the first team."

"Like hell you will," Rogers said. "I'll lead the first team, and I'll pick my mates."

Moon argued but realized that the divers were not going to yield the point.

"Fine, but it's against my recommendation. If any of you get into trouble I won't be there to help you out of it."

"We'll take our chances," Rogers said.

"We'll still have audio contact with the ship, right?" Ling Wu said.

"Through seven miles of ocean?" Moon's tone was sarcastic. "You will be able to talk to each other, but you will be cut off from the ship."

"How long will it take us to get down to the site?"

"About forty minutes. You'll come up faster than that—about half an hour on the return. You'll come up a lot faster if you pull the red lever—but never pull the red lever."

"So we'll have less than five hours each shift to do our work," Sue said.

"That's it. Make it count."

They went down to the storage bay and picked out their ADEUs. There were two extra units for emergency replacements, one of which had been used for the demonstration on deck. Captain Phillips was there to meet them. They watched a crew member begin to spray their last names on the armor plates that formed the chests of the units using stencils.

Jones took a small photograph from his wallet and placed it inside the helmet of his suit up against the polycarbonate bubble-window. He saw Rogers watching him. "My wife. She goes down with me on every dive."

"You're a good man, Digger," Ling Wu said.

"I love my wife."

"Did you guys hear what happened in Los Angeles a couple of nights ago?" Scarpelli said.

"What happened?" Kowalski had her hand inside one of the waldos of her suit, and was experimenting with its arm movements.

"A whole auditorium full of people turned into monsters."

"They what?"

"I'm not kidding. They were all covered in blood and you could see their internal organs. It was fucking disgusting."

"It's the supernova," Ling Wu said. "It's evil. Weird shit has been happening all over the world since it showed itself."

"You and your Chinese superstitions," Jones said.

"I don't believe that about the people in Los Angeles," Rogers said. "It's too crazy."

"It was on CNN. Would they lie about a thing like that?"

Rogers laughed, and told them he had decided to go with Kowalski and Jones for his team.

"Nothing against you and Scarpelli," he said to Wu. "They've just had more experience."

"Great, we get to babysit Moon," she said. "Should be fun."

"The first dive is for orientation," Phillips told them. "Learn the site. Take as many photos and as much video as you can get. We'll map it out while the second team is down, and plan what our best course of action should be."

"What do we do about artifacts?" Rogers asked.

"Photograph them in situ and leave them."

"Can't I bring up just one little piece of gold?" Kowalski asked.

"No," Phillips said without smiling. "Nothing comes up. Document everything you can."

3.

Rogers' team was on deck the next morning shortly after sunrise. The ADEUs were waiting for them on their cranes. They climbed into their units and sealed them, then powered them up.

"Check your lights," Phillips shouted, then realized no one could hear him and made hand gestures through the bubble-dome while he searched for the switch to turn on voice communication.

The shoulder-mounted lights burst into life, blinding even in the bright sunlight.

"Check your waldos," he said into the speaker that was on his front console.

The arms of the suits moved up and down. Kowalski managed to extend the middle finger of the left hand of her unit. She grinned broadly through the polycarbonate window of her suit at Rogers.

"Put them over," Phillips ordered. "We're burning daylight."

Three independently operated cranes lifted the heavy units up over the rail of the ship and lowered them straight down into the ocean.

"Once the units clear the bottom of the ship, they will be released to free-fall the rest of the way," Phillips explained to Scarpelli and Wu, who had come to watch.

For those inside the ADEUs, darkness fell early. The water turned to gray and then to charcoal. Looking up, Rogers could just see the light on the surface diminishing into the distance.

"Audio check," he said. "Can you hear me, Sue? Digger?"

"Loud and clear, boss," Kowalski said.

"You're coming through, Jake."

Every so often, he heard the whine of electric motors as the gyroscopes that kept his suit vertical spun up. The air processing equipment was completely silent. He wondered how cold his feet would get before the dive was finished. His crew had worn only sneakers on their feet to have a better feel for the waldos. He had warned Kowalski and Jones to put on two pairs of socks, and wondered if they had paid attention.

After ten minutes or so, a wall of blackness extended itself up in front of them at the extreme limit of their lights, darker even than the background charcoal gray of the water. It was something they felt more than saw.

"What the fuck is that?" Jones asked.

"That must be the side of the pit we're falling into," Kowalski said.

"We've got another five miles to go," Rogers said. "Might as well turn off our lights to save power."

In the sudden darkness Rogers turned his head to look for the others, and discovered that his suit automatically rotated itself on its gyros, following the direction of his gaze. He saw the faces of the others by the internal lights inside their suits, which caused their bubble windows to glow. As they fell facing each other, they maintained a separation of about ten yards. The units had been designed to descend at the same rate.

Every so often, something would flash past their suit windows. This part of the Pacific was a virtual underwater desert, with almost no life, plant or animal, but it was not completely lifeless. That could not be said of any part of the ocean. One of their missions was to record the life forms they encountered at the bottom of the pit they were falling into.

They didn't make much small talk. They were alert to what was going on around them and closely watched the gauges on the read-outs of their units. How the systems were functioning was of more than academic interest—it was a matter of life and death.

Finally, after forty minutes of free fall, Rogers felt the feet of his suit touch solid ground. He turned his ADEU to face away from the others.

"We're down," he said. "Switch your lights back on. Don't blind each other."

The three units lit up at almost the same moment, their powerful beams extending outward in different directions. The sight that greeted their eyes made Kowalski gasp. They found themselves standing in a kind of plaza. Massive buildings towered above them on all sides. They were windowless and extended up beyond the range of their lights. It was like standing in the middle of a submerged, deserted Manhattan. Broad streets radiated away from the plaza.

"We're lucky we didn't land on top of one of those buildings," Jones said.

"Wouldn't have mattered," Kowalski said. "All we'd need to do is step off the edge."

"Some of them aren't vertical. See the way they're leaning?"

The buildings reminded Rogers of the way giant selenite crystals grow inside caves. They angled in different directions, and their sides were not exactly parallel. Looking at them made him dizzy. He found it impossible to judge which buildings were vertical and which had a lean to them.

"Start taking pictures," he ordered. "We'll meet back here before we ascend."

They separated and went in three directions, moving along the streets with ponderous steps of their ADEUs.

"I've got a fallen pillar across my street," Kowalski said. "I'm going to try out my jet assist."

"Be careful that you—" Rogers started to say.

"Wheee! That was fun."

He heard Jones laughing.

"Let's not get cocky, people; it's dangerous down here."

He didn't know exactly what danger he feared, but he felt it as clearly as he had felt the wall of the pit rising above them. There was something here that was sleeping and it was not something they wanted to wake up. He told himself he was imagining things. When he checked the carbon-dioxide level in his blood, it was normal. The suit was doing its job. Now it was up to him to do the same.

"Man up, Rogers," he murmured with his suit mike off. "You don't get the luxury of being afraid."

He walked forward between the towering blocks of stone, which were too regular to be natural, but too enormous to be anything else. For some reason he couldn't tell if he was walking up or down a slope. The geometry of the city played with his perceptions.

His lights illuminated something embedded in the soft muck under the suit's boots that gleamed dull white. He bent down and picked it up with his left waldo, then held it in the light and turned it over. It was a skull, but not human. Or if it was, it was strangely deformed. The cranium was almost cone-shaped and more than twice as large as it had any right in nature to be.

Setting the skull carefully back where he had found it, he walked forward, looking around. Skulls were scattered all over the street, along with other bones. They poked up through the layer of mud, their large eye sockets staring at him. He wondered if they represented the race that had built this city. They seemed out of scale, somehow. The massive size of the buildings demanded larger inhabitants. Dutifully, he took a series of still pictures, then made a half-minute video clip of the skulls.

Sue Kowalski's voice crackled over his speaker. "Jake, I found something."

"What is it?"

"I don't know exactly. It's a series of boxes in rows. It almost looks like a graveyard of some kind, but the tombs are way too big for human beings."

"How big?"

"Elephant-size, at least."

"Can you open one?"

"I'll try. They've got some kind of lid on the top. I don't know if it's hinged, or if it slides to the side." He heard her grunting with effort. "No, my right-hand waldo can't shift it. We're going to have to force them open with pry bars."

"Leave it, then. Take pictures. Mark down the coordinates."

"Yes, boss."

The ground vibrated beneath his feet, and through the sides of his ADEU he heard a deep boom, like a distant explosion. After a few seconds it came again, and then again.

"What the fuck is that?" Kowalski asked.

"I don't know. Some kind of seismic activity."

"Is this city stable? I'd hate to have one of those buildings come crashing down on top of me."

"Nothing's shifted where I am. I think we're safe."

"There shouldn't be any earthquake or volcanic activity where we are, Jake."

"I know that. It should be geologically stable."

"I've got something," Jones broke in. His voice was raised with excitement.

"What have you got, Digger?"

"You won't believe me if I tell you. I'm going to have to show it to you."

"What do you mean? Everything's supposed to stay in situ. Just photograph it, tag it, and leave it where it is."

"Not on your life, Rogers. You wouldn't leave it, either. I'm bringing it up with me."

Rogers didn't try to argue the point. Jones was not a man who was intimidated by bluster or threats. The scar on his bald skull was the result of a wild night in a bar in Kingston during which Jones had sent four police officers to the hospital. If he had decided to bring something up, there was no way to stop him. Rogers looked at his clock.

"It's time to start back for the plaza," he said. "We don't want to cut into our security margin."

The other two didn't argue. He was waiting for them when their lights came into view between the towering building blocks. Jones had learned how to make his ADEU unit skip. He came skipping across the plaza like a school girl. Something gleamed in the left hand of his unit.

"What is that, Digger? What did you find?"

"I don't know what it is, but it's ugly, and it's made of solid gold, I think."

Rogers examined the small statuette in the light from his suit as Jones held it out. He was certainly right on the first count. It was the ugliest little figurine Rogers had ever seen. It squatted on its haunches, leaning forward with its clawed hands on its projecting knees. Its lower face was a mass of segmented tentacles or feelers of some kind. Clusters of tiny, insect-like eyes gleamed on the sides of its elongated head. The shape of its skull resembled the skulls Rogers had seen in the mud. On its back were folded wings that looked bat-like, for want of a better comparison.

"Is it gold?" Kowalski asked.

"It's yellow," Jones said. "It isn't tarnished, and it's heavy as hell. It must be gold."

"It could be gold," Rogers agreed. "We'll have to examine it back on the ship to know."

"This thing is worth a fortune," Jones said. "Not just for its gold content, but it must represent the god of the people who built this city."

"Could be," Rogers agreed. "Anyway, let's start back up. Controlled ascents, people—don't touch the red lever."

Kowalski laughed. "Moon would have a cow."

4.

The golden statuette sat in the middle of the dining table. It had been cleaned and dried, then weighed and measured. It weighed just under thirty-seven pounds and was eleven inches long in its largest dimension. Most of it was gold, but there were traces of platinum and silver in its alloy. It was the ugliest thing any of them had ever seen. There was something inexpressibly repellent in its octopoidal head and multiple insect eyes, although its body shape was roughly humanoid. Its skull resembled closely the shape of the skulls Rogers had photographed.

They stood around the table, admiring their discovery.

"Do you think it's the god of the city builders?" Jones asked Phillips.

"Some kind of god or devil. The natives of Easter Island speak of a god named Koulou who ruled an island kingdom called R'lyeh in the Before Times. They say it was fabulously rich in gold and had many human slaves, but the race that ruled over it was not human. They interbred with their slaves to make a race of servants that were stronger and wiser than human beings."

"What did these rulers look like?" Sue asked.

"They were shaped like their god, whom the islanders claim was taller than a mountain and able to control his slaves with the power of his mind alone. He lived in a gigantic castle on the top of a hill. Most of the time he was asleep and dreaming strange dreams of alien worlds, but when he was awake he was always angry, and made the ground shake."

"Sounds like a fairy story," Jones said.

"Of course it's a fairy story," Phillips said. "All myths are fairy stories. But some have kernels of truth hidden away inside them."

"Are we going to get a cut when they sell this thing?"

"Not a chance in hell, Digger."

"That's what I figured."

"You three better hit your bunks," Phillips told them. "You've got around five hours before Moon and his team surface."

"I wonder what they'll discover inside those stone sarcophagi," Kowalski said with a yawn.

"You'll find out when you wake up."

"You should get some sleep too, Captain," Rogers told him.

"I'll sleep when I know Team Two is safe back on board."

Rogers undressed, slid into his bunk, and was asleep almost immediately. He dreamed that he was back in his ADEU in the alien city, climbing a hill toward an enormous door. It was the largest door he had ever seen, a single impossibly massive slab of stone. On it was some kind of writing that he couldn't read. It was in the form of pictograms. Something spoke to him inside his mind, telling him how to open the door. It had something to do with the pictograms, which had to be pressed in a certain order. Rogers could not quite comprehend the message, and it kept repeating itself in his mind.

Suddenly he heard a thunderous boom against the slab of stone. After an interval this was repeated, then repeated again. The booms shook him like the blasts of a cannon, passing completely through his chest and making his heart skip. He realized with a mounting sense of horror that there was something on the other side of the door that wanted to get out. Somehow he could see the supernova through the intervening miles of water, shining high overhead, lighting everything with an eerie red glow. He realized that he must be dreaming and felt an urgent need to wake up. He could not move or even open his eyes.

He watched in mounting horror the great door slowly begin to swing upward from the bottom. A kind of monstrous hand extended itself through the widening gap and felt along the edge of the opening. The fingers terminated in great claws that were like the talons of a bird of prey. Something began to squeeze itself out from the darkness on the other side of the door. He wanted to run and hide from it, but instead he found that his ADEU was walking forward, carrying him with it against his will. He began to see what was in the shadow and emerging into the light, and a scream rose in his throat.

5.

Rogers came awake suddenly to find Jones shaking him by the shoulder.

"What's up?" he said. He wiped his hand over his face. It came away cold and wet.

"Team Two didn't surface when they were supposed to."

Rogers was on his feet before the other man finished speaking. "We need to get down there. They'll be running out of power."

"The suits are prepped and ready to drop."

"Let's go, then."

The descent was a nail-biting nightmare. When they finally reached the floor of the pit, Rogers tried the audio.

"Moon, do you copy? Ling Wu? Scarpelli? Do any of you hear me? If you can hear me but can't answer, try flashing your lights."

He turned in a complete circle with his shoulder lights off, scanning the darkness. Nothing.

"Fan out," he told Kowalski and Jones. "Give a shout if you find anything—anything at all."

He didn't say any more, but he didn't need to. All three knew that the most likely scenario was that everyone on Team Two was dead. Whatever problem had prevented them from surfacing had to be serious. There was a possibility that they were alive but unconscious. But why would all three ADEUs fail at the same time?

Kowalski's shout sent him striding toward her location. "What have you got?"

"They opened one of the sepulchers," she said. "The lid is off to the side on the ground. The box is empty."

"Any sign of any of the team?"

"Nothing."

For some reason the open tomb made him uneasy, but he could not have told why. It reminded him of something in his dream, but when he tried to remember the dream it slipped away. It wasn't as if anything could still have been alive inside the stone box after countless aeons beneath the ocean. Probably all the boxes were empty. There were thousands of them, maybe tens of thousands, stretching away as far as he could see to the limit of his lights. Who could know what their real purpose might have been?

The ground shook under his feet, and a moment later he heard a dull boom. This was followed by two more booms. It almost sounded like a giant fist hammering in slow motion on a locked door. Rogers snorted and shook his head. He had to focus on reality. He couldn't afford to let his imagination run away with him, not under these conditions, not with a team missing.

"I found one of them," Jones said in a dead voice.

"Where are you? Flash your lights."

He started to stride toward the faint flicker he saw reflecting against the side of one of the massive buildings, then cursed and hit his jet assist. The ADEU lifted off the sea floor and floated forward through the water in what amounted to a giant leap. He hit the assist two more times before he reached Jones, who was bent over something on the ground. With a sick sensation Rogers saw that it was an ADEU. Stenciled in white on its chest was the name "Scarpelli."

"Something smashed in his view window," Jones said.

"How? These windows are stronger than the steel armor."

"See for yourself."

Rogers leaned forward and was able to view the broken portal in the unit. It appeared to have been smashed inward by some great force. He whistled softly to himself. It would have taken the power of a battering ram. The suit was empty—there was no body inside.

"Whatever did it must have pulled him out through the hole."

"That hole doesn't look big enough to fit a body through."

"Not in one piece."

Again he heard the booms and felt their vibrations in his feet through the waldos of his ADEU.

"Find the other units," he said.

It took them three hours to locate the other ADEUs, which

were close together behind a fallen pillar. The bubble-ports of both suits were smashed in, and both were empty.

"Why am I thinking of cooked lobster?" Kowalski asked.

"I was thinking of peanuts in the shell," Jones admitted.

"Obviously something took them out of their ADEUs, after staving in the ports." Rogers told them. "Whether we find the bodies or not, they are all dead. That's certain."

"Captain Phillips isn't going to like this," Kowalski said.

"It's the end of the exploration of the city. We can't come down again without knowing what killed Team Two."

"Do you think it came out of the sepulcher?" Kowalski asked him.

"Right now I don't think anything. We don't have enough information to form conclusions."

"I'm thinking we should get the hell out of here," Jones muttered. "Whatever happened to them, it could happen to us."

"We'll keep looking for the bodies until our time is up," Rogers told him.

"Whatever you say, boss."

The booms came again, just three of them like the last time, but they sounded louder to Rogers.

"Whatever that is, it wants out," Jones said.

Rogers said nothing. He was thinking the same thing.

They were gathered in the center of the plaza in preparation for their ascent when they were attacked. The creature was roughly the size of an elephant, but glided through the dark water like a shark on its small black wings. When it flashed through Rogers' lights, its image was burned into his retinas. It was identical in appearance to the golden idol.

"Emergency ascent," he yelled. A split second later, the ADEUs of the other two shot upward as though fired from a gun. He pulled his own red lever. Nothing happened.

"Shit."

The monster closed its talons around the arms of his suit and drew it close. Its multiple insect eyes, so like the eyes of a spider, peered at him. The segmented tentacles on the lower part of its face gingerly felt over the ADEU's window. He tried to use the power of the suit to break free from its grip but the thing held it as if it were a child's doll. He wondered why it had not killed him? Was it curious about him? He hit his jet assist and the ADEU slipped out of the monster's claws for a moment. It quickly rose after him.

Something moved in the water behind the monster. Rogers recognized it in the lights of his suit, black against the blackness of the water. It was a giant squid, one of the few creatures of the ocean that could withstand the pressure at this depth. It was almost invisible. He saw it only by the way the light from his suit glistened at the edges of its long tentacles, so much longer than those of an octopus. Each of those questing tentacles was studded with hooks that were almost as hard as steel.

The winged monster did not sense its presence until it was too late. The squid touched the monster on the back between its wings, then swiftly flowed around it and wrapped it in its tentacles. The monster forgot about Rogers. It struggled in the tightening grasp of the squid but could not escape. The sinuous tentacles slid over its body like saw blades, and the water around Rogers turned a blue color. The blueness spread and obscured his vision, but not before he saw the monster come apart into several pieces.

As he watched in horrified fascination, a tentacle extended from the mass of bluish blood and touched the chest plate of his ADEU. It clung to the steel as though glued in place. He heard the suit groan in protest as the creature tugged at it in an experimental way. He suddenly realized it had not been the winged monster from the opened sepulchre that had killed the members of Team Two, but the squid. Only its tentacles had the power to pull their bodies through the small holes in their transparent domes.

Frantically he reset his emergency ascent lever. Saying a silent prayer, he slammed it down hard. The suit began to lift, but slowly. The weight of the great creature that clung to it was almost too much for the suit to overcome. Even so, the rate of ascent gradually increased. He watched the numbers unroll on his screen as the ADEU shot upward. The squid wrapped itself around the suit, and Rogers saw its giant eye staring in at him through the suit bubble. Close to it was the creature's beak, which was shaped like the beak of a parrot.

As they continued to rise with increasing velocity, the squid began to exhibit signs of discomfort. It squirmed around and squeezed the suit, making the metal groan where its pieces were joined. Rogers realized the deep sea creature did not like the rapid drop in pressure. Without warning it released the ADEU, which began to tumble in the water. The screaming gyros gradually leveled it out and brought it back upright. When the suit broke the surface of the sea, it flew into the air a dozen yards before splashing back down onto the waves, where it bobbed upright, the viewing dome above the water.

Rogers breathed a sigh of relief when he saw that the other two ADEUs had been lifted safely onto the *Courser*. Jones and Kowalski stood at the rail, watching him as a boat team attached cables to his suit, so that a crane could winch it up. Kowalski gave him a thumbs up. Then her expression changed. Something was happening. He tried to look around but the suit was half-suspended above the waves and he could not turn it. He saw the crew of the ship shout frantically to each other and run from the rail. The ship lurched, making his suit swing like a pendulum and bang against the hull.

All around him the sea began to boil. There was a deep rumbling that came from below, in the ocean. Steam rose and turned the world outside as white as milk. The ship lurched again and he was slammed so hard into its hull that his head rebounded from the side of the instrument cluster in his suit. He felt himself slipping into unconsciousness and tried to fight it, but a black well of oblivion rose up and engulfed him.

Rogers blinked and squinted. He took his right arm out of its waldo and used it to shield his eyes. Through the viewing dome the sun shone brightly. He realized his suit was lying on its back and wondered if he was on the deck of the *Courser*. How long had he been out? The sun was still high in the sky, so it could not have been too long. He tasted blood and realized he had bitten his own tongue when his head had struck the gauges at the side of the suit's bubble dome. He forced himself to relax and waiting for a crew member of the ship to open his suit.

When minutes passed and no one came to help him get out, he realized that something was wrong. The suit wasn't moving. Always on board a ship there is movement, even when the sea is calm as it was today. There was no motion beneath his back. He tried to remember the protocol Moon had run through for opening the suit alone, from the inside. After fiddling around in frustration, he managed to unlatch the entrance hatch and push the heavy steel plate aside. It clanged open against the suit. He crawled out through the opening, only then realizing that his entire body ached as though it had been beaten with clubs, in addition to a headache that pounded in the side of his head that had struck the panel.

What he saw made him forget his pain. The suit rested on a slope of smooth black rock that was covered in black slime. He stood swaying on unsteady legs and looked all around. Beside him lay the *Courser*, canted over onto its port side, high and dry. The cables that had been hoisting him onto its deck were still attached to his suit. They ran from the shoulders of the suit to a crane that thrust straight into the air from the rail of the ship, like the beak of gigantic dead bird.

He looked past the ship, and realized he was on the side of a mountain in the midst of what appeared to be a large island, to judge by what he could see of it. The lower slope of the mountain a considerable distance below him was covered with enormous stone buildings. With a sense of shock he recognized its slanting oblong blocks and angled corners as those of the undersea city his team had been exploring. Beyond the city stretched row upon row of stone boxes, tens of thousands of them. They looked tiny in the distance. Near the horizon he saw the thin blue line of the ocean.

Somehow the island had risen up through the depths. That seemed impossible, but he could not doubt his own senses. He felt the slime of the ocean floor under his sneakers as they slipped on it, a cooling breeze against his sweating face, and smelled all around him the dark scent of wet mud. Steam was rising at intervals from fissures in the rock. It gave the entire macabre scene a hellish appearance. In all that stretch of land there was not a single tree or bush, not even a blade of grass.

Using one of the steel cables attached to his suit as a climbing rope, he managed to work his way up the hull of the *Courser* and slide over its rail. He began to search the ship for survivors. In his heart he knew it was useless. He had survived only because he had been encased in the almost indestructible ADEU. Nobody else on the ship had been wearing a suit. He went through the cabins methodically, keeping his emotions suppressed. When he found the body of Kowalski wedged between the rail and a crane that had broken loose from its anchor bolts, he stood looking down at her in silence for several minutes. Her chest had been crushed—her face was not disfigured.

He pulled her loose and carried her body into her cabin, which was tilted on its side. Laying her gentle down, he covered her with a blanket from her bunk bed. He continued his search and located Captain Phillips on the bridge. The side of the older man's skull was crushed. Rogers left him where he lay. There was no one else on board. The others must have been washed overboard in the violence of the upheaval that had stranded the vessel so far from the water's edge.

He crawled his way over the walls into the galley and found a bottle of water in the fridge, still cold, then a chair.

He sat drinking the water, thinking about what he must do. Every instinct told him to get off this unnatural island as quickly as possible. He had seen no signs of any other life, but somehow he knew he was not alone. He needed a boat. The lifeboats attached to the rails of the ship would have been too heavy to move, even if they had been undamaged. He remembered seeing an emergency life raft stowed in one of the ships lockers. It inflated with compressed air automatically when a release was pulled.

He found it where he remembered it to be. The thing was awkward and heavy even in its compressed state. He could lift it, just barely. He knew he could not carry it very far, but he could drag it by attaching rope to it and pulling the rope. The slope of the ground was all downhill to the sea, and the slick mud, which had not yet had time to dry, would grease the thing along, making it easier to pull.

After he got the raft to the rail and tipped it over onto the ground, he found a backpack and filled it with food and water. The raft had a built-in homing beacon that would activate itself when the raft inflated. It might take a few days for the beacon to be detected, given the remoteness of his location, but he knew he had a good chance of survival. Foremost in his mind was the need to get off this island.

As he was preparing to climb over the rail, he remembered the golden idol. He hesitated, then with a curse, went back into the ship, found it where it had fallen, and shoved it into the backpack. If he ever managed to get off this island alive, at least he would have something to show the world he wasn't insane.

Rogers was fitting around his shoulder the loop of the drag rope he had attached to the inflatable raft and the backpack when he heard the booms. They came at measured intervals, as they had under the sea, but this time he heard them with his naked ears. They came down from the mountaintop. He stood listening until they stopped, then quickened his preparations. Whatever made the sound, he had no wish to meet it. He began to drag the raft and pack away from the ship. It was easier than he had imagined it would be. Hope lifted his spirits. It could not be more than a few miles to the edge of the ocean.

Something touched his brain. It was tangible, like fingers moving around inside his skull. The fingers probed, then dug deeper. He realized there must be thousands, maybe millions, of them. They began to squeeze. He cursed and threw down the drag rope.

"Get out of my head!"

COME TO ME, a voice said. It was so strong, so loud inside his skull, it made him stumble to one knee. He forced himself back onto his feet.

"Fuck you."

The voice did not repeat itself, but Rogers felt a kind of tugging at his brain. It began and did not stop, not even for an instant. For many minutes he resisted and defied it. He cursed and shook his fist at the mountain peak. He tried to pick up the drag rope, but somehow it seemed unimportant, and he couldn't find the will to loop it over his shoulder. He let it fall from his fingers.

Without meaning to, he found himself climbing the side of the mountain. There was a road cut into it which made this task easy—so much easier than dragging the raft to the sea, the voice whispered. The raft forgotten behind him, he climbed and climbed until he reached the crest of the mountain. Upon it were buildings that slanted and leaned at impossible angles. They reminded him of a tumbled pile of gigantic children's blocks. Rogers picked his way between them, dizzy with their shapes which his mind refused to comprehend.

In their midst, at the very summit of the mountain arose a stone monolith that stretched hundreds of feet into the sky. At its base stood a vast upright slab of stone set in the wall of a building. Rogers realized he had seen it before. It was the door in his nightmare. As large as the door to an aircraft hanger, or maybe larger, it towered above him, yet seemed to grow and shrink by turns as he considered it. He became unsure whether it was upright or set flat in the surface of the rock under his feet. On its surface were carved alien pictograms. The fingers in his brain told him to press certain of the symbols in a particular sequence. He used all his will to resist the command.

A boom like thunder knocked him off his feet. He clapped his hands over his ears, and when he took them away, they were wet with his blood. The sound had ruptured his eardrums. The boom was followed by a second, and a third, which he felt against his beating heart like blows from a fist as they passed through his chest. They came from the other side of that cyclopean door. He continued to sit on the rock, hands over his ears, eyelids squeezed tight together. A second series of three thunderous booms sounded, quicker this time, more demanding.

RELEASE ME! commanded the voice in his head.

Rogers opened his mouth and screamed. He screamed over and over, shaking his head from side to side in a futile effort to throw the voice out of his skull. After a while, he stopped screaming and let his hands fall from his ears. He stood and approached the door, which now seemed to tower over him like the looming face of a cliff. No longer resisting, he touched the pictograms in the order he had been shown.

At once the pressure left his brain. He blinked in surprise and backed away from the door. Once more his will was his own. He felt a single imperative—to run. A great cracking noise from the door made his turn and pause when he was several hundred yards away. It was beginning to move. Unable to help himself, Rogers watched in fascination. It open from the bottom, tilting outward and upward. As the gap widened, a hand slid under the edge of the door and grasped it, pushing upward. The hand spanned almost the full width of the door. It was rough and covered with bumps like the back of a toad, and from each finger curved a long black talon. Through the shadowed, widening crack he saw something vast and amorphous slide over itself in its eagerness to be free.

Rogers turned and ran. Many times he slipped in the mud and picked himself up to keep running down the slope of the mountain. Behind him he heard massive blocks of stone sliding and falling against each other. and felt the black rock of the island shake under his feet. He did not glance behind or stop running. His one purpose was to reach the raft and drag it into the ocean.

Something was happening on the slope below him. The boxes that so much resembled Egyptian sepulchers were opening, their stone lids sliding to the side and dropping away. From them arose creatures who were all of a shape similar to the thing that had grabbed Rogers' ADEU before the squid had torn it to pieces. They were enormous beings ,but looked as tiny as insects in the distance. Their bodies were flabby and somehow insubstantial, as though made of some gelatinous substance. Cluster of feelers hung from their faces below their beady spider-like eyes. They milled around as more and more of them left their tombs.

Suddenly, as if directed by a single will, they rose into the air and flew together like a flock of bats, swirling and rising in a column that contained tens of thousands of them, or perhaps hundreds of thousands. They flew toward Rogers but ignored him, passing over his head on their way to the mountaintop. In spite of his terror, Rogers could not resist an impulse of curiosity to look behind.

The thing that had emerged from the door stood upright, its flabby legs straddling the peak of the mountain. Its body must have been soft and jelly-like, because there was no possible way such a vast creature could have fitted itself through the doorway, in spite of the enormous size of the opening. It was a colossus. In appearance it resembled the individual members of the swarm of flying monsters that ascended toward it. Its body was thick and shapeless. Its arms, longer than its legs, ending on clawed paws. As he watched, it raised them above its massive domed head. The dense cluster of feelers hanging from its face spread wide like the legs of a spider, and from its mouth it let forth a kind of howl. In spite of his damaged eardrums, Rogers recognized it as a bellow of triumph.

The thing spread its membranous wings, which were broad and wide enough to cover a city with shadow. The

The dense cluster of feelers hanging from its face spread wide ...

swarm of lesser creatures flew around its head in a halo and began to circle it, their wings flashing with points of light in the reddish glow of the setting sun. They formed a kind of flying serpent that coiled around its vast body three times before extending itself upward into the clouds. There seemed no end to the swarm that continued to issue forth from the opening stone boxes on the plain below. A bolt of lightning flashed out of the clear sky around the monster's shoulders, and seconds later Rogers heard the thunder.

He tore himself away from this nightmare vision and continued down the slope until he reached the ship. Taking up the drag rope from where he had dropped it, he began to pull the life raft and pack behind him. It was not until after the fall of darkness that he reached the shoreline and managed to get the raft inflated. Working by moonlight, he climbed carefully into it, stowed away his provisions, and found the oars. He decided not to activate the homing beacon until he was out of sight of the island, for fear the signal might attract the swarm, or the towering thing that still stood in their midst, savoring its freedom. High in the starry night sky above his head, the red eye of the supernova glared down.

He rowed with a constant rhythm. He had taxed his body almost beyond its limits, but he was a fit man. He did not dare to pause or rest until the horror on the island passed below the horizon of the moonlit ocean. Then and only then, when he could see it no more, he turned on the homing beacon, lashed down his oars, stretched out his aching limbs, and slept.

YIG

Serpent Mound

1.

In an otherwise empty expanse of desert hills, a line of four hikers struggled up a rock ridge that was covered in loose stones. Their boots slid back at each step, raising a cloud of fine white dust that hung in the air around their bare legs. All wore packs on their shoulders. Both women had their long hair tied back in ponytails to keep it off their perspiring faces. One was blonde and the other dark. Both men were lean and fit; the muscles of their upper arms stretching the sleeves of their T-shirts and were sharply defined in their calves. They had the look of college athletes, and carried themselves with the confidence that only a life of uninterrupted prosperity instils in the young.

The blonde unslung her pack and took a bottle of water from it. She drank deeply before tucking it away.

"Better go easy on your water, Steph" one of the young men told her. "You have to make it last."

"Fuck you, Brian," she said without rancor. "I'm thirsty. We don't even know where we are."

"Exactly my point."

"Maybe if we backtrack, we can find the trail again," the dark-haired woman suggested.

"Where's your sense of adventure, Dee? I'm glad we're off the trail," the other man said. He stretched his arms behind his back with a lazy motion. "I never like following a trail."

"We could get lost, Chris," Brian told him, stressing the words as though speaking to a child. "This is the desert. It only takes a few hours to come down with heat stroke. This is dangerous."

Chris laughed and punched the other man in the shoulder. "Relax, amigo. We can't be more than a couple of hours away from the highway."

"Do you know where the highway is? Because I don't."

"If only we had some cell reception, we'd know where we are," Stephanie said. She took out her phone. "No bars. It's ridiculous. How can there be a place this close to the highway with no reception?"

"Shit, girl, don't say we've got no cell," Chris told her.

"Why?"

"Don't you watch horror movies? The minute someone says that, the monster comes."

"I hate horror movies, Booger, you know that."

He frowned at her. "I told you not to call me Booger. I don't like it."

"Oh, I'm sorry, Christopher. Did I hurt your feelings?"

Brian looked at Deedee, who rolled her brown eyes.

"Let's just hike on for another hour or so, than turn around," Brian said.

"It's so hot," Steph said. "It wasn't this hot when we started."

"That's because we started early in the morning," Chris said with a sarcastic edge in his voice. "This is the desert. Right Brian?"

"Right," Brian said without looking at the other man.

He wondered how he had allowed himself to be talked into hiking the Superstition Mountains with Chris and Steph. They couldn't go more than ten minutes without arguing with each other. How they managed to stay together as a couple was a frat-house mystery at Arizona State. Physically, they were made for each other. Steph was a cheerleader, and Chris was backup quarterback for the football team. Maybe they liked needling each other, he thought. They seemed to do it most when they had an audience.

"Let's keep following this ridge," Chris said. "The ground looks flatter down in that little valley."

Brian took a moment to admire the beauty of the desert. It might have been a scene of utter desolation, but recent rains had caused it to bloom with wild flowers. They grew around the bases of cacti as if planted there by a landscaper, and pushed up from cracks between boulders. He found himself trying to avoid stepping on them as he trailed after the other three.

They spent some time exploring the valley, through which ran a dry creek bed. High above their heads, birds with broad wings lazily circled in the cloudless blue sky. Brian caught Dee's eye and pointed up.

"You think they know something we don't?"

"I think we'd better get back to the highway."

"Yes, the truck," Steph said, overhearing the exchange. "Air conditioning, I could die for air conditioning right now."

"What do you think, Chris?" Brian said. "Time to head back?"

"What's your rush? Let's see what's down over here."

Brian shook his head and followed the other man. They spent twenty minutes clambering over boulders and poking around in the sand. Steph amused herself by picking wildflowers. When Brian was finally able to talk Chris into heading back, the sun hung low in the west.

"We better hurry if we want to get back before dark," Brian said.

"Don't worry, I know the way."

"Maybe if we follow this dry creek bed . . ." Dee said.

"I told you, I know the way. Follow me, minions."

Chris set off with confident strides between two hills. Dee looked at Brian, who shrugged.

"Wait for me, Booger, don't walk so fast. I've got sand in my boots," Steph complained.

Chris did not turn, but he raised his right hand with his middle finger extended.

"Oh that's really sweet, Booger," she said struggling to catch up.

Dee and Brian trailed some distance behind her.

"How does she put up with that asshole?" Dee murmured.

"Who else could stand her?" Brian said.

"I heard that," Steph said without turning.

They followed Chris for another hour before his strides became less confident. They found themselves moving more and more slowly, and pausing.

"Does this look familiar?" Chris asked.

"It all looks the same to me, Booger," Steph said.

Brian glanced down at a patch of loose dust. There were footprints leading across it. He made another print. It matched one of the prints in the dust. Chris was watching him.

"Fuck," Chris said.

"It's almost dark," Brian said quietly. "We're going to have to camp for the night."

"Are you crazy?" Steph said. "There are poisonous snakes out here."

"You're not afraid of snakes, are you, baby cakes?" Chris unsnapped the loop on the knife sheath at his waist and drew out a Bowie knife. Its fourteen-inch blade gleamed red in the dying sun. "Thelma and I will protect you."

"He named his knife?" Dee said.

Chris made a quick slashing motion through the air. "I hate snakes. I'll kill any snake we see."

"We don't need to kill them, we just need to avoid stepping on them," Brian pointed out.

"I always kill them. Every snake I've ever seen in my life, I've killed it."

"Very Rambo of you," Dee said.

"Rambo didn't kill snakes, except for food," Steph pointed out.

"We're supposed to kill them," Chris said earnestly, looking at each of them with his knife raised.

"How do you figure?" Brian asked.

"It's God's command in the Bible. Snakes are supposed to try to bite us on the heel, and we're supposed to grind them into the dirt."

"I don't think there's an actual biblical command that we have to kill them."

"It's in the Bible, somewhere in Genesis. Look it up."

"Sure, whatever. Let's find a good place to sleep," Brian said.

"Can we build a fire?" Steph asked nervously. "I've heard snakes come out at night."

"They're drawn to your body heat," Dee said.

"Shit. We need to make a fire, Booger."

He sheathed his knife and spread his hands. "Do you see any wood around here, Steph? Anything that will burn?"

She looked around. The long shadows of the cacti and shrubs painted themselves across the rocks. A lizard jumped onto a boulder with a quick motion, stared at them for a second, then was gone so fast they weren't sure where it had disappeared.

"We'll find an exposed ledge of rock that faces west," Chris said. "It will hold the heat of the sun for a while. We can lie back against it and huddle together for warmth."

"Are you crazy? It must be close to a hundred degrees," Steph said.

"It gets cold fast when the sun goes down," Brian told her in a quiet voice.

He took off his pack and opened it. He had started out with four bottles of water. Two were empty, the other two were full. They had stopped at a gas station just before beginning the hike, and with forethought he had made the others buy four bottles of water each.

"How much water have you got left?" he asked Dee.

She opened her pack. "A full one, and about half of one."

"Don't drink any more unless you really need to."

He looked across at Chris and Steph, who were tucking their packs against a rocky outcropping to act as pillows for the night.

"Are we in trouble, Brian?" Dee asked.

"I don't know."

He wanted to tell her something encouraging, but found himself repeating the words. "I don't know."

Darkness came on abruptly, and the sky exploded with stars. The moon had yet to rise, and the blackness was absolute. Brian held up his hand directly in front of his face and wiggled his fingers. He saw nothing.

"Look at that red star," Steph said as she snuggled closer against her boyfriend's side. "Isn't that pretty?"

A single red star, much brighter than any of the others, shone down on them like a baneful, bloodshot eye.

"It's bigger than it was last night," Dee said.

"It probably just looks that way because it's so dark out here in the desert," Brian suggested.

"No, I heard on the television that it keeps getting brighter. Scientists don't know why. They say that supernovas usually fade away after a few weeks."

"Did they name it yet?"

"I don't think so. If they did, I haven't heard."

They lay looking up at the supernova, hugging each other for warmth, until sleep took them.

"Look what I've got."

The words woke Brian from a troubled sleep. He opened his eyes and saw that it was early morning. The sun was just beginning to paint the crests of the hills with an orange glow. Chris stood a few yards away, holding something in his hand that undulated and wriggled. It struck toward his side and he extended his arm to keep it away, laughing with excitement. Brian realized it was a rattlesnake that he held by the tail.

"Are you crazy?" Steph yelled. She rubbed her eyes with her knuckles and blinked to clear them.

"Throw it away, Chris," Dee said, huddling back against the rock ledge.

"Watch this. I bet none of you has ever seen anything like this in your life."

He repositioned his hand on the tail of the snake, and the sound of its rattle was clearly audible in the still air. With a quick motion of his arm, as though cracking a bullwhip, he flipped the snake. It suddenly curled up and began to bite itself, then after a few seconds, went limp.

"What happened to it?" Dee asked.

"I broke its neck. It's what I learned to do to snakes when I was a kid. I used to hunt them and kill them all the time."

"You could have been bitten," Brian said.

"Naw, not if you know how to handle them. People think snakes are fast because of the way they strike, but the truth is, they have slow reflexes. That's how a mongoose can kill a cobra every time."

He pulled out his Bowie knife and struck off the head of the snake with a practiced motion. "Breakfast, anyone?"

Steph and Dee both make sounds of disgust in their throats and turned their faces away. Chris laughed at them. Flipping the body of the snake around, he cut off the rattle and shook it. He extended it to Steph.

"This is for you, baby."

"Get that thing away from my face, Booger. Get it away."

He laughed again and threw the body of the snake between some rocks. The bloody rattle he put into his pocket.

"I collect them," he told Brian. "I've got over a hundred."

"Shit, Chris, you're a regular snake terminator," Dee said.

He did not seem displeased by the reference.

"We better start back for the truck while it's still cool," Brian said.

"Yeah, I guess. I'm out of water. We don't want to spend too many hours wandering around out here."

They slung their packs onto their shoulders and followed him.

Why the fuck are we following him? Brian thought as he marched along. *He doesn't know where he's going any more than I do, yet we are all following him, and nobody is following me. What is up with that, anyway?*

For a while he pondered to himself that mysterious human quality that is leadership, which Chris possessed and he lacked. It had nothing to do with intelligence, or even with being right. No one ever seemed to follow his lead. Even as a boy, whenever he had suggested some activity to the other school kids, he had ended up doing something else along with the rest of them. Eventually he had come to realize that no one ever did what he wanted them to do, and had stopped trying to be a leader.

Around noon they came to a small plateau between ranges of hills. Brian wasn't sure if they'd walked there before or not—everything was starting to look the same to him.

"Hey, babe, give me a sip of water," Chris said to Steph.

"Drink your own water."

"It's all gone, babe, I already told you that."

Reluctantly, she passed over a clear plastic bottle that was less than half full. "Don't drink it all. That's all there is."

Brian and Dee glanced at each other, but said nothing.

"Look at this," Chris said, pointing at a low ridge of earth that was covered in new green brush and wildflowers.

Brian glanced at it but saw nothing special about it.

"We're too low to the ground," Chris said. He pointed at a slope of rock. "You'll see it better from up there."

Reluctantly he followed Chris up the side of a hill. His legs ached and he was tired of climbing. When they reached the crest, Chris turned and pointed down. At first Brian saw nothing. When finally he perceived the shape of the ground, it jumped up at him and he could see nothing else.

"It's an Indian serpent mound," he said wonderingly.

"It looks just like a snake," Chris said. "Look, that round part is the head, and that spiral is the tail." He raised his voice. "Steph, come up and look at what I found."

The women glanced at each other. Steph shook her head and shrugged. They climbed the hill wearily and stood beside the men.

"It's beautiful," Dee said.

"I bet we're the first to discover it," Chris said with excitement.

"You would never notice it if it wasn't covered with plants and flowers," she pointed out.

"I've got to tell the anthropology department about this. Maybe they'll name it after me."

"Snake Mound Booger," Steph said. She giggled and dodged his hand when he tried to swat her.

"How old do you think it is?" she asked Brian.

"No way to tell," he said. "I once heard that the giant serpent mound up in Ohio may be more than two thousand years old. But they really don't know its age because nothing was ever buried inside it."

"I wonder why a bunch of savages would make something like this?" Chris said. "I mean, look at it. That's a lot of work, a lot of man-hours of labor, you know what I mean? What's the point?"

"The Indians worshipped some kind of serpent god," Brian said. "The tribes of the Great Plains called it Yig, but it probably had a different name here."

"That means they worshipped the Devil," Chris said. "In the Bible, the serpent is Satan."

"It's funny how all the peoples of the Americas worshipped the serpent," Brian went on. "They had different names and different myths, but they all worshipped a snake god."

"It was a natural response to the landscape," Dee said.

"What do you mean?"

"Think about it. What is a river? It's a serpent of water, right? What is a road? It's a serpent of dirt. No path ever ran straight between these hills. Everything in Nature undulates. When a volcano erupts, it sends out serpents of fire across the ground."

"That's water, earth and fire," Brian said with a smile. "What about air?"

"That's easy," she said. "A tornado is a serpent of the air."

"Shit, that's really deep, Dee," Steph said. "No, I mean it. You should change your major."

"Look, down there," Chris said, pointing.

Brian glanced toward the head of the serpent mound and glimpsed a flash of bright color. It was like the iridescent colors you see in the tail of a peacock, but it was gone before he could really look at it.

"What was that?"

"I don't know, but it was wicked quick."

They went down the hill to explore the serpent mound. Chris said they should start digging into the head, but none of the others had the energy to even pretend to agree, and no one carried a camp shovel, so he dropped the idea.

It was Stephanie who found the entrance to the cave. She had wandered to a rock where she could sit and empty her hiking boots of sand when she noticed a deep shadow against the side of a hill. When she put her boot back on and went over, she saw that it was an opening.

"Look at this, guys," she called out.

They stood studying it.

"How deep do you think it goes?" Brian said.

"Could be deep," Chris said. "The opening is small, but that doesn't mean anything. Some of the biggest caves in the world have tiny openings you can barely squeeze through. I used to explore caves when I was in high school."

"The head of the serpent mound is pointed right at it," Dee said. "Do you think that means anything?"

"We won't know until we look," Chris told her with a broad grin.

"No," Steph said. "You've got to be kidding, Booger. It's probably full of snakes."

"I'll go first. Give me your flashlight, Brian. We're lucky you brought that along."

Brian started to say that luck had nothing to do with it, that when he went on a hike he always went prepared, but he bit his lip and handed the flashlight over.

"Maybe we'll find water in there," Chris said.

He took off his backpack and dropped it. The cave mouth was too small to crawl into with the pack on his shoulders.

"I'll yell and let you know when it's safe."

"Be careful," Brian said. "That thing we saw may be in there."

"I've got Thelma," Chris called back cheerfully.

They waited, listening to the scratch of the toes of his boots against the rocks until the sound diminished to silence.

"Booger?" Steph called into the hole. "Booger? Are you all right?"

"Come on in," his voice echoed back faintly. "You aren't going to believe this."

They slid their packs off their shoulders. Steph went first, followed by Dee. Brian took the rear. They had to feel their way. The women got out their cell phones and used them as makeshift flashlights, but their screens didn't cast much light.

"Watch your heads," Brian said. "You don't want to bash your brains out on a rock."

As they progressed, the cave became wider. It even acquired a kind of floor that had been created over millennia by bat droppings and detritus that the wind had blown in. The dust choked Brian's throat and made it spasm. He coughed, wondering how unhealthy bat dung might be to breathe.

What was a cave, he thought to himself, other than a serpent under the ground? It was a kind of negative serpent in the sense that it was hollow, its shape defined by its void. Dee had named the serpents of the four elements of Nature. Now they were crawling through a fifth serpent, having entered by its mouth. What would they find inside its belly?

They saw the reflections of the flashlight beam ahead and went forward more confidently. The cave opened into a cavern tall enough to stand up in without ducking. The roof had a natural vaulted shape. The far end of the cavern narrowed and continued deeper into the hill. From a hanging stalactite dripped water into a bowl-shaped depression in the rock. The basin looked like it was covered in white wax, but Brian realized it must be stone, deposited over thousands of years by the constant drip.

"I tasted it," Chris said. "It's good. A little chalky, but I think we can drink it."

Steph went to the basin and filled her cupped hands with water. She brought them to her lips and drank.

"I don't think that's a good idea," Brian said. "There could be arsenic in it, or lead, or anything." No one was listening to him.

The walls of the cavern were covered with paintings in black charcoal and red earth pigment. Some depicted animals, others human beings. The paintings of humans had strangely elongated skulls.

"Look at this." Steph bent to pick up a half-buried skull from the dirt on the cave floor and shook the dust off. It was shaped like the heads of the humanoid figures in the wall paintings. There was a jagged hole in its crown.

"Whoever these Indians were, they must have been deformed," Chris said. He took the skull from Steph. "This one had his head bashed in."

"It was Colonel Mustard, in the library, with a candlestick," Steph said, giggling.

"This place is amazing," Dee said, wandering around. She stopped suddenly. "Come over here, Brian."

She was pointing the light from her cell phone at a kind of table of stone that rose from the floor of the cavern. Into its flat surface a coiled serpent had been carved. The detail was amazing. Every scale was visible, and the eyes seemed almost alive. In the center of the coil lay a pair of large eggs that were about the size of pineapples. They flashed with rainbow hues as the light from her cell phone played across them.

"Are they real eggs?" Steph asked, coming over to look. She reached out and touched one of the shells. "They look real."

"They must be made of some kind of ceramic," Brian said. "No real egg ever had colors like that. Besides, they're as big as ostrich eggs."

"We need to take them back with us," Chris said. "I bet they're worth a lot."

"We shouldn't touch or move anything," Dee told him.

"This is an important archaeological site."

"I found it," Chris said. "I say we can take what we like."

Brian felt a wave of dizziness pass through his head. For an instant his vision doubled, then came clear. He wondered if he was having an allergic reaction to the dust.

"We should leave everything as it is and get out of here. We still need to find our way back to the truck."

"Babe, go out and drag our packs in here. We'll fill the empty bottles with this water, and we'll stuff an egg into each pack."

She nodded and ducked her head into the opening from which they had emerged.

"I'll come out with you," Dee said. "This place gives me the creeps."

Chris glanced at Brian. "You and Dee can take some of the bones, if you want them."

"I don't think you guys should drink that water," Brian said. "We don't know what's in it."

"Easy for you to say," Chris said. "You've still got water. Steph and I are out."

"We all started with four bottles."

Chris didn't answer.

A distant cry echoed from the walls of the cavern. It was impossible to tell if it came from the opening that led to the outside, or the opening that led deeper into the hill. The two stood holding their breath, listening. It was not repeated.

"What the ever-loving fuck was that?" Chris said in a low voice.

"It didn't sound human," Brian said.

"It was probably just the wind," Chris said, relaxing. "The wind does funny things in caves. Sometimes you can almost hear it talking to you."

Brian rubbed his eyelids and shook his head. He had to hold onto the wall of the cavern until the dizziness passed.

"I have to get out of here," he told Chris. "I don't think the dust we kicked up from the floor is good for me."

Chris didn't answer. He had one of the rainbow eggs in his hands, and was turning it and caressing it in the beam of the flashlight. Brian shrugged and bent to crawl into the dark opening that led to the outside.

Carrying the egg to the basin of milky water, Chris dipped his fingers in and used the water to wash its smooth surface clean of dust. He returned it to the serpent coil, then carried the other egg to the basin and washed it in the same way. It vibrated between his hands. He pressed his ear against it, and his expression changed. He turned to say something to Brian, but his friend was already out of sight.

Brian emerged into the bright sunlight. He blinked and squinted around.

"Where's Steph?"

"Answering the call of nature," Dee said from the rock she was sitting on.

Brian sat beside her, breathing deeply with his hands on his knees and his head bent forward until his dizziness went away. Minutes passed.

"She's taking a long time," he said.

"Constipation," Dee said. "Lack of water will do that, especially to us girls."

He pushed himself to his feet and picked up Steph and Chris' packs by their straps.

"I might as well take these into the cavern so that Booger can fill them up."

Dee watched him with concern. "Maybe you shouldn't go back in there. You don't look so great."

"I'm all right. I'll only be inside for a couple of minutes. You coming?"

"I'm going to look for Steph," she said. "She should be back by now."

"Watch where you put your feet. Snakes, remember?"

He pushed the two packs in front of him as he crawled into the low opening.

A feeling of unease prickled between his shoulders. Pausing, he turned to look out of the mouth at the sunlit brightness of the desert. Dee was already out of sight between the hills. It was a feeling of being watched. He scanned the rocky crests and the shadows that lay between them, but saw no movement. Even so, the unease remained with him as he continued deeper into the cave.

The cavern was dark and empty. Brian dug out his cell phone and shined the light from its screen around. It cast weird, dancing shadows over the painted walls. He stopped moving the light abruptly when it fell upon the stone table with its carved serpent coil. One of the iridescent eggs was broken open. The two pieces of shell were empty.

"That clumsy son of a bitch must have dropped it," he murmured to himself.

There was only one place Chris could have gone. Brian cupped his hands to his mouth and leaned into the second opening in the back wall of the cavern.

"Chris! Can you hear me?" His voice echoed faintly, but there was no response.

Something clinked against the toe of his hiking boot. He bent and picked it up. By the glow from his phone screen he saw that it was his flashlight. Sliding the phone into his pocket, he turned on the flashlight and shined it into the opening, then began to yell Chris's name. After a while, he stopped.

Why would Chris have gone exploring deeper into the cave without the flashlight? It didn't make sense. Had he dropped the flashlight and then become disoriented in the darkness? If that were the case, he would have used the light from his phone to guide him. Unless his phone was out of power. Maybe he had crawled into the second opening thinking it was the one that led to the outside.

Brian stood wondering whether he should search deeper into the cave. A wave of dizziness decided for him. He had to get out of the cavern before he fainted. Chris would find his own way out in time, he reasoned. He was an experienced caver; he must know what he was doing. Brian decided to wait for him outside with the two women.

When he emerged from the cave, there was no one waiting. The stone eyes in the head of the serpent mound seemed to mock him. He called the names of the women, then walked through the surrounding hills, still calling them until his throat became hoarse and dry. Returning to the mound, he took a bottle from his pack and drank deeply, then squinted at the sun. It was past the zenith.

He considered his options. He could wait here for Dee and Steph to return, or for Chris to emerge from the cave. There was no telling when, or even if, either of those things was going to happen. He could search through the hills for the women and maybe get himself hopelessly lost as night came on. He could go back into the cave and try to find Chris, who might be lying unconscious with a cracked skull or a broken ankle, and then try to drag him out. Or he could leave most of the water for the women in case they returned, and strike out on his own across the desert to try to find his way back to Chris's truck, so that he could drive to the gas station for help.

Brian knew he had to do something. He couldn't just sit there waiting. None of the others had water. Whichever course of action he chose, it had to be the right one, because he would be forced to live with that decision for the rest of his life. He toyed with the idea of taking all the remaining water and trying to walk out of the desert. The water would give him a good chance of finding the highway. If the others returned, they would have the milky water in the cavern. Even if it did contain poison, it would keep them from dying of thirst. The open sun could kill a person without water in only a few hours.

In the end, he took a long pull on the water bottle, slid it back into his pack, and crawled into the cave.

The smell of the dust hit him almost immediately, making him dizzy and sickening him. The cavern was as he had left it, empty. He took a tighter grip on his flashlight and went forward into the dark mouth of the opening in its back wall. The plastic and aluminum flashlight felt light in his hand. He found himself wishing that he had a knife, or almost anything else to use as a weapon. There weren't even any loose rocks in the passage.

The cave descended ever deeper into the hillside, widening as it went. He could feel the slope with his feet. The ceiling was high enough that he seldom had to duck his head. In places it dripped with water, and small pools that had collected between slabs of stone reflected the flashlight beam like mirrors. From time to time, the single passage branched into side channels. It was little wonder Chris became lost without the flashlight, Brian thought. Whenever he encountered one of these branch passages, he left a silver coin on the ground to indicate the way he had come.

There was no trace of Chris, not even footprints. Brian knew in his heart the other man would never have come so deep unless he was lost. He stopped to bend over and cough, then held onto the side of the passage until the dizziness passed. Nausea became a constant companion. Even after he threw up, it did not go away. Still he kept on, pressing ever deeper into the bowels of this hollow stone serpent.

An eerie cry cut the stillness, long and drawn out, similar to the cry he had heard before in the cavern but this time much louder. It was not the cry of a bird or a coyote, of that he felt sure. He found it impossible to characterize, but he knew there was no way it came from a human throat. He blinked hard to clear his vision, which tended to double up unless he concentrated. The air was not good for him. How long he could tolerate it before it overcame him he did not even want to guess. At intervals he cupped both hands around his mouth and shouted Chris's name until his throat burned with fire.

When do I quit? he asked himself. *When do I admit this is futile?* How many minutes of this torture was his friendship for the quarterback worth? Had Chris ever really even been a true friend to him? He remembered all the times Chris had treated him like shit and taken him for granted. It would be so easy to just turn around and go back the way he had come. He could take all the water and make a try for the highway. In spite of these thoughts, he pressed deeper.

His flashlight beam wandered over the rocks and down a side tunnel. At the extremity of its reach he saw a flicker of bright colors. It was as if a bird of paradise had flown past. He remembered the similar flash of color he had seen near the cave entrance. Undecided, he looked into the new opening, then back the way he had come. He took a deep breath, dropped a dime onto the floor of the cave, and went into the side passage.

It twisted and wound like the belly of a snake and began to narrow. He found himself forced to duck his head, then walk at a crouch, then finally to crawl on hands and knees with the flashlight between his teeth. Just as he thought the passage was getting too tight to follow any further, it widened into an enormous open space.

He stood up and stretched his back, then shined the light around. The echoes of his footfalls on the stone floor gave him some sense of the vastness of the cavern, but the beam of his flashlight would not reach far enough up to illuminate its ceiling. Going cautiously forward over the unnaturally flat floor, he came upon buildings made from large blocks of cut stone, and realized with wonder that he was in some kind of subterranean city. There was no sound but the sound of his own steps. In the dust of the streets, lying up against the walls of the buildings, were bones and elongated skulls similar to the skull Steph had found in the small cavern. This was a city of the dead. He wondered what cataclysmic event had killed all its inhabitants so quickly there had not even been time to gather up the corpses?

At the end of a narrow street he came upon a building of black stone with a round, open doorway. A soft rustling came from the darkness within. The hairs on his neck crawled up the back of his head. The sound was of something dry sliding over the dusty stones.

He forced himself to turn the beam of the flashlight through the doorway and entered. The interior space was large with a ceiling so high, the flashlight would not show it. It felt like some kind of temple or church, although he could not have explained what gave him this impression. At the far end of the room something moved on the floor, and he heard a soft hissing. He gathered the threads of his courage and advanced, but was unprepared for what the flashlight revealed.

The thing on the floor turned its pale face toward him, and he recognized Chris. The other man lay naked on his stomach. Scratches covered his bare skin, which was strangely mottled with dark and light patches. He held his arms at his sides, and while Brian watched with concern he undulated his body across the paving stones.

"Chris, what's wrong?" He stepped forward.

Something else moved in the darkness. He shifted the flashlight beam and recognized Steph's long blonde ponytail. She lay beside Chris with her face turned away. She was also naked. One of her legs was covered in blood. He called her name, and she rolled slowly over and stared at him with wide, uncomprehending eyes that were void of humanity.

As he watched, the thing that had been Chris slid toward the blonde woman on its belly and nuzzled its bloody face into the wound on her thigh. Its throat began to move, and with a sick feeling Brian realized that it was drinking her blood. She shivered but did not resist. The horror of the sight made Brian stagger, but he caught himself with a hand against the floor and pushed himself back up on trembling knees. He took another step forward.

The thing raised its head and hissed a warning at him. Something moved in its open, blood-filled mouth. At first Brian thought it was a tongue, but as it extended itself further out, he realized it was some kind of brightly-colored snake five or six feet in length, covered with what appeared to be small feathers instead of scales. Its wedge-shaped head resembled that of a rattlesnake. For an instant it paused and stared at Brian with glittering eyes. Then it sent its slender body sliding up over Steph's stomach. She did not appear to notice its presence. The feathered serpent fixed its fangs into the whiteness of her left breast, and

It undulated its body until it was between them and the door.

Brian saw its throat work rhythmically. He realized it must be sucking her blood.

Something else moved in the darkness. He took a trembling step, then another. The beam of his flashlight lit Dee's face. She blinked slowly and looked from side to side, propping herself up on her arm. Brian saw that she was still clothed, and for some reason this caused a flood of relief to wash through his heart.

"Dee."

"Brian? What happened? Did I fall down?"

He worked his way with care around the serpent, which still had its fangs locked in Steph's breast. Her face remained blank, as did Chris's face, and with a part of his mind Brian realized they must both be drugged by the serpent's venom. He helped Dee to her feet. She staggered and almost fell but he grabbed her arm.

"My head hurts," she said.

"We need to get out of here, right now," he told her.

He started to guide her around the interlocked forms on the floor and toward the open doorway. The feathered serpent released Steph's neck and lifted its head. It undulated its body until it was between them and the door. A drawn-out, eerie cry came from its throat. After a moment, it was answered by a similar but deeper cry from somewhere else in the city.

"Dee, can you walk?"

"I think so," she said in a weak voice.

Releasing her, he sent the beam of the flashlight bouncing off the walls and floor as he searched for some kind of weapon to use against it. There was nothing. The snake slid closer. He swallowed his fear and pushed Dee behind him.

The snake reared its head and hissed, opening wide its mouth to show its fangs. With a lunge forward he grabbed it by the tail. The creature's weight surprised him. Its slender body was all muscle.

Jerking it straight to keep its head from turning to bite him, he tried to snap it the way he had seen Chris snap the rattlesnake. The snake resisted the motion and continued trying to set its fangs into his arm, so that he was forced to shake it out repeatedly to keep the head at bay. Finally it began to tire, and its body drooped limp with fatigue. He snapped it hard like a bullwhip and felt something break at the other end. It twisted and let out a kind of shriek, then hung motionless. When he trained the flashlight on it, he saw that it was dead.

From high above his head there came a scream of pure rage. He heard the beat of enormous wings in the darkness, and realized for the first time that the building he was in had no roof. Built inside a cavern where it never rained, why would it need one? Grabbing Dee by the wrist, he jerked her toward the round doorway. She wrapped her arms around him to keep from falling.

"We need to get away. It's coming for us," he said.

"What is it?"

"Something that flies. Did you ever hear of Quetzalcoatl, the flying feathered serpent worshipped by the Aztecs? I think Quetzalcoatl and Yig are the same thing. I think maybe it laid those eggs, and Chris broke one open."

His words meant nothing to her.

"Where are Chris and Steph?" she asked. Her anxious face was nightmarish in the upturned beam of the flashlight. "Are they dead?"

He realized she had been too out of it to see them lying on the floor at her feet in the dancing beam of the flashlight while he had been killing the serpent.

"No, they're not dead," he told her gently. "But we have to get out of here right now."

The sound of wings descended from above. With a curse of frustration he tried to push her toward the doorway. She tripped, and her hand tore away from his.

"My ankle," she said in agony.

The air above his head filled with the beat of enormous wings. At the last instant he turned the flashlight upward and saw a rainbow of colors falling upon him. In their midst were dagger-like talons and glaring red eyes.

5.

He came to a kind of awareness slowly. Darkness still surrounded him, comforting him like a black velvet blanket. He realized in a dim way that he was lying on cold stone. The flashlight was no longer in his hand. He rolled against a warm body, and his face pressed into her hair. He recognized the familiar scent of Dee's shampoo. Trying to speak her name, he found that he could not form words. What came out was only a kind of hiss.

"Brian? Are you there?" she said in a weak voice. "What's happening?"

He felt a sudden urge to vomit. Something undulated from between his parted lips, then slid across his bare skin toward Dee. It felt smooth and soft. He heard her cry out when it struck at her, then heard the creature sucking her blood.

Dimly, he remembered the other multicolored egg that had rested in the coils of the stone serpent. He tried to raise his hand to tear the vampirish thing away from her, but his arm would not move. All he could do was slither. The sound of the creature sucking her blood triggered an intense thirst within him that overpowered his thoughts. He nuzzled his face into Dee's bare side. Biting into her soft flesh and tearing her skin open with his teeth, he began to suck.

YOG-SOTHOTH

The Knot

1.

The weekly seminar consisted of internationally famed academic Professor Charles Hinckley, and five very bright and eager graduate students intent on displaying their intelligence in the most advantageous way possible. The subject, philosophy; the topics, unconventional and chosen to spark creative original thinking.

Hinckley's hands were folded into a tight ball of fingers on the conference table. He was a little man. His hunched shoulders only half-filled his brown tweed jacket, which was wrinkled as a result, and a disordered pile of greying hair tangled itself like a rain cloud on the top of his head.

"What can we say about the portal?" he asked with a disarming smile.

"Which portal?" George Deeping asked. He played football and had the build of an athlete.

Always forthright, Hinckley thought. *Ever the materialist, that boy.*

"Any portal. Any doorway. Any gate. What can we say about it that is universal?"

"You pass through it," Patricia Sims said.

Pretty girl in a brittle sort of way, Hinckley thought. *Short hair doesn't suit her. A pity she only likes other women.*

"Yes. What else?"

"It leads from outside to inside," the eager exchange student from Uganda, Kinto Klee offered. His accent was British.

"And?" Hinckley said.

"From inside to outside," Klee added.

Why are exchange students from Africa always so keen? Hinckley thought. *They try so hard, it's almost painful.*

"It has a threshold that you must step over," Godfrey Goddard volunteered with his habitual clipped precision.

The best mind at the table, Hinckley thought. *But a prig.*

"What about that threshold? Think about the threshold."

"What about it?" Deeping asked. "It's usually made of wood. You step over it when you transition from outside to inside, or vice versa."

Hinckley fixed his penetrating gray gaze on the boy. "But is it actually there?"

"I guess it is," he said with a nervous laugh. "I've tripped on enough of them after keg parties."

"Professor means to suggest that the threshold is really just an abstract concept," said Monique Legrand.

That girl has such a delightful accent, Hinckley thought. *Pure Parisian French.*

"Very good, Monique," he said.

"Well, if it comes to that, all portals are abstractions," Sims pointed out. "The actual thresholds and jambs and lintels and whatnot are only there to represent their abstract equivalents."

"You mean like Plato's ideal forms," Goddard said.

"What else can you say about the portal?" Hinckley urged, ignoring Goddard's comment, which was too self-evident to require a response. "Come on, people; you've barely broken the surface."

They stared at him in silence, thinking.

"Well, if we're talking abstractions," Goddard said, "then it has no thickness."

"Explain."

The skinny young man pushed his wire-rimmed glasses back up his long nose with the tip of his index finger. "I mean, it doesn't really exist, does it? A portal is the transition between one place and another, and as such it has no thickness."

"Expand."

"You're never actually in the portal," he said. "You pass into it and out of it, but you're never actually in it because it doesn't really exist."

"Very good," Hinckley said. "Now apply that thinking to time. What can you say about the present moment?"

"It has no duration," Klee offered.

"It is the transition between past and future, and does not exist," Goddard said.

"It's a portal," Deeping said with sudden insight. He looked sheepish when Sims and Klee laughed, but Legrand smiled at him encouragingly.

"Yes, exactly, Mr. Deeping."

"But aren't we all supposed to be living in the present moment?" Deeping said.

"So the Buddhists tell us," Hinckley said. "But given what we have deduced about the portal, what would your response to them be?"

Deeping frowned in thought, which caused his sandy brush cut to move forward. "I guess I'd say we can't be living in the present moment because the present has no existence—no thickness or duration. We pass through it on our way from the past to the future, but we are never really in it."

"Time does not exist," Legrand said suddenly.

"Explain."

"If the past is gone and done, it has no existence," she said carefully, thinking as she spoke. "And if the future is not here yet, it has no existence either. That leaves only the present, but if the present is an infinitely thin interface between the past and future, it can't have any existence either."

"That's ridiculous," Klee said. "We are living in time. Look at my wristwatch." He drew back the sleeve of his white turtleneck to expose his left wrist. On it was a stainless-steel Rolex.

"Let's go back to the portal," Hinckley said. "We've deduced that it is a transition between two places. Outside and inside, for example. What are some of its characteristics?"

"It has a boundary—a line that runs all the way around it, I mean, like a circle," Sims offered.

"Like a circle, yes," Hinckley said, his deeply-creased face beaming. "Very good, Patricia, very good."

"A hole is a portal," Deeping said.

"Correct. More, people; give me more."

"I don't know if it's intrinsic to its definition," Klee said slowly, "but portals in the physical world have doors that can be closed and locked."

"What do the rest of you think?" the professor asked.

"I don't think a door, or closure, is a part of the basic abstract description of a portal," Legrand said with hesitation in her delightful accent. "They are two separate things, *n'est-ce pas?* Just as a door and a lock are two separate things, even though doors usually have locks."

"Can we say that a portal is always open for as long as it exists, but that it can be obstructed by a door or gate that may be locked or unlocked?" Klee asked.

"What would be the consequence of a door on a portal?"

"You couldn't just pass through it," Deeping said. "You'd need to open the door first."

"If the door were closed, wouldn't the portal cease to exist?" Goddard said.

"But it would come into being again when the door was opened," Sims said.

"And if the door were locked?"

"You'd need to unlock it before you could open it."

"And for that you would need—?"

"A key," several students said simultaneously.

"The only purpose for a door is to obstruct passage through a portal," Goddard said. "Without a lock, a door has no meaning."

"And yet the interior doors of houses often have no locks," Hinckley pointed out. "Why, then, do they exist?"

"Privacy," Deeping said. "You close a bathroom door so that no one can see into the bathroom when you take a shower, or do other things."

Sims giggled.

Hinckley ignored it. "So a portal can be looked through, like a window."

"That's right."

"Tell me how a window differs from a doorway."

"Windows are made to look through, but doorways are made to walk through," Deeping said.

"What happens to a window if you climb through it?"

"It becomes a portal," Sims said.

"Was it ever really a window if you could climb through it?"

This question made them pause for a while.

"If it is an intrinsic part of the definition of a portal that you pass through it, and if you can pass through the window, then it must be that it was always a portal, not a window," Klee said.

Hinckley took a sip from the coffee mug that sat by his elbow and made a face. It was already room-temperature.

"How many of you know what a Möbius strip is?"

Three showed their hands.

"Only three? I live among the Philistines. No matter; I will explain. A Möbius strip is a strip of flat material, such as paper, that is twisted once and then the two ends are joined so that it forms a continuous loop. Who can tell me the primary characteristic of the Möbius strip? Monique? Patricia?"

"It only has one side," Klee said.

"Exactly right, Mr. Klee. "It is a physical object in our material world, that to all appearances seems to possess two sides, but when examined it becomes apparent that this is an illusion, and it has only a single side."

"How can a loop of paper have only one side?" Deeping said. "I don't get it."

"Because, Mr. Deeping, it is twisted through a higher dimension, very much like a Klein bottle, although in a simpler and more satisfying way."

"I don't buy into that higher-dimension crap," Deeping said in a tone of disgust. "I mean, it's all theoretical, right? Nobody's ever proven higher dimensions exist."

"Without higher dimensions, mathematics would be a very limited discipline," Goddard told him.

"See, that's what I mean. Numbers are just made-up things. Numbers don't really exist."

"And yet, engineers who build bridges and skyscrapers rely on numbers to keep their constructions from tumbling down," Hinckley pointed out.

"You are confusing the hell out of me, Professor."

"You are in a philosophy seminar, Mr. Deeping. You are supposed to be confused."

The students laughed. Hinckley took the opportunity to get up and pour himself fresh black coffee from the machine on the side table. He brought his mug back to the conference table.

"Who among you has heard the name Yog-Sothoth?"

They stared at him with blank expressions.

"Nobody? Mr. Klee? Surely you've heard some mention of the myth in your native Uganda?"

Klee shook his head.

"Very well, I shall explain. Yog-Sothoth is a god who was worshipped in diverse parts of Africa and Asia thousands of years ago. He is said to be the god of portals."

"Like the Roman god Janus, you mean."

"Not quite like Janus, Mr. Goddard. Yog-Sothoth is said to embody the essence of all portals. He is the way itself. No one can pass over a threshold without calling upon Yog-Sothoth to open the gate, even though that call is usually subconscious. This god holds all the keys to all the gates in the universe."

"I don't call upon Yog-Whatever when I go through doorways," Deeping said.

"Are you so sure?

"Pretty sure, Professor."

"When you pass across a threshold, don't you think your mind takes on a specific shape, if only for the briefest instant?"

"I don't follow."

"You think to yourself, below the level of words, I am now passing through a portal. You have the concept of passing through in your mind, even if you don't realize it."

"I guess, maybe. So?"

"So maybe the shape of your mind in that instant is a call upon Yog-Sothoth to open the gate."

Deeping laughed. "You mean if this god didn't open the portal, I'd run into an invisible wall or something?"

"Perhaps. But there are different levels of portal, and some open much more easily than others. Most offer no resistance. Some require effort. And a few demand a very special key."

"Are we still talking abstractions, Professor?" Sims asked. "Because you've lost me."

Hinckley reached down beside his chair and lifted his battered briefcase onto the table. He opened its flap and dug inside, then pulled forth what looked like a round, woven placemat. It was made of knotted gray thread or fine twine. In its center was a small round opening. The thread was looped and woven and knotted in an intricate pattern around this hole.

"What's that?" Deeping asked.

"This, Mr. Deeping, is a knot. I purchased it the last time I was in Morocco."

"A knot? You mean just one knot?"

"Exactly." He slid the woven mat across the surface of the table toward Deeping, who picked it up and examined it.

"It looks old, like maybe it's an antique," he said.

"Pass it around to the others," Hinckley told him.

Deeping handed the placemat over to Patricia Sims, who studied it closely.

"It is known as the Key of Yog-Sothoth," Hinckley said. "Pass it around; I want each of you to get a good look at it."

"What are we supposed to do with it?" Deeping asked.

"Your class assignment is quite simple. You are to untie the knot. You must not break the thread or cut it during the process. This is a group project. You will all receive either a pass or fail on the assignment, depending on whether you are successful. You have until our next seminar, one week from today."

"We can't just cut it open?"

"No, Mr. Deeping. Put that thought out of your mind. You are not Alexander the Great and this is not the Gordian Knot. If you bring it back cloven asunder by a sword, you will surely receive a fail."

"You mean we have to untie it completely?" Legrand asked. "Every bit of it?"

"Until you have only a single loop of thread, which for convenience you may overlap multiple times. I was assured by the priest who sold it to me that the thread is continuous and has no ends."

Deeping looked at the mat doubtfully. "There isn't anything like a curse on it, is there?"

"Don't tell me you're superstitious, Mr. Deeping?"

"Not normally, but since it's so old, and connected with that god—"

"Yog-Sothoth."

"Yeah, Yog-Whatever. I just wondered if it was bad luck. What's supposed to happen when we get it unravelled?"

"You gain a little practical experience in the geometry of knots, and get a pass on your assignment," Hinckley said.

"Why haven't you untied it?"

"Because I was saving it for you, Mr. Goddard. For all of you. Take it away with you when you leave. Bring it back in a week, whatever state it may be in. But do not cut or break the thread. That is imperative."

Patricia Sims paused on the stone steps of the philosophy building and looked up at the sky. Night had fallen. Most of the stars were washed out by the bright campus lights, but high overhead a single crimson point blazed.

"It was supposed to start fading out," Goddard said, looking up as he stopped beside her. "Astronomers don't know what to make of it. They say it's the wrong color for a supernova, and it should be getting dimmer instead of brighter."

The young woman lifted up the knotted mat she was carrying under her arm and peered at the supernova through the hole in its center. "There's something not right about it," she said.

"That's what I just told you."

"No, I mean it doesn't feel right. Every time I look at it I get creeped out. Don't you feel it?"

"Not really," Goddard said. "It's just a stellar phenomenon."

"I know what you mean, Pat," Monique Legrand said, coming up behind her and looking up at the new star. "It's like the eye of an angry god glaring down at us. *Mon dieu*, I don't like to look at it."

"What are we going to do with that?" Deeping asked Sims, pointing at the woven knot.

"Let's take it to the coffee shop and look it over."

The others followed her across the street to a little privately-owned coffee shop on the corner called The Bean, which served as a hangout for the grad students at the university—the undergrads tended to gather at a Starbucks two blocks away. They sat at a square table and Sims positioned the mat in its center. Klee pulled up a fifth chair and straddled it with his arms on its back.

"We all know Professor Hinckley is insane, right?" Klee said.

"That's a given," Deeping told him. "What does he care—he's got tenure."

"All that crazy talk about portals, and now he gives us this old Moroccan knot puzzle," Sims said. "What's he thinking?"

"Maybe it's a joke," Legrand suggested.

"He's not the joking type," Sims said. "Insane, yes; a comedian, no."

"I don't like it when somebody jokes around with my grades," Deeping said. "They're not high enough as it is."

"So we untie the knot," Goddard said. "It's a puzzle, right? That means it was designed to be untied. We're not stupid, we can figure it out."

"Look at it," Klee said.

"They all stared at the mat in silence. It was incredibly complex. Its single strand of thin twine twisted and looped and wove through itself in a way that bewildered the eye. There were thousands of smaller knots within the single large knot.

"I can't trace the thread," Deeping said. "I keep losing it."

"I'm good with puzzles," Goddard said. He picked up the mat and took off his eyeglasses to examine it more closely, squinting at its pattern.

"We need to be careful," Sims said. "If we get it tangled up in a ball we'll never untie it."

"Just let me look at it for a while," Goddard murmured.

"When I get back to the dorm, I will research Moroccan knot puzzles," Klee said. "Maybe there is a key to untying it."

"Good idea," Deeping said. "I'll look up this old god Hinckley mentioned. What was his name again?"

"Yog-Sodoff," Klee said.

"Yog-Sothoth," Goddard corrected.

"Right, Yog-Sothoth. Maybe he's a clue as to how this knot is untied."

"I don't think Hinckley is that devious," Sims said. "It's worth investigating, though."

"I want to take this back to my apartment, if it's all right with you people," Goddard said in a meditative tone. "I need to spend some time studying it."

"Fine with me," Sims said.

There was no dissent. Goddard folded the mat in half and slid it into his portfolio.

"Just be careful with it," Deeping said. "If you break the thread, Hinckley is going to fail us all."

"I'll treat it like a Fabergé egg," Goddard assured him, sliding his glasses back into place on his head.

"Let's get together here tomorrow afternoon and pool whatever information we're able to gather about this thing," Sims suggested. "We can start working on untying it."

They left the coffee shop and went their separate ways.

Goddard walked back to his off-campus one-bedroom apartment. It was in the attic of a house that was owned by an elderly Jewish couple named Kleinman. They rented out the attic apartment to university students for extra money. It was a quiet house where Goddard could research and study to his heart's content. He got on well with the owners, who appreciated his lack of visitors and the early hours he kept. They had started to treat him almost like their own son, which faintly embarrassed the shy scholar.

Switching on the lamp at his desk, he pulled out the knot, unfolded it, and pressed it flat on the desk blotter pad. He opened the top drawer and took out a magnifying glass, which he held over the knot. The intricacy of the weave work was incredible. The knot was composed of layers of smaller knots surrounding the central hole, and those had yet more layers of still smaller knots. *It's like looking into a Mandelbrot set,* he thought. Could the knot be fractal?

His mind drifted as he continued to study the knot, searching for some place where he could begin to untie it. He noticed a repeating pattern and began to count the smaller knots. Two, three, five, eight—the groups of small knots repeated in this numerical sequence over and over. It was the start of the Fibonacci sequence, in which each number was the sum of the two numbers that preceded it. He examined the groups of knots more widely and realized that the sequence continued to higher Fibonacci numbers with larger and larger clusters of knots. It could not be a coincidence.

He took a sheet of paper and scribbled down his observations with a pencil so that he would not forget any of them in the morning. He was brain-tired, and his mind was half-conscious. As he looked into the knot, he could see curious shapes that moved and withdrew into shadows.

"I've been staring at this thing too hard," he murmured to himself. "I need to get some sleep."

He stood up, stretched, and started to turn out his desk lamp, then hesitated, gazing down at the knot. Going into his kitchenette, he took a bamboo shish-kabob skewer out of a drawer and brought it back to the desk. Sitting, he bent over the knot and with painstaking care began to tease the thread loose from the smaller knots with the point of the skewer. He continued in this way past midnight, forgetting his fatigue and losing all track of time.

Little by little, the knot was coming undone from the center. As it did so, the diameter of the hole increased and the knot expanded outward as the interwoven thread shifted to compensate. The knot seemed to absorb the loose thread like a living thing, in a manner that Goddard could not understand. He realized that his efforts were changing its shape in subtle ways.

He chanced to look at the hole, and pulled his hands away quickly. The hole was black, like a pool of black ink. It seemed to extend down through the top of his desk. Timidly, he leaned over it and peered into its depths. There was nothing to see, only darkness. No, wait; something moved deep down. It shifted ponderously, and he got the impression of immense size and crushing weight.

I really do need to get some sleep, he thought.

Even so, he could not bring himself to stop when he was making such good progress, at least on the inner ring of the knot. The Fibonacci sequence had been the key. He tried to ignore the darkness at the center, but now and then the movements in its depths drew his gaze. He took off his glasses, rubbed the corners of his eyes with his thumb and finger, and put them back on.

I can solve this puzzle on my own, he thought. *I don't need the others.*

He imagined their surprise and admiration when he brought them the coiled thread of the unbound knot. It was a pity they were all going to receive equal grades when he was doing all their work. It didn't seem fair. Somehow he had to make sure Professor Hinckley knew that he, and he alone, had solved it. Not that it was untied yet. He was almost through the first ring, but the second ring was tied in a way that he had not yet been able to understand. One by one the small knots of the inner ring loosened and slipped open, until only a dozen or so remained. Eagerly he untied them one after another.

As he loosened the final knot of the inner ring, he noticed a red spark deep in the depths of the central hole, which was now larger than it had been originally. It looked like a red star and reminded him of the supernova.

My brain is playing tricks, he thought with a satisfied smile. *I'm punchy with fatigue. I need to get to bed.*

But he continued to sit and stare into the hole. It seemed to him that the red star was coming closer, or maybe it was growing larger. Without thinking, he put his hand into the hole and extended his arm downward until his shoulder was resting against the surface of his desk.

This is crazy, he thought. *There's no hole in my desk. So where did my arm go?*

Something grasped him by the wrist and pulled hard.

4.

"Thank you for letting us into Godfrey's apartment, Mrs. Kleinman," Patricia Sims said with a broad smile.

"Not at all, my dear," the elderly woman said. "I know how you students are. Always forgetting things and missing deadlines."

Sims and Deeping entered the small apartment. Sims noted that the bed had not been slept in.

"Here it is," Deeping said, going over to Goddard's desk. The desk lamp was still turned on. He reached under the shade and switched it off. Bright afternoon sunlight glowed against the closed curtains of the window, filling the room with soft light.

"Well, I wonder where he's gotten himself to," Mrs. Kleinman said, looking around curiously. "He's such a nice young man."

Deeping studied the knot. "He's done something to it."

"What do you mean?" Sims said.

"It's bigger than it was, and the hole in the center is larger."

"He must have untied some of it," she said. "Look, here's a sheet with his notes."

"You better take that," Deeping said, folding the knot and putting it over his arm.

She slipped the sheet into the pocket of her jeans, than looked around the apartment while the old woman stood beside the open door.

"His clothes are all still here, along with his suitcase," she said, opening the closet.

"His wallet is on the dresser," Deeping said.

"Where would he go without his wallet?" Mrs. Kleinman said.

Neither of them had an answer. They took the knot back to the coffee shop, where they found Klee and Legrand waiting for them.

"Can either of you make anything of this?" Deeping asked, spreading the penciled sheet out on the table.

"It looks like mathematical formulas of some kind," Klee said.

"No shit, Sherlock. What about you, Monique?"

She studied the numbers. "This is the Fibonacci sequence, or the beginning of it anyway."

"What does 'fractal' mean?" Sims asked, leaning over the table to look at the paper.

"That I know, sort of," Deeping said. "A fractal is a pattern that repeats itself in a general way on larger and smaller scales but never actually repeats exactly. There are always differences. Look, he wrote down 'Mandelbrot set.' That's an example of a fractal pattern. They are defined by mathematics."

"This is way beyond me," Klee said. "I'm no good with math."

"Goddard had more math than all of us combined," Deeping said.

"Why isn't Godfrey here?" Legrand asked.

Sims explained how Goddard had left his apartment.

"That doesn't sound like Godfrey," Legrand said. "He's always so regular, so scheduled."

"He might have gone out to celebrate getting some of the knot untied, gotten drunk, and could be sleeping it off in an alley or a drunk tank," Deeping suggested.

"Not Godfrey," Legrand said. "That's just not how he is."

"Well, what do we do?" Deeping asked. "None of us know mathematics. We aren't going to be able to replicate what he did. Without him we're never going to get this knot untied."

"I'm sure he'll show up later today," Klee said. "Something must have happened for him to leave his apartment."

They ordered cappuccinos and settled themselves at the table.

"I was able to get some information on that old Sumerian god at the university library this morning," Deeping said. "Much good it will do us."

"Let's hear it anyway," Sims said.

Deeping opened a folder containing some sheets of jotted notes. "Nobody knows the origin of the myth, but it's old. Yog-Sothoth is what the Sumerians called him. The name appears on about a dozen clay tablets inscribed with cuneiform writing that were unearthed nine years ago in Mesopotamia. Of course the god is mentioned in many other places, sometimes under different names. He is a god of portals, just like Professor Hinckley told us. He is named Opener of the Ways in some ancient texts, which is a term used in Egyptian mythology in a different context, but in other sources he's just called the Way.

"As near as I can make out, Yog-Sothoth is not just the god of portals, he is portals, all portals, everywhere of every kind. The myth states that in the times before men walked the earth, he opened the way for alien races to descend through

". . . wheels within wheels and shining bubbles of many colors."

the dimensions to this planet, where they ruled for millions of years."

"What happened to all these aliens?" Sims asked.

"The stars went wrong."

"Wrong how? How do stars go wrong?"

"That is not clear in the surviving literature. It seems as though they somehow changed position, or maybe it had something to do with their colors. Anyway, they changed, and all these alien beings could no longer tolerate living on the surface of this planet, so they hid themselves away."

"You mean they are still here?" Klee said with a smile.

"That's what the myths tell us. Some of them went under the ground, and some hid in the deep oceans. Others retreated into the spaces between the stars, whatever that means. I think it has something to do with inter-dimensions. They're all still there, waiting to return and reclaim the earth once the stars come right again."

"Creepy," Sims said.

"Maybe they are coming back," Legrand said with a smile. "After all, the stars have changed."

"How's that?" Deeping asked.

"The supernova. It's never been there before."

"Not in recorded history, at least," Sims murmured.

"That's not how supernovas work," Legrand said. "They only blow up once."

"If this is a supernova. I remember seeing on the news that astronomers don't know what to make of it. So far it hasn't done what they expected it to do."

"The other day I read on a UFO website about a ship in the South Pacific being pulled under the waves by a giant hand," Klee said. "Maybe it was Yog-Sothoth."

"Yog-Sothoth doesn't have hands," Deeping said. "There's no actual description of the god, but some myths talk about wheels within wheels and shining bubbles of many colors."

"The report said an island has appeared where no island is supposed to be."

"I don't see what any of this has to do with our knot," Sims said.

"Neither do I," Deeping agreed. "But I thought I might as well do the research."

They sat in silence for a time, staring at the knot, which was laid out in the middle of the table.

"We could just cut the thread, unravel it, then tie the ends back together," Deeping suggested.

"I don't think that would fool Professor Hinckley," Sims said.

"I'm going to read up on knots in the library," Legrand said. "On how they are tied, I mean. Maybe I can figure something out."

"Take the knot with you, and the sheet," Deeping said. "I have to get to class."

"Me too," Klee said.

"I'll go with you," Sims told Legrand. "I've got the whole afternoon free."

They spent the next two hours locating books and essays on knots and studying them. Most involved multidimensional geometry and were beyond their understanding. They tried finding references to the various number series Goddard had jotted down, but found nothing useful.

"Who knew there was a whole literature on the topography of knots," Sims murmured, leafing through a mathematical text. It was filled with complex mathematical formulas. "Maybe we should find a mathematician to help us."

"I used to date a mathematician," Legrand said.

"What happened?"

"He was absentminded. One day he forgot to lock his door."

"You caught him with another woman?"

"With a guy."

"Do you think he'd help us?"

Legrand shrugged. "He might, if I play on his guilty conscience."

They left the library and made their way across the campus to the dorm where Legrand's ex-lover was living. A look of surprise came over his face when he opened his door and saw her, followed by an expression of pleasure.

"Walter, this is Patricia Sims. Patricia, Walter Leviston," Legrand said by way of introduction.

"Monique, it's so good to see you again. I never thought, after what happened, I mean I didn't expect—"

"May we come in and talk to you, Walter?" Legrand said sweetly. "We need your help."

"Yes, sure, of course," he said, stepping aside to admit them into his room.

Legrand looked around. The room was tidy to an obsessive degree. "Is Simon still staying with you?"

Leviston took off his eyeglasses, which were framed in heavy black plastic, and blushed. "No, he left. I haven't seen him for weeks."

"I'm so sorry to hear that," she said. "You two seemed so happy."

"Yes, well, things change. How can I help you?"

"We need your mathematical expertise. We have a puzzle and don't know how to solve it."

She sat beside him on a worn leather sofa that had a knitted Afghan blanket thrown over its back. Sims took a nearby armchair. Legrand drew the knot carefully out from her briefcase, unfolded it, and showed it to him, explaining the situation. He turned the knot over and ran it through his hands, studying it intently.

"This is fascinating," he said. "I've never seen anything like this."

"If we don't get it untied before our next seminar, we all get a fail," she said.

"And you believe this Goddard guy untied some of it?"

The women nodded. She gave him the sheet of notes Goddard had made. He studied it with a frown.

"I think I see where he was going with this. He must have applied an inversion of the Fibonacci sequence."

"Can you do the same to the rest of the knot?" Sims asked.

"I don't know." He peered closely at the woven disk, picking at it with his fingernails.

"Don't break the thread, or we fail the assignment," Legrand warned.

"Sorry. I was just thinking. I may be able to extrapolate what Goddard was doing and apply it to the rest of the knot.

It's hellaciously complex, though. Honestly, I don't know how he got as much untied as he did."

"Maybe it was intuitive, like solving Rubik's Cube," Sims said.

"I wouldn't know. I cheated and looked up the solution."

"I swapped the labels," Sims admitted. She put her hand on his knee and squeezed. "You're the first person I've ever told."

He shifted uneasily and drew his knee slowly away. Beside him, Legrand smiled at Sims.

"Can you help us, Walter? We've got no one else to turn to," Legrand said.

He looked at her and swallowed, making his prominent Adam's apple bob up and down.

"I can try. Leave the knot and the paper with me and I'll have a go at it."

They stood up.

"I know you need to get to class, Patricia," Legrand said.

"No, I don't—wait, yes, that's right I do, I'd forgotten."

"Why don't I stay with Walter and help him? I'll see you tonight at the coffee shop and tell you if we've made any progress."

Sims stepped out into the dorm hallway and caught the flash of Legrand's grin as the French woman closed the door gently behind her.

"The boys have lost one from the team," she murmured to herself.

The members of the seminar met at their usual hour of eight in the evening at the Bean. When Legrand failed to appear by nine, Sims decided to go back to Leviston's room to check on her.

"Leviston didn't strike me as the axe-murdering type, but you never knew with these shy introverts."

"I better come with you," Deeping said. "In case you need some muscle."

"I'll come too," Klee said. "You know, in case you need some brains."

Sims laughed, but was glad the two men had decided to go with her.

They walked across campus to the dorm building. The red supernova burned in the night sky overhead.

"I read on the Internet that something weird happened in Los Angeles a while ago," Deeping said.

"Weird how?" Sims asked.

They followed her into the dorm and up the stairs as he talked.

"A bunch of people in some concert hall had their skin torn off, or something like that, but they were still alive. Can you imagine that?"

"I'm trying not to," she murmured.

"Weird shit is happening all around the world," Deeping said.

"This is the door," Sims told them.

They looked at the door, saying nothing. All of them were listening for sounds from the other side.

"Maybe she just fell asleep," Klee suggested. "Sex can be tiring."

"For you men," Sims said. "Not for us women."

Deeping rapped on the door. They waited. He knocked again, looking at the other two. He tried the doorknob. It was not locked. It turned and the door opened.

"Monique? Walter? Are you in there?" Sims said. Not a sound came from the dorm room.

"I'm going in," Deeping said. "You two can stay out here if you want to."

"We'll all go in," Sims said. "Strength in numbers."

"You both realize this is illegal?" Klee said.

"How? The door was unlocked. That's practically the same as open," Deeping told him.

Then went in cautiously, looking from side to side. Deeping found the light switch and turned on the overhead lights. Legrand was lying across the bed in the corner on her back. Her throat had been torn out, and her long hair was surrounded by a halo of blood spatter. They found Leviston behind his desk. He lay on his face, but his back had been shredded by something with claws. Sims saw the white bones of his spine and almost threw up. She choked and coughed.

"Don't touch anything," Deeping said. "We have to call the police."

A low growl came from an alcove off the main part of the room that was filled with wall-to-ceiling book shelves. It sounded like the growl of a large dog. Before any of them could move, it bounded around the corner to the middle of the floor and glared at them. It was not a dog, although it was similar in size to a mastiff. It had colorful scales like those of a snake, and a ridge of bony plates along its back. The end of its tail was barbed. Its body rippled with muscle when it crouched, and its mouth was filled with needle-like teeth that were stained with blood.

Deeping cursed and spread his arms, pushing Sims behind him as he backed toward the open door. Klee pressed himself against a wall. The beast did not give them time to leave the room. It roared, then leaped onto the top of the desk and vanished.

"What the fuck?" Deeping said.

He approached the desk with cautious steps, assuming the creature had jumped behind it, but there was nothing behind the desk except Leviston's corpse. On the top of the desk lay a loose coil of gray thread. It was the same color as the knot, and Sims suddenly realized that it must be the knot.

"Where did that thing go?" Deeping asked. "Did you all see it?"

"I saw it," Klee said. The whites of his eyes were visible all around the pupils.

"They did it," Sims said. She went to the desk and picked up the coiled thread to study it closely. It looked unbroken. She held it up to show the others. The single thread had been looped over and over on itself so that its open center was about two feet across. It hung from her hands like a skein of gray yarn. No knots remained along its length.

"Leviston must have figured out how to untie it," she said.

Deeping was not paying attention. His eyes roved nervously around the room. He went toward the alcove and peeked cautiously around the corner. It was empty.

"Where did that thing come from?" he asked.

"More importantly, where did it go," Klee said.

"I think I know," Sims said. "Untying the knot must open a portal of some kind."

"Are you saying that thing came through a hoop of thread?" Deeping asked.

"I'm not definitely saying anything, it's just an idea."

"I say we get out of here and call the police from outside the building," Klee said.

"They are never going to believe what we saw," Deeping said. "They will think we killed them."

"Don't get any blood on you," Sims said. "Let's just get the fuck out of here. We can make an anonymous call to the police later. Wipe off the doorknob, it's got your fingerprints on it."

They went into the hall. Deeping wiped the inner knob with his unbuttoned denim shirt sleeve, closed the door, then wiped the outer knob. They crept out of the dorm. There was no one in the lobby. Sims carried the untied knot under her arm.

They went to her dorm room. She hung the knot from a coat peg on the back of the door. The twine was stiff, so it did not hang limp but assumed an oval. She sat down on her bed. Deeping leaned his hip over her desk while Klee paced nervously.

"Professor Hinckley must have some idea what's going on," Sims told the others. "He wanted us to untie the knot and open the portal."

"Why didn't he just untie it himself?" Klee asked.

"Maybe because he had some notion of what might come through," Deeping said.

"That's what I'm thinking," Sims said. "Professor Hinckley used us. He probably knew what would happen if we succeeded in untying it."

"We need to see him and find out what the hell is going on," Deeping said.

"I agree. But first, I want to try an experiment. You remember how Professor Hinckley made a distinction between a door and a window?"

"Vaguely," Deeping said. "What about it?"

"I want to see if we can use it as a window."

"That might be dangerous," Klee said.

"You can leave if you want to, Kinto. No shame," Deeping told him sincerely.

"I think that would be best," Klee said. "All this is too much for me."

He walked toward the door and reached for the knob. As his hand came near the loops of thread, something black and shining darted out from the loop and grabbed it. Klee cried out and tried to pull his arm back, but the black appendage, which was covered with bristles and had an insect-like quality, pulled him off balance. His head vanished into the loop, followed by his shoulders, torso and legs. One of his leather penny-loafers dropped off his foot and clattered on the floor.

Sims and Deeping stared at each other.

"Fuck!" he yelled. He went to the window and put his face close to the glass to look down. "Does this open?"

"No. The room is air-conditioned. Anyway, we're three floors up."

"I will take my chances," Deeping muttered. He picked up her desk chair and raised it in preparation to smashing out the window.

"Wait. We need to find out what's going on."

"I don't need to find out anything, except how to get out of here."

"We're too involved in this to just drop it. What if that dog-like thing comes around later, looking for us?"

He paused and stared at her. "Do you think that's possible?"

"I don't know, Georgie. But it must have smelled us. It has our scent."

"It wasn't a fucking dog," he pointed out.

"I'm just saying, we don't know anything, and we're in too deep to risk just running away."

He exhaled slowly, glanced at the window, then set the chair back into its place behind the desk. He eyed the loop of thread as he came over to the bed where she sat as though it were a sleeping tiger.

"What do we do?"

"Try my experiment. Maybe we can learn something about what is happening."

"OK, I'm game. Let's do it."

"I'm going to dim the light," she said. She approached the door cautiously from the side, pressing her back against the wall. Gingerly, she reached out and moved the slider on the light switch downward. The overhead light dimmed. She backed away.

"So far, so good," she said.

"Now what?"

"We sit and look into the knot, or thread, or whatever it is now."

"What are we looking for?"

"It's not just a door, it's a window, right? We should be able to see something through it."

"Why didn't it kill us in Leviston's apartment?"

"How should I know? Shut up and look into the circle. Try to look through the circle. If you see anything, tell me. I'll do the same."

"We don't know how far away from it is a safe distance," he murmured, eyes on the loop.

"I realize that," she said.

They sat in the dimness, staring at the door. Before long, Sims felt her eyes begin to burn. She blinked and held them shut for a few seconds, then opened them. Instead of shadow, the loop of thread was filled with an image of a desert landscape. Sand dunes rolled like waves to the horizon. The scene was illuminated, so that it almost looked like a picture on a screen. Something flashed past and she realized that the image was animated. The flying creature reappeared in the distance and wheeled in the air. It was long and scaled, with broad leathern wings and a flat tail with a barb in its end. It had a vague similarity to the dog-like beast. She heard a distant scream, like the cry of a bird of prey.

"I'm seeing something," Deeping said softly.

"Is it like a bird?"

"Yes."

"We must be seeing the same thing."

A four-legged creature loped across a slope of sand into the foreground. It resembled the dog-like thing they had met in Leviston's room. It looked at them, but did not react.

"I don't think it can see us," Deeping said.

"Maybe it has bad eyesight," she said.

The scaly beast cocked it head to one side, listening.

"Shit," Deeping whispered.

It started to advance toward the portal on stiff legs, the spines along its back standing erect and its lips pulled back in a silent snarl. Abruptly, it stopped and turned its head to the side, than darted from their view in the opposite direction.

"Thank God," Deeping said.

A dark figure stepped into view from the side. It looked like a man in a long black monk's robe. The hood was pulled up over his head so that his face was in shadow under the strong sunlight that beamed down on him.

He looked at them. There was no doubt in their minds that he saw them clearly. They felt the force of his gaze, even though his eyes were hidden. The figure took a step toward them, then another. Clearly it had some intention. It raised its arm. Projecting from the loose sleeve of the robe, its large hand was bony and thin, like the hand of a dried corpse. The skin resembled old leather. The unnaturally-long index finger was pointed toward them.

Deeping jumped to his feet and crossed to the closet where a broom stood in the corner. Grabbing it up, he turned it so the handle pointed outward and advanced quickly toward the door with his back against the wall, the broom extended. The leathery hand of the robed figure extended out through the loop of thread into the dorm room. With a quick jab of the broom, Deeping flipped the loop off the peg and onto the floor. It lay in a heap of thread. The hand had vanished. They stared at the thread in silence.

"I guess it's only a portal when it's open," Sims said.

"Good to know," Deeping said.

Hinckley opened his office door and peered at them suspiciously.

"What are you two doing here? The next seminar's not until Wednesday."

"We need to talk to you," Sims said.

"Do you know how late it is? I was just about to go home."

"This won't take long."

Reluctantly, he opened the door wider to admit them. His office was spacious. One side wall was lined with bookshelves. Open books and papers littered the surface of his antique desk, which was made of a dark mahogany and ornamented with hand-carved little faces of fawns and other creatures that stared out from behind leaves.

"Sit, sit," Hinckley said, motioning at two chairs. He sat behind the desk.

"We completed the project," Sims told him.

A smile appeared on the old man's deeply lined face. "Really? I hardly expected it. But of course I'm delighted."

"Godfrey Goddard has disappeared," Deeping said.

Hinckley bridged his fingers and pressed them to his lips. "When you say disappeared, you mean—"

"Vanished off the face of the earth. His clothes and driver's license are still in his apartment, but he's gone."

"That is troubling, but I don't see how it concerns me," Hinckley said.

"We think it very much concerns you, Professor," Sims said. "The death of Monique Legrand also concerns you."

"Monique, dead?" Hinckley shook his head sadly. "Such a beautiful girl. Such a delightful accent. How did that happen?"

They described the scene in Leviston's dorm room, watching his face for his reaction. They said nothing about the scaled beast.

"So you just found them that way?" Hinckley said. "You saw nothing else?"

"Like what?" Deeping said.

"I don't know. No clues as to what happened?" He paused. "No sign of the murderer?"

They shook their heads.

"Kinto Klee is missing as well."

"Whatever happened to Mr. Klee?"

Sims glanced at Deeping.

"He's disappeared," Deeping said in a dry tone.

"Such a tragedy," Hinckley said, shaking his head and causing the puff of his gray hair to jiggle. "Three of them, imagine that. Well, life goes on. You say the knot is unbound?"

"Completely. It's just some loose loops of thread now," Sims said.

"Excellent. Where is it? Do you have the thread with you?"

She took the wadded loops of loose twine from her leather portfolio and held it out draped over her hand.

"Just put it on the corner of my desk," Hinckley said nervously.

"I've got a better idea. Why don't I open it up and throw it over you and your desk?"

"No, stop; for God's sake, don't do that."

"So you do know," Deeping said.

The old man stared at him. Guilt was apparent in Hinckley's bloodshot eyes.

"What do you two know?"

"We know that two students, Walter Leviston and Monique, were killed by some kind of beast that came through the knot."

"It tore Monique's throat out," Sims added.

"We saw Kinto pulled into the knot by an arm that wasn't human. We can guess that something similar must have happened to Godfrey, after he managed to untie part of the knot."

Hinckley said nothing, his eyes darting from one to the other.

"You expected this to happen, didn't you?" Sims said.

He shrugged his thin shoulders beneath his tweed jacket. "It's dangerous even to untie a small portion. Each small knot reinforces the binding spell, you see. Every knot that is untied weakens the spell's power."

"You son of a bitch," Deeping said, standing suddenly with his hands clenched into fists. "I should wring your scrawny neck."

"Sit down, Georgie," Sims told him.

Hinckley regarded him with a mild expression. After a few moments, Deeping sat, his face still flushed.

"Why did you do it?" Sims asked.

"My dear, I'm not a mathematician. I didn't have the skills to untie the knot myself. But the five of you are . . . were . . . young and resourceful. I knew you might find a way."

"You should have told us the risks," Deeping said.

"To what point? You would never have believed me, and if you had, you would not have untied the knot."

"You sent three people to their deaths."

Hinckley spread his hands disarmingly. "How was I to know what would happen? I don't control the knot, or what may come through it. None if it can be placed on my doorstep."

"But you suspected what might happen," Sims said. "That's the real reason you didn't try to untie the knot yourself, isn't it?"

Hinckley said nothing.

"Tell us now what this thing is," she said, gesturing with the handful of twine.

"Isn't it obvious? It's a gateway between worlds. The Arab who sold it to me had no idea how ancient it was, or about its true function, but I recognized it at once from my researches. It's called the Knot of Yog-Sothoth. It was tied by the priest-worshippers of that god in a monastery on the Plateau of Leng five thousand years ago. They tied many such knots, only a few of which have survived. Until recently these knots were mere curiosities, but the coming of the supernova changed that. It made the stars right for the return of the Old Ones. Yog-Sothoth is their gateway, you see, and I am but their humble doorman."

"What happens if these Old Ones return to our world?" Deeping asked.

"Everything ends. They will erase all life upon the surface of this planet and move it out of its present orbit to a higher sphere, where it rightfully belongs."

"Why in God's name would you want that?"

"Look around you, young man. What do you see? Perversion. Violence. Decadence. Decay. Crime. Corruption. It's time to end it all and start anew. The earth needs to be wiped clean, the way it was by the Flood in the days of Noah."

"You're not God," Deeping said. "That decision is not yours to make."

"I disagree." He stood from his chair. They saw that he held a small nickel-plated revolver in his hand. Neither had noticed him pick it up. "Now, my dear, lay the knot on the corner of my desk and leave me. I have work to do. Yog-Sothoth must receive my prayers. The Old Ones must be called."

"You want the knot? Here, take it."

Sims threw the handful of twine onto the floor. As it fell through the air it spread itself into an irregular loop that was around six feet across. Hinckley stared at it in open-mouthed horror.

"Do you know what you just did? I haven't had a chance to set up wards. The gate is unguarded. Anything can come through."

Deeping stood from his chair slowly. "We'll just leave it with you and go."

Hinckley swung the muzzle of the revolver to point at his face.

"No," he shrieked, spittle flecking his lips. "You pick it up, now. Get over there and pick it up. Hurry, you fool, before—"

A tall figure draped in a long black robe stood in the center of the circle, facing him. It was the same being Sims and

Deeping had seen through the opened knot in Sims' dorm room. The overhanging hood that surrounded its head cast its face into shadow. Only its bony hands were in view, extending beyond the wide sleeves of the garment. Sims smelled dust. The dryness choked her throat. She resisted the impulse to cough.

It took Hinckley several seconds to notice the figure standing silently beside him. When he saw it, he shrieked and fired all six rounds from the revolver into its body. It was impossible for him to miss, yet the figure did not move or give any sign of distress. Hinckley continued to click the trigger mechanically. His face had gone completely white and his mouth hung open.

Both Sims and Deeping were too dumbstruck to think of running from the office. Deeping smelled the sharp tang of gunpowder from the discharged rounds, but his mind was blank, having become nothing more than a biological recorder of events.

The tall figure stepped quickly to the edge of the knot and plucked the revolver from Hinckley's hand. Its slender fingers tightened on it, and the revolver crumbled like wax and fell to pieces that scattered across the floorboards.

"I command you, in the name of Yog-Sothoth, god of all coming and going," Hinckley said in a shaking voice, pointing at the figure. "Depart from this place. By Yog-Sothoth, who opens and shuts all gateways, be gone! By Azathoth, the maker and unmaker of all things, I command you. *Ye-aye phang deflag azozo othazod lah-tagh . . .*"

The hooded figure extended its index finger. The black fingernail was long and pointed. Its tip touched Hinckley on the forehead. It was the merest touch. He stopped talking, and his eyes widened in horror. Then his body fell in upon itself and crumbled to dust with the soft sifting sound of falling sand. One moment he was standing by his chair, and the next he was gone.

The silent figure turned slowly to look at Sims and Deeping. Sims at last found enough strength in her legs to stand, but she had to hold onto the arm of her chair to keep her knees from buckling. Deeping felt a strange lightness in his head, as through he were floating, or watching events unfold from a distance. He put up his hands in an automatic defensive gesture, as though to ward off a blow. Warmth trickled slowly down the inside of his left thigh, and with a part of his stunned awareness he realized that he had just urinated on himself.

The black figure raised its bony, claw-like hand to its shadowed hood and pointed with separated index and middle fingers at the places where its unseen eyes must be. Then it extended its arm straight out toward them and pointed at them with the same two fingers. Sims cringed back as though struck, although she felt nothing. Suddenly, it was not there. It did not fade, it just was no longer standing in the office. Deeping looked at the floor, and realized the looped twine of the knot was missing as well.

Sims turned to him. They stared at each other. Neither felt any impulse to speak. At last, Deeping inched toward the desk and leaned forward to peer over. On the floor beside the chair was a small pile of gray ash such as might come from a cremation urn if its contents were poured out.

Still neither of them spoke. They turned and walked on stiff legs out of the office without looking behind them. Deeping pulled the door shut with a quiet click.

TSATHOGGUA

The One Who Waits

1.

Police Captain Leroy Banks sat on the front edge of his desk and bent forward to grip each of its battered corners with his scarred hands. His suit jacket hung limp on a hat rack behind his office door. The sleeves of his white shirt were rolled to the elbows, its collar open. His Hawaiian Sunset tie dangled loosely from his neck like a dead tropical fish pinned up by its tail. Banks' square face needed a shave. Beads of perspiration covered his forehead, and dark sweat patches showed at his armpits. The air conditioning was broken again, and the humidity in New Orleans more than the temperature made it almost unbearable in the Fifth District Police Station.

"What have you got on the latest one?" he demanded.

Detective James Neely glanced across at his partner, Detective Rodney White. How White managed to keep from sweating like everyone else was a mystery among uniforms and plain clothes alike that none of them had been able to solve. White had not even taken off his suit jacket. Granted, the young black man was rake-thin and bald, but that alone couldn't account for it.

"Nothing much," Neely said when White declined to speak. "We thought we had a lead when a neighbor reported seeing a man run down the alleyway behind the building, but it turned out he was just a peeper looking to get himself off."

"We have to catch this bastard," Banks said. Tension was audible in his voice.

"We know that, sir."

"The city is ready to blow up. This crazy heat wave isn't helping matters. Last night was the eighth snatch. The FBI is second-guessing my decisions. I've got the mayor's office on my back. His Honor calls me half a dozen times a day, looking for updates. What am I supposed to tell him?"

"The usual bullshit," White said. His face wore a bored expression.

"Don't get smart," Banks snapped. "I'm about to take off some heads. Unless you want one of them to be yours, find this sicko before he grabs another kid. Now get the fuck out of here, both of you."

They left him fuming in front of a fan with the streamers kissing his fleshy cheeks, and went out the back of the station house to where Neely's unmarked Ford Taurus was parked.

"When are you going to get this piece of shit repainted?" White asked.

Neely looked at the car. As far as he knew, it had never even been washed. The forest-green paint had no shine left. The driver's door was kicked in, and someone had done an artistic job with a knife on the hood. Fortunately, that person had not been able to spell.

"I like it the way it is," Neely said.

Sliding into the front seat, he folded up the sun reflector that was on the dash and put it away. In spite of the lateness of the year, the sun was murderously hot and he didn't want it melting the plastic. White got in the other side.

"Turn it on and give me some air," he said.

"You're in a sweet mood today." Neely started the car and turned the air conditioner on full blast.

"The Captain has no call to give us grief," White said. "He

knows we've got no witnesses."

"Whoever is grabbing these babies, he's like the Shadow," Neely said. "Nobody sees or hears him."

"I don't believe that. I think the mothers are scared. I think he tells them that if they say anything, he'll come back for them."

"This is their babies we're talking about."

White tilted back his seat and let the cold air wash over him. "The neighborhoods where these snatches are occurring, mothers got more babies than they need. They're probably glad to get rid of one."

Five of the kidnappings had occurred in the Lower Ninth Ward, two in Holy Cross, and one in the Desire area. The infants had been taken from lower-income homes, all but one of which was single-parent.

Neely remembered the tear-streaked face of the young mother he had interviewed yesterday. She had sobbed so uncontrollably that she had to run into the bathroom to throw up. He said nothing to White. When his partner got into one of his moods, only time would get him out of it.

"I say we interview these people again who claim they didn't see anything, and this time we put the fear of God into them," White said. "Somebody had to see something."

Neely put the car into drive and sent it cruising through the city. Boarded-up buildings were on every block. Bourbon Street might not show it, but New Orleans had fallen on hard times. Nothing was the same since Katrina. That hurricane had blown out the city's heart, leaving only a terminally sick shell that continued to cling to a kind of life, unwilling to admit that it wasn't getting better. He looked at the people walking on the cracked and broken sidewalks. Most of their faces were expressionless. A few tried to look mean. Some kept their eyes down and heads bowed, like dogs that had been beaten too often.

"I have to get out of this city," he muttered.

"You'll never leave," White said. "You've been here over twenty years. If you really wanted to leave you would have done it by now."

When he left New York to come to the Big Easy for a change of lifestyle, Neely had been a brash and confident rookie, sure he was going places. Twenty-two years later he was more thoughtful, a little slower in his movements, and starting to feel his age. His hair had gone gray at the temples, and it was taking him longer to urinate. Not that he was old yet, he thought, but White made him feel old. His new partner looked like he'd just graduated from junior college.

Neely sometimes found himself wishing that his former partner, Big Bubba Nash, had not decided to retire the previous year. Nash had talked about retiring to Florida for the entire eight years they had been together, and last year he had finally done it. He was living in a condo in Orlando with a young Puerto Rican woman. He'd sent Neely a card last Christmas. They looked happy.

"It's this case we're on," Neely said. "Little babies, for Christ sake. I lie in bed wondering what he's doing with them, and it makes me sick and I can't sleep. I've been taking sleeping pills and they knock me out but they make me feel like shit. I have to get away from all this." He waved his hand to point at both sides of the street. "I can't take much more."

"Your problem is you care too much," White said. He took sunglasses from his shirt pocket and slipped them on. "You can't care about people in our line of work."

They spent the afternoon interviewing for a second time some of the people who were in the vicinity when the snatches occurred. White tried to put a little pressure on them. He succeeded in frightening a few and pissing off the rest, but none of them gave any useful information. The kidnapper had come through the window unseen and unheard, picked the infants out of their cribs, and carried them off. Most of the houses had no air conditioning, so naturally the windows were wide open. What puzzled Neely was that none of the babies had cried. You would think being picked up by a stranger in the middle of the night and carried out a window would have set them off, but none of them had cried.

They stopped off at a rundown McDonald's for burgers and fries. Neely sat at the table, chewing his quarter-pounder without enthusiasm and staring out the fly-specked restaurant window at the human tragedy that passed on the sidewalk. Mercifully, the air conditioning was working.

"What do you think he does with them?"

White made a sound of disgust. He used a paper napkin to wipe ketchup from the corners of his mouth. "Don't go there, man."

"Best case, he sells them to women who want to be mothers, who will care for them and raise them right."

"You know that isn't happening."

"Worst case . . ."

"Yeah," White said. "I told you, don't go there."

They left the restaurant and walked around its corner toward the Taurus, which Neely had parked in the shade. Neely stopped and stared at the side of the building. Near a metal dumpster some budding street artist had spray-painted on the bricks in red capital letters "HE WAITS." Above the words was a symbol that consisted of two circles side by side, beneath which was a kind of jellyfish shape with three drooping points.

"They started popping up three or four weeks ago," White said, walking back to him. "Now they're all over the city."

"What do you think it means?"

"It means nothing. These graffiti assholes just want to get noticed."

"Don't you think it sort of looks like a face?" Neely asked.

White tilted his head to the side and pursed his lips. "I don't see it."

"The circles are its eyes, and the other shape is a turned-down mouth with its tongue hanging out."

"I still don't see it."

"What does 'he waits' mean?" Neely murmured, staring at the symbol. "Who waits? What's he waiting for?"

"Man, you really need to get a good night's sleep," White told him.

"It's going to happen again," Neely said. "He's going to take another baby."

"Maybe, but there's nothing we can do to stop him. My advice to you, as your partner, is that you should buy a quart of Jack Daniels and get drunk tonight."

Neely barely heard him. He was still staring at the symbol.

"Wasn't one of these on the back fence of the building where the last kid was snatched?"

White wrinkled his forehead in thought. His shaved head gave him a lot of forehead to wrinkle. "Yeah, I think so. What about it?"

"I want to go back over the scenes to look for this symbol. I think I remember seeing it a couple of times close to where kids were taken."

"I told you before, it's all over the city."

"I know. You don't need to come with me, this is something I can do myself. I'll drop you off at your building."

"Suit yourself," White said. "But you're chasing your tail."

Neely found the symbol at five of the crime scenes easily. The other three were not so obvious. One was sprayed on an old picket fence that was choked by weeds. Another had been placed on the side of a steel trashcan that someone had turned around so that the symbol faced the wall.

He hunted for the final instance of the symbol for over an hour as the shadows of early evening lengthened. Finally, just as he was about to give up, it jumped off the wall at him. It had been sprayed on bricks that were already covered with other graffiti, and some enterprising Picasso had come along and half-covered it with the anarchist symbol.

He stared at the paint-covered wall with excitement, his heart beating hard in his chest. This was the first lead of any kind on the kidnappings. Taking out his phone, he photographed the symbol, as he had the seven others.

An elderly black man with an aluminum walker saw

what he was doing and stopped to watch. "You like graffiti?" he asked Neely in a cracked voice.

"Not particularly. I'm just interested in this symbol." He traced its outline with his finger. "It's half covered up."

"He waits," the old man said.

The way he said it made Neely look at him more closely.

"You know anything about it?"

"I heard it's some kind of cult or church or something like that. You see them around sometimes. Little men wearing these black hoodies with the hoods up, always with the hoods up. How can they do that in this heat?"

"I don't know," Neely said. "You happen to know where they hang out?"

"Naw, I don't know anything about them. I just see them now and then, slinking along like they got something to hide. They mostly come out at night."

"Why do you call them little men?"

"Because they're short. Ain't none of them taller than this." He held his hand up at shoulder level.

Neely felt growing excitement as he made his way back to his car. Suppose the kidnappings were not the work of an individual, but of a cult? The same symbol at every crime scene had to mean something.

He slid into the car, turned it on to let the air conditioning cool, and took out his phone. Sergeant Eleanor Cheever answered almost immediately. She worked the early night shift at the station.

"This is Neely. I need some information on a cult. I'm sending you a picture now."

"I'm up on gangs, Neely, not cults," she said in mild irritation. "There's a difference."

"I need to know where I can find them. The cult members wear black hoodies."

"Well that narrows it down, doesn't it."

"The symbol I sent you is all over the street. Try to find out about them, will you? Maybe one of your gang contacts knows something."

"Neely, you know what those punks are like. They're

high on drugs half the time. They believe all kinds of crazy shit. One of them told me there were white alligators in the sewers. Another said he was cursed by Voodoo and was going to die in nine days."

"Did he?"

"What?"

"Die in nine days."

"Of course not. He broke into an apartment, raped a woman, and he's doing three to five in Angola. My point is, no matter what these punks say, you can't trust them. They don't know the difference between fantasy and reality."

"Try anyway, Cheever. It's important."

As Neely put away his phone, a loud bang rocked the car. He looked around through the windows at the darkness that had fallen so quickly and drew his Glock from its shoulder holster. Cautiously, he stepped out of the car. The street appeared to be deserted. He walked around a hedge that had been let grow wild in front of a boarded-up house, and looked down the nearby alley that he had emerged from after taking the picture of the symbol. Nothing.

Going back to his car, he noticed that a new dent had appeared in the rear fender. *At least I don't need to get a window replaced*, he thought. He searched the cracked asphalt until he found what had struck the car. It was a piece of red brick. Leaning into the car, he rummaged around in the glove compartment until he found a plastic bag, then used it to pick up the brick, which he dropped into a baggie so that it could be dusted for prints. Maybe the incident meant nothing. Or maybe he had been watched as he drove from one crime scene to another, photographing the symbol.

He put a hand behind his neck and craned it back, stretching. In the night sky overhead a bright red star burned. Around it was a fiery red ring. The resemblance to a glaring eye was uncanny. He'd been hearing about the supernova for weeks in the media. At first the astronomers had sounded excited and confident. Then they became less self-assured and said the supernova was doing things it was not supposed to. He remembered one expert who claimed that what the star was doing was impossible. Since the ring had appeared around it, they hadn't been saying anything. Neely didn't much care what they said. The distant exploded red star didn't interest him.

His phone rang. It was the station. As he listened, he felt sickness in his gut. It had happened again. This time the kidnapper had not only taken a baby, he had cut the throat of the mother. Neely sent the car through the dark streets with the lights that were hidden behind its grill flashing, but no siren. When he got to the scene, White was already there. They went into the row house without speaking to each other.

The mother lay in a bedroom doorway, her upper body in the hall. A pool of blood surrounded her head and shoulders. Neely bent his knees and studied her face. Her eyes were frozen wide open in an expression of terror. White stepped over the body into the bedroom, looking at everything. The casement window was open. It had no screen. White leaned out and looked down. As with the other kidnappings, the child's room had been on the ground floor.

"No footprints," he said.

The cool night breeze blew in and touched Neely's face. He noticed a young uniform standing nearby, watching him.

"Who found the body?"

"Neighbor," the cop said, glancing at his notebook. "A Mrs. Lee. She heard a noise and thought that maybe Sandra Jenson, the victim, had fallen down and been hurt. She had a key because she sometimes takes care of her infant girl, Mandy."

"Mandy's the missing kid?"

"Yes. Lee came in, found Jenson, then went looking for the girl, who is fourteen months old. The child was gone, and the window was open."

"Why do you think he killed her?" White asked Neely, staring down at the corpse.

"She came in, saw what he was doing, and attacked him."

"Looks more to me like she was trying to get away," White said.

"Maybe she saw something that scared her."

"This killing is a break in the pattern," White said. "He's getting careless."

"Or running out of time," Neely said.

Neely left his partner questioning a tearful Mrs. Lee and wandered out the rear door to search for the symbol. He felt as though he had not slept for three days. The sleeping pills knocked him out but they did not restore his vitality. He felt used up, like an old plastic bag that was stretched thin and full of holes. While a gaggle of curious neighbors watched in silence over the back fence, he shone the beam of his flashlight this way and that until he spotted the symbol. It was sprayed on the back of a rusting metal tool shed. He photographed it, then turned to study the faces that lined the fence.

"Did any of you see what happened here?"

They shook their heads slowly and looked at each other. There was fear in their eyes.

The next evening Neely and White worked overtime, driving down leads that all led nowhere. Neely had a sick feeling that it was going to happen again. What the fuck were these monsters doing with the kids? The question haunted him. He tried to put it out of his mind, but like an abandoned dog, it refused to go away.

He got a phone call from Sergeant Cheever that one of her contacts had found someone who was willing to meet with him and talk, but that person would not come to the station house.

"They want to meet with you at nine o'clock."

"You left a little late to call me. It's almost nine now."

"The contact didn't call me until ten minutes ago."

"Where's the meeting?"

When she told him, he got a bad feeling. It was in the Lower Ninth, and not on a good street.

"Do you think this is legit, Cheever?"

"My contact thinks it is, and he's a smart kid."

Neely put away his phone and swung the Taurus in a U-turn.

"Where are we going?" White asked.

"Lower Ninth. There's a concerned citizen who is willing to talk about that symbol."

"Again with the symbol," White said. "Did you get any sleep last night?"

"Enough," Neely lied.

"You need to forget about this symbol. It's just a bunch of street writers. It won't get us anywhere."

"It's all we've got."

The meeting place was the backyard of a burned out house. At one time, maybe fifty years ago, the house had been a beautiful wood-frame structure with bay windows and a corner tower. Now it was a shell. The fire had collapsed the roof and the floors. They walked around the back and found a black girl around sixteen or seventeen years old sitting on the concrete back step. She wasn't wearing gang colors, which surprised Neely.

"If I get seen talking to you, I'm dead. You know that, right?"

"Has someone threatened your life?" White asked.

"No, but this crew I'm with, they got some push, you know? They don't like rats."

White looked around at the tall bushes and trees that bordered the back yard.

"Who's going to see us?"

She stared at Neely with a sullen expression. "I'm only doing this for the babies. I don't like to see no baby get hurt."

"Do you know who took them?" Neely asked.

"Hell no."

He pulled up an image of the symbol on his phone and showed it to her.

"You recognize this, right?"

"So what? They all over the place."

"What can you tell us about the people who make them?"

"I can tell you they is a bunch of crazy motherfuckers. We see them at night creepin' around. They got these hoodies pulled up over their heads to keep anyone from gettin' a good look at them. One time Mitch and TreyZee caught one of them in our territory. They pulled off his hood and they say he was deformed."

"Deformed how?"

"I didn't see it, but they said his head was too big in the back. Like it stuck out way more than it's supposed to. They said his eyes were real big and his skin was pasty white—whiter than yours, even. They started beatin' on him, tryin' to get him to talk."

"Did he?"

"He kept screamin' one word over and over. Tsathoggua, Tsathoggua, Tsathoggua. Like he was a retard."

"Tsathoggua," Neely repeated. The word felt strange on his tongue. "Any idea what it means?"

"TrayZee said he was callin' to his god for help."

"Did he get help?"

"Expect not. They shot him and dumped him in the river."

White barked out a laugh.

"This is bullshit, Neely. She's just feeding us a line."

"They live underground," she said hotly, glaring at White.

"Girl, this is New Orleans. There is no underground."

"In the storm sewers. They live in the sewers and only come out at night. And there are regular people who help them."

"Help them how?" Neely asked.

"Fetch for them. Buy things for them. Keep the police or the city workers from knowin' about them."

"Why would people cover up for these freaks?" White asked.

The girl made a dismissive sound in her throat. "Same old reasons. Money and fear. They pay those who help them, and they kill anyone who crosses them, and not in a nice way."

"What do the words 'he waits' mean?"

"Don't know, don't care."

White chuckled. "She's playing us, Neely. Can't you see that?"

"Screw you, I'm out of here," she said. She stood up and started to walk toward the trees.

"Hold up there, girl, we're not finished with you yet," White said.

She started to run.

"Shit," White said. "I'll go after her. Get back to the car and circle around the block."

When Neely got to the front of the burned-out house, he saw that the hood of his car was up. Cursing under his breath, he looked into the engine bay to see what was missing. It was the battery, as he expected.

"Son of a bitch," he said, slamming down the hood of the Taurus.

He looked up and down the street. It was deserted, which was not too strange given that only half the houses on the street were lived in, and their occupants probably cowered inside at night with the doors triple-bolted and guns in their laps. He pulled out his phone and called White. When White didn't answer, he left him a text telling him what had happened. Then he started to punch in the number of a towing service to ask them to bring him a fresh battery.

Movement caught his eye under the one street light that had not been smashed out with rocks. A small figure in a black hoodie walked quickly away, only its back visible. Neely started walking rapidly toward the light with long strides. The sound of his footfalls clicked loudly in a stillness only broken by distant traffic. The figure began to run. Neely cursed and ran after it. He worked out regularly in the gym, but his durations on the treadmill were becoming briefer as his years advanced. His track and field days were definitely over.

He was able to keep the figure in black in view, but just barely. It led him across the Ninth in a direction opposite the one the girl had taken. He began to wonder if he was being decoyed away from her. The state of the neighborhood got progressively worse. It became like an overgrown ghost town, with here and there a building that looked as though it had been bombed.

He lost sight of the person in an open area that had turned back into a field. Tall grass and scrub trees grew around what was left of a concrete foundation. Panting to catch his breath with his hands on his thighs, he straightened and put White's number into his phone. No response. Where was that son of a bitch?

A noise drew his attention to a small shack at the edge of the overgrown vacant lot. It was painted flat black and built out of heavy planks. There were no windows. He walked around the edge of it with his Glock drawn, and saw that there was a door. Its heavy padlock had been beaten open. The wood of the door around it was scarred with the blows.

"Come on out. New Orleans police."

No response.

"If you make me come in and drag you out, I'm not going to be in a good mood."

Nothing.

"Shit," he muttered to himself under his breath. "I should have retired last year."

Holding the gun close to his chest at the ready, he stood to the side of the door and eased it open with the toe of his shoe. The interior of the shed was pitch black. He listened and heard nothing. The flashlight was back in the car—he shone light from his phone screen into the structure. There was nothing inside but a concrete cylinder jutting up from the floor that looked like a well. Its steel lid had been thrown back. Neely peered into the dark hole, and saw a steel ladder.

Caution warred with his hunter's instinct. It would be foolhardy to go down into that darkness alone, but if he waited, the little man in black would be long gone. Shaking his head at his own recklessness, he holstered the gun and climbed down the ladder with one hand, trying to light his way with the dismally dim glow from his phone. It wasn't a long descent. He found himself in a concrete tunnel that was just tall enough to walk in without bending over, if he kept to the middle where a trickle of water ran. He realized he must be in the New Orleans storm drainage system. The concrete pipe would lead eventually to a pumping station.

All the water in the sewers had to be pumped since there was no place to drain it. Half of the city was under sea level, and it was only the levees and pumps that kept it from being flooded by the river.

The pipe went on for what seemed like miles. Here and there other smaller pipes opened into it, sending their trickles of dirty water to join with the stream he was following. He wondered how long the battery in his phone would last. After walking for what seemed like an hour, he saw dim red light ahead and heard the hum of electricity. He approached the glow cautiously, gun in hand.

The pipe ended in a large square room that was illuminated by red lights in wire cages high up on its walls. It was a pumping station, as he had expected. The pump was enormous, a leviathan of cast iron painted bright yellow. The floor around it was covered with steel grates. When the water below the grates rose to a certain level, the big pump would probably cut in, he thought.

On the other side of the room was a concrete ledge about three feet above the grates that formed its floor. Trash had accumulated on it, as was to be expected. Every time it rained, discarded junk would be washed down the pipes into this room and caught by the grates. The city workers must have to clean them regularly. They were not doing their job, he thought. That was a large pile of debris on the ledge. It was black and rounded at the top. Where it caught the red light, it glistened wetly.

He reasoned that the force of storm waters rushing in must have washed all the trash up into one big pile and left it there. He started toward it across the grates, his metallic footfalls echoing from the concrete walls above the background hum.

When he got closer he saw the symbol painted in red on the wall. There were dozens of thick unlit candles stuck to the ledge on either side. They looked like church candles. The wax accumulated at their bases testified to frequent use.

There was something about the black heap of trash and dirt. Its shape was regular, almost as though it had been

It had a corpulent roundness, like a squatting frog or toad.

sculpted. Neely wondered if the cultists had shaped it into a crude representation of whatever god they worshipped. It had a corpulent roundness, like a squatting frog or toad.

"Drop the gun, Neely."

4.

Neely turned quickly. White stood at the mouth of the large pipe with his Glock in his hand, pointed at him. Beside him stood the girl they had been interviewing. She stared at him, her face expressionless.

"How did you get here?"

"I said to put down your gun." There was a hard edge to White's voice. "I'm not saying it again."

Neely slowly bent to lay his Glock on the grating under his feet. He straightened with his hands raised to shoulder level. The girl came forward and cautiously picked up the gun, never taking her eyes off him, then backed away.

"You're in with them," Neely said to White.

"I tried to steer you away, but you are one persistent son of a bitch."

"All this time you've been trying to keep me from following up on the symbol."

"So quick. Guess that's why they made you detective."

Neely looked at the girl. "This whole thing was a setup. You lured me here."

"You were getting close," White said. "We can't risk that. Sorry, Neely, but you have to go. Just so you know, it's nothing personal."

"It's pretty damned fucking personal with me," Neely said between his teeth.

A sound behind him made him turn his head.

"Keep those hands up," White barked.

From the mouth of a pipe above the ledge some distance from the sculpted heap of trash, four figures in identical black hoodies crawled forth. Their faces were shadowed by their hoods. Neely could not tell if they were male or female, but none of them were more than five feet tall. He wondered if they were children. One of them proceeded to light the candles on either side of the idol with a cigarette lighter.

"They've been here for thousands of years," White said in a conversational voice. "Since before New Orleans was even built. Usually they keep a low profile, but the appearance in the sky of the supernova has got them all excited. That's why they've been so active lately."

"I hope they pay you well, baby-killer."

White chuckled. "Yeah, they pay well, and in gold. I don't ask where they get it and I don't watch what they do with the babies. They pay me to protect them from people like you, which is what I'm doing."

"What about you?" Neely asked the girl standing beside White.

"The same," she said. "I make sure nobody gets close. They pay me good."

"We're all over the city, Neely," White said, grinning. "Hell, half the city council knows what's going on, or at least has heard rumors about it, and they don't care. They know not to ask questions."

"They care now. Too many kids have been snatched."

"Maybe." White shrugged, and the gun sagged lower in his hand. "It doesn't matter. Nothing's going to change."

Neely wondered if he could catch his partner off balance. There was around ten feet between them. The girl was holding his Glock by its barrel. *Maybe if I was twenty years old,* Neely thought. *Not today.*

More of the little men emerged from various pipes in the walls of the pumping chamber. One of them slid back his hood and took off his hoodie. He wore a red tunic with gold trim on the collar and sleeves. Neely saw that his head was bulbous and elongated in the back. Instead of hair, it was covered with a fine gray fur. The fur extended over his face and down his neck. It was even on the backs of his hands. Only his tiny ears were naked. He looked at Neely with black eyes twice as large as they should have been. His tiny slit of a mouth accentuated their unnatural size.

"Christ, they're not human," Neely said.

"Again with the lightning-quick intellect," White said. "Driving around with you for the past year, listening to your bullshit, and not being able to tell you to shut the fuck up was like living in hell, do you know that? I did it because I was told to do it, but you don't know how many times I wanted to put my fist in that blabbering mouth of yours."

Neely turned and faced him. He clenched his fists and spread his arms. "I guess now's your chance, hotshot."

White raised the Glock and gestured to the side with its barrel. "Over there. I don't want to hit any of my patrons."

The wail of a baby made them look toward the ledge. One of the little men jumped out of a pipe with a wadded blue blanket cradled in his arm. From the blanket a tiny pink hand emerged and waved in the air. The baby cried with those short, hard cries that demand attention, the cries no mother can ignore.

"Are they going to kill it?" Neely asked.

"Guess so. I've never watched it being done before."

"Just shoot him so we can get out of here," the girl said.

Neely had moved around the chamber so that the ledge and the little men were on his right side. White and the girl stood with their backs to the great yellow pump.

"I think we'll let Neely watch," White told her.

The little man with the baby passed it to the one who wore the red tunic. He held it cradled in his left arm and made a series of gestures over it with his right hand, muttering in a low voice. Neely could not distinguish the words, and realized he was speaking in some foreign language. The baby stopped crying. The other little men slid back their hoods. Their heads were elongated and covered in gray fur, just like the head of their priest, who stopped talking and extended the baby in both hands. With a slow reverence he walked toward the idol and laid the baby on the portion of the concrete ledge in front of it, then backed away. He knelt and bowed his head. All the other little men did the same.

The cutting-in of the pump made a sound like thunder. Neely leaped forward and grabbed White's gun hand. White was caught off balance. Neely forced him back against the vibrating pump and banged White's hand against the cast iron. The girl rushed to them and started to beat Neely on the head and shoulders with the butt of his Glock, which she still held by its barrel. Neely felt wetness on the side of his head and realized it was his own blood. He tried to protect himself by hunching his shoulder.

As the three struggled, the gun went off in White's hand. Neely barely heard it above the rumble of the pump. The girl staggered backward and fell to the floor grates. Neely did not look at her. All his attention was focused on holding White's gun hand away from his face. White was younger and stronger. Neely knew that if he weakened for only an instant, he was dead.

None of the little men tried to help White. As the two straining men came nearer the ledge, the alien creatures separated to either side and watched. The thunder of the pump made speech impossible. White had his back to the idol. He managed to kick Neely away and leveled the Glock at him with both hands.

The pump stopped. In the sudden silence the gurgling of the baby could be heard. Neely took a step back and spread his hands, wondering where his gun had fallen on the grates. He did not dare take his eyes off White to look for it. White straightened up slowly. He seemed to relax.

"Nice try, Neely. No cigar."

Behind him, the enormous round eyes of the black idol slowly opened. They were like the eyes of a toad. It stared down at White. A sound of reverence went up from the throats of the little men on either side. As White's finger began to tighten on the trigger, the wide, lipless mouth of the idol opened like the mouth of hell, and a shining black tongue darted out. It looked to Neely like a stream of black oil. It wrapped itself around White's shaved head and covered his face. Smoke rose from where it touched his skin. Neely heard muffled screams. The gun went off three times, but the bullets struck the concrete ceiling. White was dragged back off his feet and lifted into the air, his arms flailing and legs kicking. His torso disappeared into the mouth of the thing, followed by his legs and feet. The mouth closed.

Neely darted forward toward the living idol and grabbed up the baby in its blanket with both hands. He felt the thing's black eyes on him, but its tongue was occupied with White. He ran back across the grates and snatched up his Glock from where the girl had dropped it, then turned to confront the little men who had begun to close in behind him. He shot one of them in the stomach. The others stopped and stood looking at him.

"This isn't over," he said.

The little men said nothing.

The escape through the pipe was a nightmare. When he was a little way in, he got out his phone and used its screen for light, cradling the baby with his left elbow. Every time he passed an open side pipe, he wondered if they were going to come pouring out at him, but all the side pipes were empty. He had to stick the Glock into its vest holster to climb the steel ladder with the baby tucked under his left arm, but somehow he managed it. All the while it never stopped crying.

He felt the cool night air on his face as his head emerged from the mouth of the concrete cylinder. Something slid around his left ankle. It tightened, then burned like acid through his sock, making him scream. It began to pull downward with a force that was slow but irresistible. Holding on to the top iron rung of the ladder with his right hand, he shifted the still-squalling baby against his chest so that his left hand was beneath it, and threw the blue bundle up and over the lip of the cylinder. As he was dragged down the ladder and back into the sewer pipe, he heard the baby's cry.

Someone else will hear it, he thought. *When morning comes, someone walking by will hear it and investigate the black shed.*

The cries of the baby diminished to silence as he was dragged farther and farther away from the ladder. The water in the bottom of the pipe soaked through the back of his suit as he slid along in the slick mud. The pain in his ankle was beyond anything he had ever experienced. He found himself screaming and could not stop. He screamed his throat raw. The darkness was absolute.

After an eternity a red light became visible. He found himself dragged into the pumping station, across the floor grates, toward the concrete ledge while the little men stood on either side of their black god and watched in silence. Tears provoked in automatic reflex to the pain blurred his vision. Blinking them away, he saw the glistening toad-like thing, its wide mouth gaping, its tongue a black ribbon that dragged him ever nearer.

Someone will find the kid, he thought. When the light comes, someone is bound to walk by the shed. They'll find the baby and turn it in to child services.

He pulled his Glock from its holster and shot the god-thing in the face several times. One bullet went through its right eye. It blinked slowly but did not otherwise react. He shot the little priest in his red tunic and had the satisfaction of seeing him stagger and fall. The other little men in their black hoodies scattered silently into the open pipes like rats.

As he was lifted off the grates toward the gaping mouth of that expressionless gigantic caricature of a face, he put the muzzle of the gun to the side of his head and shot himself.

THE HAUNTER OF THE DARK

DARK LIGHT

1.

Harold Dobbs smelled the salt tang of the sea before the man who had just entered through the plate glass door of the antique dealership reached the counter. It was mingled with traces of tar and rotting fish. The scent was out of character for the upscale Providence establishment. Tailor-Dobbs was more likely to attract customers who smelled of Chanel No. 5 or lavender water. He waited with curiosity for the other to speak. The man cleared his phlegmy throat and swallowed. Dobbs tried not to wince.

"People say you buy things they find." His swamp Yankee accent was thick enough to spread on toast.

"Do they?"

"I want you to take a look at this and tell me what you'll give me for it."

Something rustled and thumped on the glass countertop. There was silence for several seconds.

"Well?" the seaman said.

"Describe it to me."

"What for? It's right in front of you."

"That may be so, my dear man, but I cannot see it."

"Maybe if you took off those dark glasses, you could see better."

Dobbs sighed patiently and smiled with the corners of his thin lips. "I've tried that. I'm afraid it doesn't work."

"Wait, what? Are you telling me you're blind?"

"As the proverbial bat."

"Well, shit, I never meant anything by what I said."

"No offense taken. Describe the item, please."

"It's a metal box. Me and my crew fished it up from Narragansett Bay along with our lobster pots. It looks old-like, and it's got some kind of writing on it and weird designs."

"How large is it?"

"About eight inches, I'd reckon."

"What metal is it made of?"

"You got me there. I was hoping you could tell me. It looks sort of like brass, only it's got no corrosion and it's so damn hard, a drill won't even leave a mark on it."

Dobbs raised his eyebrows behind the dark glasses. "You tried to drill a hole in it?"

"We couldn't get it open and thought maybe it was full of gold or jewels or something. Then Charlie—that's Charles Snider, my mate—says, 'What if the box itself is worth more than what's inside it?' That made us think."

"I would imagine so."

Dobbs reached out his slender white hands and touched the box. He jumped slightly as a kind of electric shock went into his fingers, but gave no other sign of surprise. He picked the box up and turned it over several times, tracing the bas-relief letters and symbols on its surface. It was heavy for its size, and there was something odd about the angles of its corners. With care, he felt for the crack between the lid and the body. He had to use his fingernail before he found it, the gap was so tight. It must be almost invisible, he thought. The metal had a kind of oily feel and drew the heat out of his fingers. With care, he shook the box gently and listened. There was no rattle, but something heavy inside made it feel unbalanced.

"Have you shown this to anyone else?"

There was silence. Dobbs visualized the lobster boat captain shaking his head. People often did that when they forgot he was blind.

"I was told you give good money for things people find."

"That's true, but only for things of value."

"This is old. Got to be. No telling how long it's been down on the bottom of the Bay. Maybe a hundred year or more."

"What you have is a white elephant," Dobbs said. He did not emphasize his words, merely stated them as fact.

"What's that?"

"That's something odd that nobody wants."

"This has to be worth something. That carving looks real old. And the writing is foreign. I never seen nothing like it, and neither has my crew."

Dobbs set the box down and tapped the top several times with a manicured fingernail, pondering to himself. It was an unusual item, of that he had no doubt. Maybe an art piece of some kind, or a relic stolen from a museum or a private collection. It felt ancient to his practiced touch. The edges of the letters were worn round. Only centuries would do that. Likely whatever was in the box had spoiled long ago, but it was strange that the box itself was not corroded. And there was just a faint possibility that it contained something of real value.

"Did you clean the box up? Polish it?"

"Didn't need to. It come out of the ocean like this, shining like a new quarter. Whatever metal this is, it don't rust."

"Possibly electrum," Dobbs mused, still considering.

"Elec-what?"

"It doesn't matter. I will buy it from you right now, for one thousand dollars cash money in your hand. What do you say?"

"A thousand? Damn, you got yourself a deal."

The man had expected Dobbs to try to bargain him down. This was not the antique dealer's way. He detested haggling, and always gave what he considered a fair price. This had made Tailor-Dobbs a byword in Rhode Island among those with old family treasures to sell.

Dobbs knew he was taking a chance. If he had misjudged the man or the box itself, he would be out a thousand dollars. But money was not a pressing issue. Not only was the business doing well, but he was independently wealthy due to a family inheritance. He could afford to be generous, and to take a risk. He rang the little silver bell that sat on the counter and waved with his hand in the air. The high-heeled shoes of his young assistant, Andrea Newcastle, clicked across the marble tiles on the floor.

"Yes, Mr. Dobbs?" Her accent was cultured British upper-class. That was the main reason he had agreed to let his partner, Julian Tailor, hire her. He enjoyed listening to her crisp diction. It reminded him of college days at Oxford.

"Withdraw one thousand dollars from the safe for this gentleman, will you please, Andrea. And take this box into the office and set it on my desk."

"You won't be sorry," the lobsterman said with enthusiasm. "It's a real strange box. No one ever seen anything like it. I bet it's worth a whole lot more than you paid for it."

Dobbs did not bother to answer. He had lost interest in the man as soon as he had agreed to the transaction. Maybe his story was true, or maybe the box was stolen and the story a lie. Dobbs did not particularly care one way or the other. His curiosity was aroused by the electric shock he had received when he touched it. That, he had not imagined. The texture of the metal and the shape of the elevated letters, if letters they were, felt very old, and alien. And the shape of the box itself was wrong, somehow. That puzzled and intrigued him more than anything else.

"You paid a grand for this? Have you gone insane, Harold?"

Dobbs winced at the withering tone in his partner's voice. He had not expected Julian to be pleased about the purchase, but he disliked being scolded like a truant schoolboy, even by his lover.

"It's my money, Julian," he said with an excess of the Boston drawl he tended to fall into when annoyed. "I'll spend it in whatever way I see fit."

"Sure, but a thousand dollars? I bet that fisherman would have sold you this for a hundred. Hell, he probably would have let it go for fifty."

"You may be correct, but I believe it to be worth more. What do you make of it?"

He waited while Tailor examined the box. They were in their shared office at the back of the store. Two desks faced each other beneath a wall of tall, naked windows. The items on Dobbs' desk were neatly arranged. Tailor's was almost buried beneath scattered documents and receipts.

"Well, it's unusual, I'll give you that. The bas-relief was cast in place when the box was made, I'd say. Probably a lost-wax casting. The characters looks vaguely Phoenician or Etruscan. I'm not familiar with any of the symbols."

"What do you make of the corners?"

"You mean their angles? They're a little off, but that's not unusual with ancient castings."

"Did you feel anything when you picked it up?"

"It feels oily, if that's what you're getting at, but I think that's just the alloy itself. It looks like some kind of electrum. It may have a significant gold content."

Dobbs hid his disappointment. Evidently the box did not shock everyone who touched it.

"Have you opened it yet?" Tailor asked.

"The lid's frozen shut."

"It's hinged, I think. Hard to see the hinges, they're recessed and integrated with the design. There's no latch."

"I'm going to try penetrating oil and heat before I resort to anything more drastic," Dobbs said.

"Whatever's inside it is probably slime by now," Tailor said.

"Yes, Julian, I know that. Even so, I am going to try to coax the lid open before I start hammering on it like a coked-up baboon."

"Whatever you say." Dobbs heard the box being set down on his desk. "This is your toy to play with, Harold. God knows, you paid enough for it."

"There's no point in having money unless you can spend it unwisely. You should know that. What's the name of the new car you just bought?"

"Roma."

"That's it. Roma."

"It's a Ferrari, Harold. A driver's car. What can I tell you, I like to drive."

"So did I, before the accident." Dobbs could not keep bitterness from his voice.

He had lost his sight thirteen years ago in a boating accident while serving as a crew member on his late father's World Cup racing yacht, the *Kismet*. It had not been anyone's fault, just one of those little things that happen and change your life forever. A squall blew up, the sheets got fouled, and a rogue wave sent his head into the stainless steel capstan. It was a miracle the crew managed to keep him from being washed overboard. After seven weeks in a coma, he had awakened with nothing to show for the incident but a scar across the back of his head and eyes that no longer served as windows on the world.

"You know I'll always take care of you, Harold," Tailor said. There was a note of tenderness in his voice.

"I know that, Julian, my love. Where would I be without your eyes and . . . other body parts."

Julian laughed. Dobbs felt a strong hand squeeze his shoulder.

Julian had come into his life, blond, muscular and tanned, nine years ago when his spirits were at their lowest ebb, and talked him into using some of his family money to open a store so that he could turn his passionate hobby for antiques into a business. He had wanted to call it Dobbs & Tailor, but Julian had convinced him that Tailor-Dobbs sounded more professional.

"Leave me alone, now, will you, Julian? I want to play with my toy, as you call it."

"Whatever you like. I've got to look after that auction we've got on for tonight. There are going to be some big players in the audience. The crème de la crème of Providence social life. This is how we make our money, kid."

Dobbs forced a smile. He was thirty-eight, five years older than Tailor, but Julian persisted in referring to him in that patronizing manner, which, if he were honest with himself, Dobbs had to admit he found somewhat endearing.

"Before you go, tell Andrea to come in and take photographs of this box so she can research it online. Maybe she can come up with a match."

"Will do, kid. Have fun."

3.

Despite his intention to work on the box immediately, business affairs occupied Dobbs until after closing time. The windows beside his desk were black rectangles and the store an empty, silent tomb before he was able to get out the can of penetrating oil and the hairdryer he used to free up the mechanisms of delicate metal antiques.

He need not have bothered taking them out of their drawer. When he tried the lid of the box experimentally before applying the oil, it opened with ease and stood wide on its hinges.

As he gazed into the box with his blind eyes, he saw that it contained an irregular egg-shaped crystal some four inches on its longest diameter that was suspended by wires. He continued to stare at it, feeling numb.

It was impossible. He could not see anything, not so much as a fuzzy blur or a shadow. The best specialists in Boston had repeatedly assured him that he never would see anything again. Yet he was looking down at the crystal, and seeing it in a kind of black-and-white, negative image way. It flickered with white fire that crawled along its edges. Bending his head closer, he saw that it was some translucent crystalline mineral, black with lighter striations running through it like veins in black marble.

Wonderingly, he looked around the office, and realized that the crystal was the only thing he saw. It seemed to float against a black velvet curtain, or more accurately against a curtain of no color at all, because the darkness within him was the absence of all light, color or form. He saw its edges clearly, but the metal band that surrounded it and the wires that supported it were a dim gray. The wires, seven in number, faded to nothing as they extended away from the crystal, as though illuminated only by the radiance thrown off from stone itself. The interior sides of the box to which the wires were attached remained invisible.

He could not take his eyes off the crystal. It was the most beautiful thing he had ever seen. He removed his glasses and wiped the inner corners of his eyes with his fingers, realizing that it made no difference when his hand passed in front of his face. His view of the crystal was not obstructed. This meant he was not really seeing it with his eyes. Of course not, his eyes were dead. Then how was he seeing it?

He tipped up the lid of the box and allowed it to fall shut. The crystal disappeared. he opened the lid wide and it reappeared against what he thought of as the darkness.

"What the devil are you?" he murmured under his breath, squinting reflexively down at the irregular facets of the stone in a futile effort to see it more clearly.

Something stirred in the depths of his mind. It was not a voice or a touch, or any sensation at all, but a feeling of awareness, a kind of response that he intuited on some level below language.

Dobbs sat back in his chair, listening to the silence. He tried to sense the stirring but felt nothing.

"Hello? Is something there?"

No response came.

Leaning forward, he let his fingertips flutter over the smooth facets of the crystal. It appeared to be naturally formed, but its crystalline structure was unfamiliar to him. It drew the heat from his fingers as if made of ice. Why was it suspended within the box? Maybe it was some cultic object, and the crystal had a sacred significance. This he could readily believe, since it gave sight to the blind—a limited kind of sight, at least.

After staring at the stone for many minutes and caressing it like some wondering child, he finally closed the lid and put the box into the floor safe behind his desk, then went up to the living quarters he shared with Tailor above the store. Julian had still not returned from the auction. Dobbs made himself a light meal in the microwave, undressed, showered, and slid into bed, all the while his mind filled with wonder. To see again, to see anything, was a miracle. Before falling asleep he found himself giving thanks in a spontaneous prayer, without knowing to whom he prayed.

4.

"You may have been right about it being a cultic object," Andrea told Dobbs.

"What have you been able to find out?"

Dobbs sat at his desk, leaning back in his swivel leather chair. The open box rested on the desk. The girl sat beside the desk with a notebook and pencil in her hands. She wore her dark hair gathered at the back of her head in a French twist to reveal the lines of her slender neck. He studied the angles of her high cheekbones, her straight nose, her full lips. It was a pity her features did not match the beauty of her voice.

Four days had passed since the purchase of the crystal. Each night he had sat at his desk for hours, gazing into it, and had been both shocked and delighted to realize that his field of vision was expanding. Now he could see not only the crystal itself, but dim outlines of the faces of other human beings. As yet they were like chalk drawings on a blackboard, edged in fine lines of white fire against shadow, but each day they became clearer, and just this morning he had begun to make out the outlines of hands as well. Whatever quality in the crystal had restored his sight was strengthening it, expanding its field.

He had said nothing about this miracle to Julian. In part it was because he dreaded that his lover might dismiss him as a self-deluded blind man. But mostly it was an instinct that told him to keep the change private. He remembered fairytales his grandmother would read to him when he was a young child. If someone questioned a fairy gift, it always vanished away. He could not bear to think about losing this gift of sight.

He realized the girl was speaking and focused on her words.

"There were no photographs, of course. I didn't expect to find any due to the object's apparent age, but I had hoped for a drawing or engraving. No such luck, I'm afraid. I did locate a textual description in an old newspaper article that matches the object."

"Read it to me, please."

She consulted her notebook. "It was in an article about a religious cult that operated from an old church on Federal Hill in the latter part of the 19th century. The building was torn down decades ago. They called themselves the Church of Starry Wisdom. There were rumors of child abductions, and the local people drove the cult out of Providence. Many years later, in the nineteen-thirties, when the article was written, this box or something very like it was discovered in the church spire. The article describes it, and I quote, as 'a roughly cubical box of strange yellow metal with raised letters of an unknown language and occult symbols covering its surface.' Nothing was written about its contents."

"What became of it?"

"Apparently it was cast into Narragansett Bay and never seen again. Until now, that is."

He saw the corners of her lips move as she smiled at him. She might have been beautiful, he thought, if only her face were not quite so gaunt and drawn. An unkind critic might even describe it as haggard.

He recognized Julian's footsteps before he breezed into the office to stand beside Andrea. Dobbs found his partner's features equally disturbing. A kind of shadow seemed to move across them, and his eyes were dark and sunken. Had Julian always looked like this? Or could it be that he was ill?

"Any luck?" Julian asked brightly. He put his hand on Andrea's shoulder. She glanced up at him but did not draw away.

"What do you know about the Church of Starry Wisdom?" Dobbs asked.

"Never heard of it."

"Andrea has been telling me this box and the stone it contains had some sort of religious significance for this cult."

Julian glanced down at her notebook, his lack of interest evident.

"I don't see how this helps us with the sale of the box. It's mere speculation that what we have is the same as what is described in the article."

"It doesn't matter. I'm not selling the box."

"Suit yourself," Julian said with a shrug. "I just dropped in to remind you about the cocktail party in the Sutherlands' townhouse on Thursday."

"I wish you hadn't. I'd forgotten about it."

Tailor shook his head. "You have to be there, Harold. The Sutherlands are our biggest buyers."

"So you've told me. You know how I like to leave that side of the business to you."

"The name on the storefront is Tailor-Dobbs. They want to see the Dobbs side of the business at their party. You're the great antiques expert of Rhode Island. They're showing off that bronze they bought from us last month."

"The Remington. I remember it."

"Nine o'clock, kid. I'll get you there and back home. Andrea's coming, too."

"Did the Sutherlands ask for Andrea?" Dobbs said in surprise.

"No, but they might have questions about our inventory, and she knows what we have better than we do."

Andrea reached up to her shoulder and laid her hand lightly on Julian's hand.

"It's just that I believe a separation should be maintained between owner and employee, as a matter of decorum."

Julian looked at the girl, who started to laugh and put her hand over her lips to stifle the sound.

"Of course, Harold, but Andrea is practically a partner, wouldn't you say?"

Dobbs said nothing. Inside his heart a small flame of anger ignited and continued to burn there like a drop of acid.

5.

Later that afternoon a man of strikingly unconventional appearance entered the store. Dobbs watched him approach the counter. He was several inches over six feet in height, broad in the shoulders but thin and angular, with a cadaverous face. A solid block of chin jutted out from under a hawk-like beak of a nose. He wore a gray Homburg hat with a black band and a herringbone wool topcoat, although the weather was mild. When he spread his hands on the glass counter, Dobbs saw that they were enormous, their knuckles swollen with arthritis, the fingernails square-cut. On the back of the left hand was a small star tattoo in blue ink.

Movement attracted his attention to the tall man's shoulder. Dobbs reflexively drew back. Something peered at him from behind the man's neck and slid forward. It was sinuous and elongated, like a weasel or ferret, with bright little eyes that did not blink. It was a bizarre pet to carry about in public on one's shoulder, Dobbs thought. There was something sinister about it that he did not like.

"May I help you?"

"You have something I want." The man's lips barely moved. The voice seemed to echo in his chest.

"I certainly hope so. That's why we're here," Dobbs said, forcing a bland smile.

"A box. A seaman sold a metal box to you several days ago."

"I don't seem to remember such a sale."

"It is here," the man said. "I wish to buy it."

"I can have someone examine our inventory, if you will leave your name and number."

"Whatever you paid for it, I am prepared to give you ten times the amount."

Dobbs felt his face harden. "I'm sorry, but no such item is for sale."

The man said nothing. He continued to stare at Dobbs.

"Now if you will excuse me, I have other business to attend to."

"I will pay you one hundred times what you paid for the box, and its contents."

"We have no box for sale," Dobbs said sharply.

The tall man nodded. The creature he carried poked its furry head around his neck and hissed softly, showing sharp little teeth. He reached into his coat and took out a business card, then laid it on the counter without shifting his dark eyes from the antique dealer's face. He touched his fingers to the brim of his hat.

"If you do decide to sell it, you can reach me at this number, day or night. Mr. Dobbs, believe me when I say it would be in your best interest to sell the box."

"Is that a threat?"

The man smiled coldly, turned and walked out of the store. Dobbs picked up the card. His vision was still not good enough to read what was printed on it. He rang the silver bell and motioned for Andrea.

"What does this say?" he asked, passing her the card.

"Where did you get this?" she asked in surprise.

"The gentleman who just left gave it to me."

"It says only 'Church of Starry Wisdom.' And there is a phone number."

"Nothing more?"

"No, that's all."

That night, Julian stayed out late, something that was happening with greater frequency since the hiring of

Andrea. Dobbs sat alone in their bedroom, naked on the queen-sized bed with his thin legs folded under him, the box resting open in his lap. He had not turned on a light. Why bother, when he knew the position of every article of furniture by memory? In any case, he had begun to see inanimate objects. The edges of the matching bureaus and the old French wardrobe that stood in the corner shimmered with pale fire.

As he gazed at the black crystal, vistas opened not only in space but in time. He felt himself falling into the past through aeons and aeons as though down a dark well. Panoramas formed and dissolved in front of him. The visions were colorless, with white edges against a dark background. He watched primitive creatures that looked almost human battle reptilian beings that were not human in any degree, and saw great towers of black stone raised into the heavens in alien cities. Whirling back through time made him dizzy, but he could not turn away. The ancient prehistory of the world, as it had been long before the rise of humanity, rolled before him in reverse like a black-and-white silent movie.

Abruptly, he became aware that he was no longer alone. His sensitive nose detected a whiff of sulphur on the air. Something slid across the floor of the dark bedroom, something large. A fear more intense than any he had ever felt gripped his heart and stopped his breath. He did not dare look up from the crystal. A kind of static in the air crackled and made the hairs on his bare arms and legs stand up. He forced himself to whisper.

"What are you?"

Dobbs knew he would have shrieked out loud if the thing had spoken. Mercifully, there was no answer. This was what the ancient Greeks meant when they wrote about panic, the primal fear experienced by a mortal when in the presence of a living god.

"Do you come from the crystal?"

There was a sense of affirmation at the base of his skull.

"Is it you who gave me back my sight?"

Affirmation.

"Thank you."

No response.

Slowly, he forced his gaze up from the crystal and looked beyond the footboard of the bed. He received a chaotic impression of an asymmetrical form that ceaselessly rolled in upon itself and reformed from moment to moment, like a billow of smoke. Along with it came the sense of great wings.

"Why did you not show yourself earlier?"

A flash of blinding white light seared his vision for an instant. It was like a bolt of lightning. Dobbs sensed fear, hatred, revulsion, anger, bitterness, agony.

"I think I understand. You cannot tolerate light."

Affirmation.

"That's why you waited until tonight to show yourself. You needed a place of total darkness."

Affirmative.

"The French wardrobe," Dobbs said. "The one standing in the corner. It has a lock, and only I possess the key."

The enormous, ornate walnut wardrobe was empty. Julian had never liked it, and Dobbs had always found it inconvenient due to its height. It stood over eight feet tall. He watched as the roiling mass of smoke slid over the floor with a soft rustle. The doors of the wardrobe opened. The darkness poured itself into the oblong cavity. Two shadow appendages that reminded Dobbs of the great taloned claws of a bird of prey extended out and gently drew the doors shut with a small click of the latch.

His heart pounding with mingled terror and wonder, Dobbs eased himself off the edge of the bed and inched his way to the wardrobe. An antique key stood out from the keyhole in one of the doors. He reached toward it, his hand shaking, and gently turned it. In the dead silence he heard the lock click into place. Withdrawing the key, he carefully slid the ornate little silver cover on the keyhole closed.

"Is it suitable for your purpose?" he whispered.

A sense of affirmation came from inside.

"You have given me back my sight. I will not reject your gift."

If the thing of darkness heard and understood, it gave him no sign.

7.

Everyone at the cocktail party wore a mask of nightmare. All the faces were sallow, pale, gaunt, the haunted eyes surrounded by dark circles, or they were bloated and florid with blood.

Dobbs sat in the middle of a white leather sofa, a cocktail glass in his hand, looking around at the other guests from behind his dark glasses. He had begun to realize that the sight granted him by the black crystal, or more properly by the god of the crystal, was shadowed or tainted in some way. He saw the character flaws and vices of other people reflected in their facial features as various kinds of deformities or diseases. It was as though everyone he looked at wore a semi-transparent mask of ugliness.

A few of the guests, who were among the wealthiest and most prominent members of the Rhode Island social circle, has grotesque creatures crawling over their bodies. Only Dobbs saw them. Some of these things looked vaguely like small animals and were similar to what he had seen on the shoulder of the man from Starry Wisdom. Others were more insect-like, or so completely alien they defied characterization. When he had tried to touch one of them in passing, his hand went through it. He speculated that they were spiritual parasites of some kind, and that they expressed the sins of those who bore them. Periodically, they sank their sharp little teeth into the necks of their hosts and seemed to feed.

Julian and Andrea stood across the room, chatting with Eleanor Sutherland, an elderly woman with a giant spider clinging to her breast. It had its grotesque round head nuzzled into her scrawny throat. From time to time its bloated, bristle-covered body pulsed and trembled with a kind of ecstasy.

Julian looked over at him and said something into the ear of the English girl. She laughed and put her arm around his neck, then kissed him on the cheek. She looked at Dobbs with a self-satisfied smile on her gaunt face. Neither of them carried astral parasites. Maybe they had not yet fully materialized from whatever nightmare dimension spawned them. Or maybe neither of them had yet committed crimes heinous enough to warrant their presence.

The man sitting next to him on the sofa was talking.

"I really wish you could see the supernova, Harold. It is spectacular, as red as a ruby and absolutely huge. It dominates the entire night sky. They say it's going to fade away in a few weeks, but it just keeps getting brighter. Superstitious people are calling it a bad omen. I don't believe in astrology myself, but you have to admit, there have been a lot of bizarre happenings around the world since it showed itself. Religious nuts are even talking about the apocalypse, if you can believe that. They think it's the Wormwood of prophecy."

Dobbs stood up, his gaze never leaving his partner and his assistant. He picked a knife off the coffee table and tapped it repeatedly against the rim of his glass. Heads turned to look and the room fell silent.

"I have a party trick that I would like to show you," Dobbs said. "Do you wish to see it?"

Murmurs of assent came from a number of people. Dobbs removed his dark glasses and stared around the room.

"As most of you know, I am stone-blind. I have been blind for thirteen years, ever since a boating accident took away my sight. None the less, lately I have been studying the esoteric secrets of the adepts of India, and I have developed the ability to see without eyes."

Amused laughter rippled around the room. They thought he was making a joke of some kind.

"I'm going to ask you to challenge me to identify the items you hold up or point to. To make it absolutely certain that I cannot see, I will blindfold myself."

He took a handkerchief from his suit pocket, shook it out, then twisted it and tied it over his eyes.

Tailor came over to him with a frown and touched his arm. He leaned close. "What in God's name are you doing, Harold? Are you trying to make yourself into a laughingstock? You look like a fool."

Dobbs pushed his partner gently aside. "Who has an item they wish me to identify? Yes, you? Hold it up, please, so that I can sense it."

A young woman giggled and bent to remove one of her high-heel shoes. Balancing unsteadily on one leg, she held it above her head. Several others laughed.

"I sense a woman's shoe. Is that correct?"

There were murmurs of surprise.

"Who else? Hold it up."

A well-dressed older man with a potbelly silently held up a pen.

"Yes, I sense it. A pen, is it not? And unless I am wrong, it is a fountain pen."

"That's right," the man said in a gruff voice. He looked around. "He's right."

"It's a trick. He can see," someone said.

Mrs. Sutherland held up her hand. "I assure you all, Mr. Dobbs spoke the absolute truth. He has been completely blind for many years."

"Harold, stop this," Tailor whispered harshly into his ear. "You're creating a spectacle."

"Really, Julian. It's not as if I'm fondling a woman in public, is it?"

Tailor's face registered surprise, then confusion. He said nothing.

"My partner wishes me to stop," Dobbs said to his audience. "Perhaps that would be for the best. Some mysteries are better left in darkness."

With a flourish he pulled off the blindfold. A spatter of puzzled applause occurred. He sat down and picked up his unfinished drink. Tailor sat beside him.

"How did you do that?"

"It's just a party trick, Julian. As I said at the beginning."

"But how could you know what would be held up? Did you make a prior arrangement with the people who held up the items?"

"No."

"Then how? It was almost as if you could really see."

"A magician never reveals his secrets. If I told you, I'd have to kill you."

He laughed. After a moment, Tailor joined in, but his laughter was uncertain. From across the room, Andrea continued to stare at him with wide, nervous eyes.

8.

"Why are you saying these things, Harold? It isn't like you." There was hurt in Tailor's voice.

They sat at their desks facing each other, as they had sat through all the years since Dobbs had bought the business. He was no longer wearing dark glasses. His clear gray eyes regarded Tailor without emotion.

"I am dissolving our partnership. I want you to move out of our apartment. You can keep the things I've bought for you over the years. Everything else stays in the store. By the way, you can inform Miss Newcastle on your way out that her services will no longer be required. Perhaps you can find a place for her."

Tailor's face hardened. "You can't do this, Harold. We are legal partners. I own half of the business and half of the inventory. I don't know what's got into you, but I'm not going anywhere."

Dobbs relaxed back into his swivel chair and smiled. "I think you are, Julian. The other day I examined the books you've been keeping and discovered a number of shocking anomalies. You have been cheating me out of most of the profits of Tailor-Dobbs for years, and that's not all. You have been siphoning off my savings at the same time. The police would be very interested."

A shadow of uncertainty had fallen across Tailor's features.

"You couldn't have examined the books. You're blind."

"I was blind. But now I see very clearly."

"If that's true, it's wonderful, Harold. No one in the world would be happier for you to regain your sight."

"You don't need to pretend any longer, Julian. I should think that would be a relief, after all the years you've fleeced me while sharing my bed. My bed, Julian. I bought this business. I furnished our apartment. I acquired our inventory."

"The business would have gone under long ago without me," Tailor said with a savage note in his voice. He scowled at Dobbs. "You know nothing about people. Buyers and sellers alike would have robbed you blind." He laughed, realizing that he had made a cruel joke.

"That may be," Dobbs admitted. "You are good with people, Julian, I'll give you that. But everything you know about antiques, you learned from me."

Tailor stood up and leaned forward. "I'm not just going to walk out. This is my life, Harold. I won't let you take it away from me."

"You will do just that, and you will do it today," Dobbs said calmly. "Unless you want a visit from the police. I have the books, Julian. I have the receipts. You've left a paper trail that anyone could read—even a blind man."

Tailor started to speak, thought better of it and bared his teeth, with his knuckles pressed against the desktop.

"You'll be hearing from my lawyer," he said, and stalked out of the office, slamming the door behind him.

"I doubt that," Dobbs said softly to himself.

Something woke him from dreamless sleep. He lay in the middle of the big bed, listening. The room was dark save for a pale shadow of moonlight on the drawn drapes. The scuff of a shoe on the floor of the hall made him sit up. He slid out from under the white silk sheet and stood naked beside the bed on the cold floorboards, peering around the room through the darkness. It was empty, but someone was approaching the door from outside.

He stared at the wall and concentrated, then began to see through the wall to the hallway. Two men crouched there with flashlights in their hands. One was obese. There was no weapon in the bedroom. Dobbs had never imagined he would need a gun. The valuable items in the store were locked up downstairs and what money he kept there was in the safe, along with the box that held the black crystal.

A sliding sound came from inside the French wardrobe. The god of the crystal was aware of the danger. Dobbs wondered if it had sensed the approach of the two men on its own, or had been alerted by his anxiety.

There was only one door to the bedroom. The windows had security bars on them. He thought about hiding in the bathroom but knew they would find him, and the idea of cowering in the shower was somehow distasteful. Instead, he went to the bedroom door and opened it.

"Come in, gentlemen."

Brightness washed over his face as they painted him with the beams of their flashlights.

"It's him," the fat man said.

They pushed him back into the bedroom. Dobbs saw that the one who had spoken held a revolver. They ran their flashlights over the walls and furniture.

"Check the bathroom."

The thiner man drew a compact automatic from his waist and went cautiously into the bathroom. He emerged a few seconds later.

"Empty." His voice was high-pitched, like the voice of a child that had not yet broken.

"Is there anyone else here?" the fat man asked Dobbs.

"I am alone."

"Your name is Harold Dobbs?"

"That is my name."

"Do as I say and you won't be harmed."

"I'm not a brawler. What do you want from me?"

"Is he really blind?" The thinner man waved his gun up and down in front of the antique dealer's face.

"Do you mind if I put something on?"

"Go ahead," the fat man said. "Don't do anything stupid."

Dobbs took his bathrobe off the back of a chair and covered his nakedness.

"Do you know why we're here?"

Dobbs studied the man's round face. His cheeks were flushed to an unhealthy degree, and there were broken blood vessels in his nose. The other man, who could not have been out of his late teens, was pale and thin-faced. Both carried nebulous, semitransparent creatures on their backs. A kind of giant centipede slid over the shoulder of the fat man with a silken ripple of its many legs. The thing that clung to the youth looked a little bit like a large rat.

"I presume you are here to rob me."

The teenager chuckled. "You're not wrong."

"The box you bought last week from a fisherman. Where is it?" the other demanded.

He held the revolver in his left hand. Dobbs saw on the back of the hand a small star tattoo. He studied the hands of his young companion and found a similar tattoo on the back of the boy's hand.

"You are both from Starry Wisdom."

"You're sharp," the fat man said.

"Why else would you want the box?"

"I'll ask the questions; you just work on answering them."

With a casual gesture, Dobbs indicated the French wardrobe. "The box is in there."

The younger man went to the wardrobe and rattled the doors. "It's locked."

"Where's the key?" demanded the fat man.

"I'll get it for you." Dobbs crossed to his bureau. "Shall I turn on the overhead light so that you can see what you're doing?"

The fat man hesitated. "Turn it on. Don't try to run—you won't make it."

"I'm blind. How could I run?"

He went to the doorway and snapped on the ceiling light, which was on a dimmer. A soft yellow glow filled the bedroom. The two turned off their flashlights.

"The key," urged the fat man.

He returned to the bureau and took an antique key from its hanger, then held it out. The fat man nodded, and the youth took the key from Dobbs.

"Stand back. Don't do anything foolish or I will shoot you," the fat man said.

"I have no doubt of that," the antique dealer replied in his Boston drawl. He backed toward the doorway. The fat man kept the revolver leveled on his chest.

"Get the box."

The youth inserted the key into the wardrobe lock and turned it.

"What is that stink?" he said.

Dobbs reached behind him and snapped off the ceiling light.

The screams of the two men were gratifying, although brief. Overlaying the sulphur stench was a sharp scent of ozone. He watched the dark god flow around each corpse lying on the floor. It seemed to draw some unseen essence from the bodies. After a time the god slid back into the wardrobe and closed the doors with its shadowy hands. The parasitic creatures that had crawled on the shoulders of the robbers were gone. Dobbs approached cautiously, stepping over the body of the fat man, and picked the key up from the floor. He used it to lock the wardrobe.

His heart was beating hard, but not from fear. He felt a strange kind of excitement, almost an exultation. The Starry Wisdom cult had expected to find a helpless blind man. They had not anticipated encountering someone in league with their own dark god.

In the depths of his mind grew determination. The cult would never stop trying to steal the crystal. It was necessary to deal with them. He wondered if this was his own thought, or something the entity in the wardrobe had inserted into his brain? Not that it mattered. They were joined together as one. He bent and picked up the revolver from where it had fallen, then found the automatic beneath the bed.

"I'll have to dispose of their bodies first," he said out loud.

In his mind he felt impatience, then grudging acceptance.

"You will go with me?"

Affirmation.

"You will guide me?"

Again, affirmation.

"Good. We'll do it all tonight."

10.

It was a strange sensation, to be behind the wheel of a car, driving again after so many years. He had taken Julian's new Ferrari Roma, which his partner had not yet had a chance to remove from the garage. He drove for what must have been almost two hours, not knowing where he was going, but trusting the guidance of the dark god. The car left the highway and followed a deserted secondary road through a farming district that had been largely abandoned and allowed to grow wild.

As he approached an old-fashioned country church with a tall steeple, the impulse came to turn off the car's headlights. He idled closer and killed the engine. Beside the church were parked cars and pickups. Lights glowed in its pointed windows.

Dobbs got out of the car. From inside the building he heard chanting. Focusing his vision, he saw through the wall that more than a dozen men and women were gathered around some kind of altar that stood within a circle of tall sculpted figures that reminded him of the stone statues on Easter Island.

The moon had set. Apart from the light spilling from the windows of the church, there was that complete darkness that is only to be found in the countryside, far from streetlights and houses. He looked up. In the starry vault blazed the supernova. He had been told it was blood-red, but he could not see color. To him it appeared to be a shining white diamond. It had a ring around it that gave it the appearance of a great eye that glared down on the world in judgment.

He took from the passenger seat of the Roma the chain and padlock he had been instructed to bring and carried it to the doors of the church. With great care to avoid noise, he slid the chain through the wrought iron handles and clicked the padlock shut through its links. He returned to the car and took out a can of gasoline from the footwell of the passenger seat. Opening it, he walked once around the church, pouring the liquid from its spout onto the base of the clapboards as he went. When he returned to the doors, the can was empty. He drew a lighter from his pocket and used it to ignite the gasoline, which burst into flame with a great whooshing sound as the fire raced around the church.

Dobbs felt serene. He realized that his heart rate was not even elevated. He had a sense that nothing could go wrong, that he was guided and protected. Without haste, he returned to the car and took from it the handguns of the two dead robbers, then stood waiting.

Shouts of alarm came first, followed by screams of terror. There was loud pounding and kicking on the doors, which rattled on their iron hinges but did not open. The fire began to eat its way up the wooden walls of the church. It was the first time he had looked at so much fire with his new sight. He found the way it danced strangely beautiful, almost mesmerizing.

One of the church windows crashed outward as a chair was thrown through the panes of glass. A man struggled to crawl through the rising sheet of flames to escape. It was the same cadaverous giant with the long face who had visited the store and tried to buy the crystal. The man stared at him and hesitated, even though his ritual robe was burning. Dobbs saw recognition in his dark eyes. He allowed the man to reach the tall grass under the window, which was now also on fire, then shot him with the revolver. Three more cult members; two men and a woman, managed to climb through the opening with their hair and robes in flames. He shot each of them in turn with a single bullet. There was no need to use the other gun. The rest of the cultists must have been overcome by the thick smoke. They died inside.

He waited until the last scream ceased and the entire structure blazed like a furnace. The heat was so great, it blistered the paint on the hood of the car. He threw the empty gas can and the guns into the burning church through the broken window, using his coat to shield his face and hands from the heat, then drove the Roma back to Providence.

11.

Julian was waiting for him in the dark bedroom when he got home to the apartment. Dobbs saw him sitting on the edge of the bed and stopped in the doorway.

"You've got sharp ears," Tailor said in a conversational tone. "I've always found that creepy."

"Hello, Julian. I warned you not to come back."

"You can't see it, Harold, but trust me when I tell you that I'm holding a gun, and it's pointed at your stomach."

"How gauche."

"That's another thing. I've always hated that snide, superior Boston accent you affect. All these years it's been like fingernails on a chalkboard. You can't imagine how many times I've come close to screaming at you to shut the fuck up."

"I like you better this way, Julian. You're finally being honest with me."

"That's right, because it no longer matters what you think. I can't allow you to take away everything I have and ruin my life, Harold. I'm sure you can understand that."

"Are you asking me for absolution?"

Tailor's voice hardened. "No. I just want you to know why you have to die. After our years together, you deserve that much."

The gun was deafening in the closed space of the bedroom. Tailor fired six shots into the slender figure framed in the dim glow of the doorway, but Dobbs only heard the first one, which went through his heart.

Tailor stood over the body, smoke curling from the muzzle of the gun.

"Goodbye, Harold. Some of it was fun, but you really were a bit of a bore."

The doors of the French wardrobe exploded outward in fragments behind him. He flinched and whirled around. Black smoke poured through the darkness toward him and rolled over him, then past him, and he smelled the stench of burning sulphur. He stared at the shattered wardrobe in disbelief, wondering if Dobbs had hidden a bomb inside it.

A rustling noise made him turn back to his partner's corpse, which was climbing awkwardly to its feet. The blood had ceased to flow from the wounds in its chest. Harold Dobbs looked very much alive. Tailor emptied the automatic's remaining bullets into his body, but Dobbs did not fall. He walked forward with measured steps. Tailor shook his head, still clicking the trigger as he backed away.

"You can't be alive. It's not possible."

The thin lips of Dobbs curled into a cynical smile. He raised his arms and grasped Tailor by the shoulders, then pulled the other man against his body in a tight embrace.

Tailor began to struggle, then to scream. He pounded the butt of the gun against his former partner's back and head but the blows had no effect. Electricity crackled. Tailor's body gave off wisps of smoke. His suit burst into flame and his face blackened. The stench of burning meat filled the air. Dobbs continued to hold him until his body was reduced to blackened skin and charred bones. Then he opened his arms and allowed what was left of Tailor to fall into a pile at his feet.

His own clothing had largely burned away, and the smoke alarm was shrieking overhead. He turned off the alarm and opened a window to clear the air, then stripped off the blackened rags that clung to his body and showered.

Standing naked in front of the full-length mirror in the bathroom, he examined his chest. There was nothing to show that he had been shot except small white dots on his skin. In some way beyond human understanding, the dark god had restored him to life and healed him.

"I understand now."

He felt the god move inside his body.

"You needed a dark vessel in which to dwell," he said to his own image in the mirror. "A vessel into which no light could ever intrude."

His head nodded.

"That's why you chose me, a blind man."

Another nod.

"Now you need something else. A sacrifice to replace the vitality you expended in healing me. You need a human life."

The head nodded.

"I believe I know the perfect woman for you."

DAGON
The Sea Pillar

1.

The great storm that swept over our island took away half our beach, but it did not get our fishing boats. Our chief elder, Daniel Batamba, is a wise man who has been through many such storms. He ordered the men to drag the boats into the forest and lash them down to the roots of the palm trees. Then we lashed ourselves to the palm trees as well. The waves rolled over the boats, just as they rolled over our village, but when the storm left, the boats were still here, and we were still here. But it took away with it half our beach. Daniel says that some day the sea will bring back the part of our beach it took from us. That is the way of the sea, which both takes and gives.

In the days of our father's fathers we worshipped the sea, and the sea god. We prayed to him for full nets. We prayed to be cured from disease. We prayed for our gardens and fruit trees to prosper, and our children to be healthy. Then the Jesuits came to our island, and we all were made into Christians. The Jesuits told us that our god was called Dagon, and was a god of evil. Now we pray to Jesus the Christ and to Mary, the mother of Jesus.

The Jesuit priest who stayed on our island lives in a little house made of wooden boards beside the red brick Catholic church. He is called Father Ignatius, but that is not his true name, only the name he took when he became a priest. He is a tall, stern man with wind-blown black hair and pale blue eyes who frightens me when he speaks. The brick church was not washed away by the storm. Every Sunday we gather in the church and listen to Father Ignatius talk about the Gospels, and about what a good man Jesus was during his life.

My name is Aleeu. I am fifteen and a half years old. I go to the school the Jesuits made for the children of the island, and I am learning to read French. Our teacher is Sister Magdalene, who is short and plump, with reddish hair and pink skin that burns in the sun when she forgets to wear a hat. She says that when I have learned to read and speak French well, she will teach me English, but I will be married soon and then I will have no need for English. I will have my own house with my own children, and that is enough.

When the waves of the storm departed from our island, the men found a strange greenish stone washed up high on the remaining half of our beach. It was long and square and very heavy, but my father says the waves can move anything, even a great stone. Pictures were carved into its sides. Some of them I recognized, but others were strange to me. There were fishes and birds, and the great whale, and the octopus, and shells like the giant conch. One carving showed a monster fighting with a whale. The whale looked small in its arms.

Father Ignatius was so excited when he saw the stone, he started talking very fast. He said it was a pillar and had once belonged to a pagan temple of Dagon that had been lost under the waves ages ago, before my people came to live on this island. He said it must be very old, older even than Christianity itself, and he wanted the men to drag it back into the sea, because he said it was an evil thing. But the men laughed at him, and told him that the sea pillar was a token of good fortune and would bring large catches of fish. They tied ropes around it and dragged it up to the top of the highest hill on our island. There they dug a hole and set it upright.

Father Ignatius was furious with them and told them that it was a blasphemy that would damn their souls, but they only laughed at him again. They faced the task of repairing or rebuilding their homes and needed all the good fortune they could get. It was luck that no lives had been lost in the storm, they said. The sea pillar had protected the people of the island. I think it was the foresight of our elder, Daniel Batamba, that saved our lives, but it is not the place of a fifteen-year-old girl to contradict the words of her elders.

I watched the young men pulling the stone on log rollers up the hill. They were stripped to the waist and streaming with silver sweat that dripped from their noses and chins and elbows. One of the youths, Ben Renu, cast his eyes at me with a shy smile, but another of them, Hector Kelepa, stared at me boldly and grinned. My cheeks became warm and I turned my face away, but a smile was on my lips. I bleed like my mother, and when a girl begins to bleed it is said to be a sign that she is ready for marriage. Both young men wanted me, but I had yet to choose between them.

As twilight gathered into darkness, the sounds of saws and hammers gradually ceased. The house of my father had survived almost intact. My family was more fortunate than most of our people, some of whom had lost almost everything they owned. Father Ignatius and Sister Magdalene made places for them to sleep on the floor of the schoolhouse until their roofs were repaired. I sat with my mother on our little porch, listening to the sounds of the night as the stars came out above our heads. The new red star with the ring around it shone down brightly, as it had for several weeks, but in the last few nights the sky had become crossed with brightly colored banners that slowly waved like curtains in a breeze.

"It's so pretty," my mother said as she knitted. She did not need to see her hands to knit.

"The Sister told us it is called the aurora borealis," I said, pronouncing the strange words slowly. "It has never been seen so far south as our island in all of history."

"I like to watch it," she said. "But I don't like so much that new red star. It is an evil omen. I think it brought the storm."

"A storm comes every year. This time we were ready for it, because Father Ignatius heard about it on his radio and warned Daniel."

"I think Father Ignatius is going to leave us the next time the big boat comes to the island."

I looked at my mother with surprise, but could barely see her outline in the darkness. "Why do you say that?"

"The poor man is unhappy. A woman knows these things. He looks at Sister Magdalene the way a man looks at a woman when he wants to lie with her."

"Priests are not allowed to lie with women."

"I know. That is why I say he will leave us. He is not content here. It makes him angry, and they say he is drinking rum before he goes to bed."

I thought about my mother's words. It is true that Father Ignatius had been growing short-tempered with Daniel and some of the other men of the village, but he always smiled and spoke softly to the children. His voice was so deep, the children would stare at him with wide eyes when he spoke, and then run away. What would we do if he left the island? There would be no one to hold mass at the altar in the brick church. Would he take Sister Magdalene with him? Then there would be no one to teach us spelling and geography in the school house.

Father Ignatius had been on our island as long as I could remember. Would the Pope send another Jesuit priest to take his place? I had always thought Father Ignatius would perform the ceremony when I got married. The fear of the unknown touched my heart with its chill fingers. What would a new priest be like? Would he change things on the island? I was content with the way things were, and did not want anything to change.

"I am going up to the sea stone to pray that Father Ignatius does not go away," I told my mother.

"You must leave something there, if you want your prayer to be answered," she said.

"Why is that?"

"There are other gods besides the Christian god Jesus, gods who are older. When you ask something from them, you must give something in return. It's just the way it works—if you don't give an offering, your prayer will not be answered."

Heeding my mother's words, I picked wild flowers as I followed the path up the hill to its crest. The pillar of stone shone with a green glow as I approached it. At first I thought it was the light of the sky curtains reflecting from its smoothly polished sides, but then I realized the glow came from the stone itself. Approaching it with my head bowed, I laid my bouquet of flowers at its base, then pressed my hands against its side. With my fingers I traced the lines of the symbols carved deeply into its surface. It felt warm to the touch.

"Do not let Father Ignatius leave our island," I whispered. "We are happy with things the way they are and do not want anything to change. If he leaves, outsiders will come and they will want to change things. That is always the way with men who come from across the sea. They never stay long, but they always tell us we are doing everything wrong and want to change our ways. Then they go before they can make us change. But if a new priest comes, he will stay, and he will want to change things. That is why I ask you to prevent Father Ignatius from leaving us. I have brought you beautiful flowers in return for the fulfillment of my prayer."

When I finished, I felt foolish because there was no one to answer me. How was it different from the prayers I spoke in my heart to Jesus in the red brick church? Those also received no answer.

I turned from the stone to walk back down the hill and heard a rustle in bushes that grew near. Stopping my breath, I listened. Something moved against the leaves with a soft sliding sound.

"Who is there?" I tried to keep my voice from trembling. "Is that you, Hector? Did you follow me up here? Don't play jokes on me."

A shadow stood upright behind the bushes. From its size I knew it must be a man, but something about the outline of his shape frightened me. I turned to run down the hill, but he moved quickly and took me in his hands, hugging me to his bare chest. I smelled the salt of the sea. What pressed against me was damp and chill. I felt myself lifted off my feet and carried behind the stone. I fought to get away, but the one who held me was too strong. He laid me onto the grass like a child and covered me with his body. I felt a sharp pain between my legs and knew he had violated my honor. When I tried to scream, his large hand covered my face so that I could not breathe. The hand felt strange against my lips and nose, and I realized there was webbing between its spread fingers.

When I woke, he was gone. It burned between my legs. I touched myself under my skirt and felt sticky wetness. Putting my hand near my face, I smelled the coppery scent of fresh blood, and something else. I felt like weeping but I did not weep. I thought about what my father would say if I told him I had been spoiled before my wedding night, and resolved then to say nothing about it to my parents. Feeling around in the darkness, I found some leaves and used them to wipe myself. Then I went down the hill and made my way to the beach, where I washed the blood from my thighs and hands in the warm lapping waters.

The next morning, before the sun was fully above the eastern horizon, the men went out upon the sea in their boats to cast their nets. When they drew them in, they cried out in wonder, because the nets were filled with dancing silver fish. Daniel said that never in all his years had he seen such a large catch. The boats could not hold it all, so that some of the catch had to be released back into the sea. The men told each other that it was due to the magic stone they had set up on the hill. It had brought them more good fortune.

Some men said they were going to carry bread and milk up the hill to lay at the base of the stone, but Daniel told them Father Ignatius would be very angry if they did so, because it would be a sacrilege. The older men whose hair was turning white listened to him, but the younger men did not.

When Father Ignatius saw what the young men were doing at the stone, his face got red and he choked when he tried to speak, so great was his rage. He ran to the stone and kicked the offerings away with his boot and trampled on them while the young men watched in silence. When he ordered them to go back to the village, none of them dared to defy him, although Hector cast daggers from his eyes. I know because I had followed the young men up the hill to watch them from behind the trees.

Father Ignatius preached against the stone that Sunday, but on Monday when he climbed the hill he found fresh offerings laid around its base. Not only the young men, but older men and even women and girls were climbing the hill at night when they would not be recognized by the priest and making prayers to the sea pillar. People began to call it the wishing stone, because they said it granted the wishes of anyone who gave offerings to its unknown, nameless god.

Father Ignatius took Daniel Batamba into the office in his house beside the church and talked to him for a long time. I could hear his voice through the walls because he was shouting in anger. Daniel answered him in a humble voice so that I could not hear his words, but the priest ordered him to have the stone torn out of the ground and dragged back into the sea. He said it many times, but when Daniel at last emerged from his house, Father Ignatius stood at the door with a scowl on his face, watching Daniel walk slowly into the village, and I knew our elder had not promised to obey him.

My people would never have allowed Daniel to pull up the stone and cast it back into the sea. Each day was more prosperous than the last. In addition to fish, the men began to find objects in their nets that were made of gold. There were gold coins with the heads of kings stamped on them, and jeweled rings. Some of the objects were strangely shaped. They resembled adornments such as a woman might wear on her head or neck, but none would fit our heads or our necks. The woman hung the smallest ornaments on woven threads and wore them as pendants.

When Father Ignatius heard about the golden trinkets found in the fishing nets, he told Daniel to collect them all from the men and bring them to the church. This Daniel was able to do, but some of the women were reluctant to part with them. They asked Daniel why they should give them to the priest when he had made no offerings at the wishing stone? The golden things were gifts to them for their prayers, and did not belong to the Jesuits or to the Pope. Even so, Daniel was able to gather the golden things, and Father Ignatius put them all in a trunk which he locked and kept at the foot of his bed in the sleeping room of his house.

When the day of the moon arrived for me to bleed between the legs, the blood did not come. I asked the other girls what it meant when the blood does not come, and they laughed at me for my ignorance and told me it meant a baby was growing inside of me. When I learned this, I went into the forest by myself and thought long about what I was to do. Then I put on my best dress, wove flowers in my hair, and went to Ben Renu where he was seated beside his boat on the beach, mending his net with a large ivory needle. I stood close and talked softly to him, touching him on the cheek with my hand. His face became flushed. He dropped his eyes, then looked up at me with meaning in them. I nodded, and we embraced and kissed.

Our marriage took place in the red brick church a week later. Everyone was happy for us except Hector Kelepa, who did not attend the ceremony. The women said he had offered prayers to win me at the wishing stone, and was angry that his prayers had not been answered. Now he had gone up the hill to curse me and my husband, and even my future children. I could well believe it to be true. Even as a small child Hector had never been able to control his temper. That is why I chose Ben over him. My husband was a quiet man who thought before he spoke, and was always gentle with dogs and small children.

As the weeks passed, more gold was found in the nets, which continued to overflow with fish. This time the men would not give the gold to Daniel when he asked for it. They began to avoid the glaring wrath of Father Ignatius, and as the Sundays came and went, the oak pews in the red brick church had more and more empty places. The young men and some of their wives and daughters began to hold a kind of prayer service around the wishing stone. They did this while services were being offered in the church, because they knew Father Ignatius could not climb the hill while he was conducting the Catholic mass. None of them wanted to confront his anger, but none of them were willing to obey his order to stop praying at the stone.

No one knew when the people of the sea began to visit the stone pillar on the hill. We saw them from our windows late at night, walking on the hill like misshapen shadows against the stars. They said nothing and moved with hardly a sound. In the mornings after their visits, we would climb the hill and find precious jewels and gold coins left at the base of the stone. Daniel said they must have come from the treasure of some ancient wreck. None of my people dared to touch these things. They feared the sea people. The gold in their nets was given to them as a gift, but the gold around the sea pillar was an offering to the god of the sea. Father Ignatius would climb the hill and gather up the gems, coins, rings and other golden offerings the sea people left, and put them all in his locked chest.

He began to drink rum during the day. When I walked past him on the road I could smell it on his breath, and sometimes he staggered from side to side and talked to himself, as though talking to people only he could see. His thin face became even more gaunt, and dark shadows formed below his bloodshot eyes. He forgot to shave his cheeks for days at a time. When he stared at me, I was frightened. My people began to avoid meeting with him so that they would not need to look at him or speak to him. On Sunday, only a few of the more faithful older women and men attended mass in the brick church. Most of the village sang songs on the top of the hill, gathered around the stone pillar, then gave their offerings of flowers, food and rum to it.

News of our prosperity was carried across the sea. Men from other islands began to bring their families in their boats to live on our island so that they could share in that bounty. At first Daniel welcomed them, but eventually there were so many he was forced to turn them away, saying we had no place for them. The young men of our village drove off with sticks and stones those who would not leave willingly. They pushed their boats from the beach back into the waves, cursing us.

The baby in my belly grew with unnatural haste, so that after only a little more than four months from the night it was conceived behind the stone, it was ready to come forth. My husband was quiet when he looked at the dome of my belly, so that I felt ashamed and could not meet his eyes. He did not question me or speak harshly, and in this way I knew he had accepted the baby even though he understood it was not his own.

The women who helped me during my labor shook their heads and muttered among themselves, but when the baby at last came out, they smiled and nodded. It was a boy, perfectly formed in all his parts and normal in every way, or so it appeared to them. I knew otherwise, but I kept my thoughts to myself, and gave thanks to Mother Mary that my son looked normal in outward appearance, except perhaps for his eyes, which were round and stuck out from his head just a little, like the eyes of a fish.

At night, when I would wake from sleep and slid from the side of my husband to walk outside and cool myself with the night breeze, I would hear voices softly talking in the darkness. Some of those voices I recognized as men of the village, but the voices of the others were strange in my ears. They spoke in a kind of choking cough that was hard to understand, even though the language was French. I knew these were the voices of the sea people, who had come onto the island to trade with my tribe.

It was said that some of the women lay down with the

men from the sea without needing to be forced, in return for gifts of gold and jewels. They began to hang the trinkets around their necks during the daytime, as they had done before Father Ignatius had forbidden it. By this time the priest had given up trying to collect the gold found in the nets or left at the base of the pillar. He had stopped doing all the things he had once done, except only the weekly mass, which he continued to hold in his nearly empty church.

The night sky was so bright with dancing colors that it almost hurt the eyes to look at them. Some of the elders became frightened, and told us not to look at the moving lights. They said they must be a bad omen since nothing like them had ever been seen before. The young men laughed, and told them it was a good omen, because the colors in the sky had come shortly before the finding of the wishing stone. The green stone pillar on the hill also glowed more brightly, so that it was possible to see it at night from the village, its green glow reflected from the trunks of trees and the leaves of bushes. Around the base of it, the grass started to turn brown and die in a perfect circle that every day became a little larger.

3.

It was then that the big boat came to visit our island. The big boat comes two times every year to pick up the craft goods we fashioned for sale to those who live across the sea, and to drop off supplies that were ordered by Daniel, Father Ignatius, and others on its previous visit. It is too large to land on our beach, but it anchors in our bay. When he heard the great horn of the boat sounding across the sea, Father Ignatius got very excited. He ran from the church down to the beach and waved his black hat in the air over his head, shouting loudly even though the boat was still too far away for the people on it to hear him.

There is always a celebration in our village on the first night after the big boat arrives. The sailors come ashore in their little boats and there is dancing and singing and music. Many people get drunk on rum. The captain went with Father Ignatius back to the priest's house and they did not come out, not even when the bonfire was lit and the pig was roasted. I did not drink the rum. My husband is a modest man and stayed away from the sailors, who flirted with the young girls in their loud voices and gave them candy from Australia and plastic combs from China.

The sailors got very excited when some of the girls showed them the gold pendants they wore, but the girls would not tell them where the gold came from, and after a while they were too drunk to care. Many of them took girls into the forest to lie with. Daniel disapproved of this practice, saying it was not Christian, but it had been going on for generations and he could not stop it. Above the feast, the sky shimmered with many colors and the big red star burned down like a glaring eye, but we had seen the same thing for so many weeks, we no longer took notice of it.

The next morning, the men did not go out in their boats to catch fish. Most of them were too sick from the rum. They lay on the beach asleep or groaning from the pain in their heads. Later in the day, men from the big boat set up tables in the open air and the villagers began to trade with the sailors, and to order things from a catalog shown to them by the officers. Money and gold changed hands. The officers of the big boat were amazed at the amount of gold suddenly available for payment. They asked where it came from, but the men of the village only winked at them and said nothing.

I saw the officers get angry and argue among themselves, and knew they would not rest until they understood where poor fishermen had found so much gold. My heart was filled with foreboding as I held my baby close to my breast and soothed him. My husband said little, but from the frown on his face I knew he had the same worry that was in my own heart.

In the afternoon, I saw two sailors carry the trunk into which Father Ignatius had put all the gold from the sea he could gather, before people stopped giving it to him. The trunk was heavy. The bare arms of the two strong men bulged with muscles, but they were almost unable to lift it, and in the end they dragged it across the sand of the beach to one of their boats. Other men helped them put it into the boat, and the little boat took it to the big boat. Father Ignatius directed the sailors to carry other trunks and boxes and racks of clothing to one of the little boats, while Sister Magdalene stood by and wrung her hands with tears streaming down her cheeks. I knew then that the priest was leaving our island with the gold from the sea people.

When night came, I let myself out of my house without waking my husband or my baby and climbed the hill. I wanted to offer a prayer for the health of my baby, that he would grow up like other children. It was quiet. The people of the village had gone to sleep early because of the drinking the night before, and most of the sailors had returned to the big boat. Only a single boat from the big boat remained on the beach, the one they called the captain's launch. The wind made the fronds of the palm trees rustle, so that it sounded as if they were laughing at me as I walked past them. It was darker than it had been for many nights. Clouds covered the stars and hid the curtains of shifting colors. I felt a large drop of rain strike my cheek. More drops began to fall.

I heard voices and realized that I was not alone on the hill. Men cursed and grunted with effort, then laughed. They were not the voices of my people, but the deeper, rougher voices of the sailors. There was the sound of picks digging in the ground, and shovels moving loose soil. A voice I recognized as that of Father Ignatius said something, but I could not make out his words.

"We need a light," someone said.

"We can't risk a lantern," Father Ignatius said. "If the villagers knew what we were doing, they would attack us."

Another voice I recognized as that of the captain said, "It's coming." Then he said, "It's almost there—pull hard, men."

Something heavy thudded against the wet ground.

I saw something that was bigger than the brick church move past me . . .

"Get the ropes around it," the captain ordered. "We'll drag it to the boat."

"Take care not to damage it," Father Ignatius said. "It's worth a lot of money."

"The mud is soft, it won't get damaged," the captain told him, and one of the sailors laughed.

As I backed off the path and into the wet bushes, crouching low to hide myself beneath them, three shadowed shapes brushed past me on their way up the hill. I smelled the sea smell and knew they were sea people. There was a cry from one of the sailors, and curses from the others. I heard the sounds of fighting, but in the darkness I could not see what was happening. A man bellowed in agony—I think it was Father Ignatius. The clear, prolonged note of a conch rang out on the night air. There was a gunshot, and the music of the conch stopped. I heard two more shots, then there was silence except for the rustling palms and the patter of the rain.

"I'm wounded," the captain said in a weak voice. "Leave the stone—we need to get back to the ship."

"I think the priest is dead," one of the sailors told him.

"To hell with the priest and his crazy story," the captain said.

From somewhere down near the beach I heard the sound of splintering wood. There was a heavy thump that I felt in the mud through the soles of my bare feet. Then came another, and another, and another, each closer than the last. I shrank back into the bushes, too terrified to run away. In the darkness I saw something that was bigger than the brick church move past me up the path. I smelled the salt of the sea. A sailor screamed. I heard gunshots, then more screams. A roar shook the air. It was so long and so deep, I felt it in my chest the way you feel the beat of a big drum. It was like the roar of the lions that I have heard on the videos of Africa that Sister Magdalene plays in the school, only much louder. Then there was silence.

The thumps on the ground came again, this time moving down the hill. They stopped when they reached the place I crouched. I put both my hands over my mouth and held my breath to keep from making a sound. In the rain I heard a kind of sniffing, as if some great animal were smelling me. I thought it would tear up the bushes and kill me, but after a time the thuds in the mud moved down the hill, going further and further away toward the beach until I could no longer hear them.

I waited for a long time, afraid to move. No one came up the hill, even though the gunshots and the roar must have been heard in the village. I realized the men were too afraid to come up in the darkness. At last, I stood on shaking legs and went quickly down to the village. My husband was awake when I slipped back into my house. He had his face near the window and was peering out. A candle burned on the table. He looked at me when I entered but said nothing. I saw that he was afraid and did not speak to him, but dried myself and undressed and went to bed. After a while he came to bed and lay beside me.

In the morning, there were many people walking around, talking in low voices about the events of the night. I looked out to the sea, but there was no big boat. Always before it waited until daylight before departing, so that we could gather on the beach and watch it leave. It would blow its horn, and we would all wave. But it had vanished in the rain and the darkness. The boat called the captain's launch that had been pulled up on the sand was smashed into splinters. The fishing boats were all unharmed.

Men carried the bodies of Father Ignatius, the Captain and the sailors down the hill and laid them on the ground in front of the church in a row. Before Sister Magdalene covered the bodies with sheets and blankets, I saw that the head of the priest had been ripped off. The men had not been able to find it, so they had laid his body down without its head. The ribs of the captain were crushed, as though a great weight had pressed on them, and one of the sailors was missing an arm, which had been torn out at the shoulder, but they did find the arm and laid it beside him. All of the corpses were covered with blood, their faces bloody and disfigured, except for Father Ignatius, who had no face because he had no head.

The bodies of the sea people were not found on the hill. I think they must have been carried away during the night. Daniel organized the men, and they went up the hill and cleaned away the blood. I went with them to watch. In the mud of the path were great footprints, each long enough to lie down in. The feet that made them had three toes with long claws, and they were webbed between the toes. The men would not walk upon these footprints, but walked around them as they made their way up and down the path. They did not look at them or talk about them.

They set the sea pillar upright where it had stood before and filled in the earth around its base so that it would not fall over. The women took flowers and rum and other offerings up the hill and laid them around the stone, saying prayers as they did so. We gathered the splinters of the captain's boat for firewood. Later that day, Sister Magdalene said a service over the bodies of the dead men, and they were buried in the graveyard behind the red brick church. Daniel ordered wooden crosses carved to mark the graves.

SHOGGOTH

What Is That Thing?

1.

Two men stood in the corridor, their heads close together as they peered through a small reinforced security window in an armored steel door. One wore the uniform of a colonel in the United States Army. He was a big man, but fit for his age, with steel-gray hair that receded at the temples. The other had on the cheap dark suit of a lower-level civil servant. A head shorter than the soldier and twenty years younger, there was a slight stoop to his rounded shoulders that suggested a career spent shuffling papers across a desk. This appearance was misleading.

"Can it get out?" the man in the dark suit asked.

"As I told you before, Mr. Jinsky, that is impossible."

"Has it ever tried?"

"Over the past two months it has probed and tested the strength of the walls of its prison every day."

"You're sure it can't get out, Colonel Breckwood?"

"The window is four-inch polycarbonate; the armor on both sides of the door is one-inch shock-resistant carbon steel; the walls, floor and ceiling are twenty-four inches of high-strength reinforced concrete."

"What about your external defenses?"

The colonel stared at the Jinsky. "What do you mean?"

"What security levels exist beyond the walls of this room?"

"I told you, external security is unnecessary."

The man in the dark suit regarded the military commander with a mild expression that somehow made the other flinch.

"Nothing in the hallways? The ventilation ductwork? The electrical conduits?"

"Exactly who are you, anyway?" the colonel demanded with a frown.

"Don't you know?"

"I was told to give you access, Mr. Jinsky, nothing more."

The man in the dark suit looked back through the window at the vast pulsating thing on the other side. It was translucent and resembled an amoeba that had been expanded to a million times its normal size. Curious opaque bodies floated within its mass as it shifted and flowed within the confines of its prison.

"I fix things," he said.

The colonel studied him up and down. Jinsky had a face you forget the instant you look away from it—small nose, receding chin, thin lips, colorless eyes, short brown hair.

"You don't look like a fixer."

"That's good."

Breckwood grunted. "I suppose it is useful at times."

They put their heads together again and peered into the window. The thing shifted, as though aware of their presence.

"Does it know we're here?" Jinsky asked.

"We think so."

"How?"

"We think it's psychic, or something like that."

"Have you tried to kill it?"

"Several times."

The little man waited for the colonel to continue.

"We've tried bullets, explosives, electricity, fire, freezing, acid, caustics, radiation. Its body just breaks apart and then reforms."

"Freezing didn't work?" Jinsky asked.

"It froze, but when it thawed out it was unharmed."

"You could keep it frozen permanently."

"Yes, but that would be expensive. We've run all the tests we can think of to run on it. We just want it gone."

Jinsky regarded the thing through the window with his mild expression. "Did it ever occur to you that it might be studying us?"

The colonel laughed. "It's not sentient. It responds to stimuli in its immediate environment the way an amoeba would, but it can't actually think."

"You're certain of that?"

"Believe me, if it knew what I was thinking right now, it would be more agitated."

As he spoke, a pseudopod extended from the gelatinous body inside the cell toward the door. When it was several feet away from the window, a spear suddenly lashed out from it that was shaped like the blade of a rapier. Its sharp point pierced through the polycarbonate window, through the colonel's blue left eye, and emerged out the back of his head, spraying blood and bits of brain onto the white concrete wall of the corridor. Jinsky stepped to the side of the door and studied the spear with interest. It withdrew itself as suddenly as it had extended. The colonel's body collapsed downward like a marionette with its strings cut.

"I guess you knew what he was thinking," Jinsky murmured.

A claxon began to sound in the corridor, and red lights flashed. Jinsky wondered how the response had come so quickly, then saw the camera in a ceiling corner at the end of the corridor. They had been monitored constantly. He heard the approach of running feet. Pulling out his credentials from the vest pocket of his suit, he stopped the soldiers before they got close to the door.

Behind him, the thing began to ooze in a thin line through the tiny hole in the window. It accumulated in the corridor with surprising rapidity, considering the large mass of its body.

"You can't stop it," he told the sergeant of the guard over the barking horn. "I suggest you get your men out of here before it kills them."

"I'm sorry, sir; I can't do that, sir."

There was a hint of pity in the little man's pale eyes. "Then good luck, Sergeant."

He walked quickly past them along the corridor toward the elevator. As the doors of the elevator slid shut, he heard the first scream.

The office of General Hale, commander of the research facility, was windowless but well lit with indirect lighting. The walls and both doors were armored with sheets of steel. Jinsky stood facing the older man, who smoked the stub of a thick cigar with vigorous puffs, his jaw clenched around it.

"What happened to the bodies of Colonel Breckwood and the security detail?"

"It ate them," Hale said. "We found their clothing discarded on the floor of the corridor."

"You're sure it's still inside the building?"

The general scowled. His eyes were ice blue and his eyebrows looked like drifts of giant snowflakes. His face might have been chiseled from a square block of granite. It was an impressive face, but Jinsky was not impressed.

"Positive, Mr. Jinsky. My men have formed a perimeter. All the exits are monitored. The body of the thing is slightly radioactive, and we're picking up its radiation signature in one of the lower levels."

"How did you capture it in the first place?"

"Cattle prods and flame throwers. It doesn't like fire, not that it hurts it much, but it doesn't like it."

"In that case, General, I would say that you have a big problem."

"We'll get it contained again," the general said with

confidence. "My men were just unprepared for its escape. Next time there won't be a window in its cell."

"I wasn't sent here to contain it, General Hale."

"No, you were not, Mr. Jinsky." The general eyed him shrewdly from under his feathery white eyebrows. "Have you got any idea how to kill it?"

Jinsky took a mint off a roll from his pocket and placed it into his mouth. He sucked it for several seconds in silence.

"No. But I may know how to contain it permanently."

"You Pentagon boys think you know everything," the general said. "But when it comes down to brass tacks, we regular army are the ones who solve the problems."

"The way I heard it, you had four years to solve this problem."

"The scientists were studying the thing. My hands were tied. But they're not tied now."

"No, they're not," the little man said quietly. "That thing, as you call it, is a shoggoth."

"How do you know what it's called?"

"This isn't the first time humanity has encountered one of its kind. There are myths, folktales, historical references from all over the world."

"What do these myths say about it?"

"Different things, some of which are contradictory. What they all agree on, however, is that a shoggoth is the strongest and the toughest creature that has ever lived. They were created by an alien race before earthly life crawled out of the sea onto the land, and they are deathless. Immortal. There is no way to tell how old this one may be, but it could have been alive for billions of years. They mostly stay on the bottom of the sea or deep in the bowels of the earth."

"The thing was captured in a gold mine, over two miles underground."

"It wasn't captured," Jinsky said. "It allowed itself to be taken. It could have escaped at any time over the past four years. It's been studying us in preparation for something, and whatever that something is, it is about to happen."

"What makes you say that?"

"It's become aggressive. It began to probe its prison, and according to my report it ate two of your scientists."

"Tims and Zachery. They thought it was dormant and went in to take readings. Good men. Tragic loss."

"It knows that what it has been waiting for has arrived."

"That's ridiculous," Hale said. "It's just a mindless animal."

"Have you been following the news lately?"

"Not particularly. Why?"

"Ever since that supernova appeared in the sky, strange events have been happening all around the globe."

"Do you think this creature—what did you call it?"

"Shoggoth," said Jinsky.

"Do you think this shoggoth is reacting to the supernova?"

"Yes."

"I always knew you boys in Special Projects were off the wall, but you're even nuttier than I was told you are."

"General, you will give me all the support I need and you will provide it wherever and whenever I say I need it. Is that understood?"

The face of the general flushed. He swallowed before replying, but his orders were clear.

"Understood."

"Good. Now show me the full plans for this installation."

Hale called in a technician. After some digging, the tech pulled up blueprints for the building on the large wall monitor. Jinsky studied it for several minutes in silence. He went to the monitor and pointed at a place.

"Are these the air-conditioning ducts?"

The tech glanced at the general, then said, "Yes, sir."

"That's its most likely choice to move around. It can squeeze through the smallest crack, but that takes time. These ducts are wide enough to allow it to flow through them quickly."

"Wouldn't it just want to get out of the building?" Hale said.

"If it were trying to get away," Jinsky said. "But we know that isn't the case. It could have escaped any time it wanted, but it stayed, studying us."

"I'd say it was done with studying us, son."

"Because I forced it to act. It can read our thoughts; it knew I was here to kill it. But I suspect it was getting ready to do whatever it came here to do in any case."

"Do you know what that is?"

"Not a clue," Jinsky admitted.

"What are you planning to do?"

"I'm going to freeze it."

"We tried that once. We can't keep it frozen. Once its temperature rises above minus 316 degrees, it regains its mobility, and its hellishly quick when it wants to be."

"I'm not planning on keeping it frozen."

He recited a list of the materials and tools he needed, and the technician wrote it down.

"I'll need two teams in protective thermal suits to deploy the liquid nitrogen."

"It will be arranged," Hale said.

"We'll have to lure it down to the sub-basement where the floor is solid concrete. Otherwise the cold is liable to weaken the structure under it and cause it to collapse."

"I can ask for volunteers," Hale said.

"I'll decoy it down there myself."

Hale's snowy eyebrows went up.

"Before I neutralize it, I want to try talking to it," Jinsky explained. "We need to know why it's studying us."

"My boys have been trying to get a response out of that thing for four years. Beyond a basic pain reflex, it gave them nothing."

"When it read my mind and learned why I was sent here, it decided to leave its cell."

"That's conjecture, Mr. Jinsky."

"I believe it is not only sentient, but highly intelligent. I need to talk to it."

"You'll get yourself killed, boy."

"It's worth the risk. We have no way of knowing how many shoggoths live in the deep places of this planet, but there may be millions of them. What if they were all to rise to the surface at the same time and attack us?"

General Hale took the cigar from his teeth and looked at its end. It had gone out. He laid it into an ashtray on his desk.

"They would wipe us out. We wouldn't stand a chance. Not even our nuclear arsenal would save us. They are immune to radiation, totally immune."

"That's why I need to talk to it."

3.

Jinsky found the shoggoth on the middle level of the underground parking garage, filling the space between two cars. He approached with caution up the ramp from the lower level, watching closely for any sign of movement. Its great, gelatinous bulk pulsed regularly, but it gave no indication that it was aware of him. He knew this must be false. If it could read minds, it must be able to sense the approach of human beings.

He stopped when he was still thirty feet away from it. "I want to talk to you."

A large round eye that was the size of a saucer formed itself in the surface of the creature. It regarded Jinsky.

"Do you have any way to communicate?" Jinksy asked. "Can you read my mind?"

A kind of mouth formed above the eye.

"Only its surface." The whistling voice was eerily unhuman. There was no emphasis, no accent on the words.

"You can only read the thoughts that are on the surface of my mind?"

"Yes."

"But you can speak. You know our language."

"Learned while studying your species."

Jinsky edged a little nearer. The shoggoth still did not move from its place. Jinsky wondered how far it could extend its pseudopods. Was it waiting for him to come close enough to be killed?

"Why did you kill Colonel Breckwood?"

"Breckwood is not dead," it said in its breathy, whistling voice.

"I saw you kill him."

Something began to form on the surface of the creature's body. With a thrill of horror Jinsky saw that it was the face of Colonel Breckwood. The face wore an expression of confusion. Its rolling eyes focused on him.

"Mr. Jinsky? What's going on?" the face said in a weak, cracked voice.

"Colonel Breckwood? Is that you?"

"What's happening, Jinsky? I can barely see you. I can't feel my body."

Jinsky said nothing. What could he possibly say to the disembodied face? A kind of ripple ran across the surface of the shoggoth as the face dissolved back into its translucent mass. Was it laughing at him?

"Are all the other men you killed inside you?"

"Yes, but not dead. They are a part of me now."

"You absorbed them to possess their knowledge and their memories," Jinsky said with sudden insight.

The shoggoth shifted itself out from between the cars, its body rolling across the concrete floor. The big eye turned like a cartwheel but remained fixed on Jinsky, who took two cautious steps backward.

"Is your race planning to conquer my race?"

Again, the ripple ran across its body. It must be a kind of laughter, Jinsky thought.

"Unnecessary. Your race will soon cease to exist."

The simplicity with which the alien creature said these words chilled Jinksy to the bone.

"If your race will not kill us, what will?"

"The stars have come right in your heavens. The Old Ones return. They will make your world their domain, and your race will be of no interest to them. You will be in their way. They will remove you."

Jinsky thought feverishly, wondering what questions to ask. He might only have seconds before the thing killed him, or became bored and decided to leave. How could he make it follow him? The teams must be in position on the lower level by now.

"What teams?" it whistled.

Jinsky focused his mind firmly on the here and now. "If you do not intend to kill us, why did you allow us to bring you here?"

"To study you. To learn about your weapons. To determine if they could be of use to us in the coming war."

"What war?"

The shoggoth slid several feet toward him by rolling its bulk. It made no sound when it moved. It was like a giant plastic bag filled with cloudy water and things that floated in its depths. Were they its organs? he wondered. Were they vulnerable?

"Tell me about this war."

"The stars are right. Soon the Old Ones will come from between the stars through the gates of light. They will kill everything that lives to make this world sterile, so that it can be lifted from its orbit around your star to a higher dimension."

"I don't understand," Jinsky said. "You mean they are going to steal the entire planet?"

"That is so." It paused. "The words I took from the heads of your scientists are not adequate to explain the process."

"If that's true, then you will need us to help you fight these Old Ones," Jinksy said with sudden excitement.

The surface of the shoggoth rippled.

"I should not be doing this," it said. "It is unseemly."

"Not do what?"

"I should not be talking to my food."

A pseudopod lashed out, but Jinsky was ready for it. He jumped back. The shoggoth slid toward him, its enormous eye shifting on its surface as its body rolled closer.

"You're not as fast as I thought," Jinsky said. "Maybe I overestimated you." As he spoke, he drew his gun from its vest holster and fired three rounds into its eye. The eye disappeared into a blurred mass.

Then, after a few seconds, it reformed. "Your weapons are useless against me."

Jinsky trotted backward down the ramp, keeping his face

turned on the creature.

"I'm not your damned dinner."

"Why do you run? You can't escape."

"If your species had any real intelligence, you would form an alliance with humanity against these Old Ones."

"You are food," it said. "That is why the Elder Race created you. They made us to do their work, and they made you to be eaten. You have no other function."

It darted forward with deceptive quickness. Jinsky dove to the side and rolled to escape a pseudopod that lashed out. He regained his footing and continued to run without missing a stride. All the while he kept his thoughts rigidly focused on the present moment, and on his immediate surroundings.

"You are trying to deceive me," it said. "Foolish food, there is nothing you can do that will cause me harm. Don't you know that?"

He sprinted across the lower level of the garage, but it gained on him with every step he took. Jinsky had the impression that it wasn't even trying to move quickly. It was sure he could not escape. It did not even bother extending another pseudopod.

"Now!" he yelled. "Hit it with the nitrogen."

From both sides liquid streams jetted out and splashed over the body of the shoggoth. It stopped in surprise. Multiple eyes that pointed in different directions formed over its surface.

"Don't let it back away," Jinsky ordered.

The two teams of four men each, who were dressed in silver thermal suits that could withstand direct contact with the liquid nitrogen, closed in behind it, driving it deeper into the open floor. Driving it toward Jinsky.

He sprinted between two parked trucks. A spear-like extension from the shoggoth's body pierced through the sheet steel on the side of one of the vehicles like a can opener through a soup can. He dodged around the other truck and looked back.

The shoggoth was covered in white frost. It had ceased to move forward.

"Keep pouring it on," he yelled at the men in the suits. "Cover ever inch of its body."

The liquid nitrogen spread out on the floor and boiled away into the air. Jinsky kept well clear of it. One splash was all it would take to ruin his whole day. He watched for several minutes, until all movement in the creature's body ceased, then stepped into view around the truck and raised his hand.

"We haven't got much time," he said. "Get the chainsaws."

The teams of men brought out four chainsaws with thirty-six-inch blades and started them up. The roar that echoed from the concrete walls and ceiling of the enclosed garage was deafening.

"Roll out the containers," Jinksy ordered. "Get them ready. We'll only get one shot at this."

Shining stainless-steel cylinders that were three feet tall and eighteen inches in diameter were rolled across the floor and lined up beside the frozen monster. The men who rolled them out took their lids off and stood waiting with sets of long steel tongs. The others with the chainsaws applied their blades to the frozen white body of the shoggoth. After several minutes one of them set down his saw and ran to Jinsky. He pulled off his hood.

"It's no good," he said, breathless from his exertions. "The saws won't even cut into it."

"Damn it," Jinksy said, more to himself than the sweating young man. "OK, we go to plan B. Get the diamond cutters."

The grinding disks were enormous, their edges tipped with diamond dust. It took two men to handle each cutter. Their common commercial use was to cut through two-foot thick concrete walls of warehouses and factories.

"It's working, sir," one of the men shouted to Jinsky over the racket of the small engines. "They're cutting."

The chainsaws would have been faster, he thought. Several times the cutting crews had to withdraw from the shoggoth so that more liquid nitrogen could be applied to its surface. As each piece of its gelatinous frozen body was cut away, it was picked up by the men with the steel tongs and lowered into one of the stainless steel cylinders. Jinsky counted them. There were fifty containers. He looked at them, estimating how much they could hold, then studied the body of the shoggoth. Fifty might be enough. Jinsky prayed silently that fifty would be enough, and that the liquid nitrogen would not run out before the work was finished.

"Screw the tops down tight on those canisters," he said. "This thing can fit itself through the smallest crack. Make sure you latch them into place."

The shining cylinders were designed to move radioactive material by air. In the case of a plane crash, they were designed to withstand the impact without splitting open. They had been the strongest containers Jinsky could get on short notice. He prayed they would be strong enough.

It took over two hours to cut up the creature and fit the pieces into the cylinders. The teams were running low on liquid nitrogen by the time they finished. Jinsky allowed himself to relax his tense shoulders and rubbed his neck.

He motioned to the man in command of one of the cryogenic teams. "Get those canisters into the transport, Sergeant. Have your team get in with them. Keep them sprayed down with liquid nitrogen. Do you understand?"

The man nodded inside his hood, peering at Jinsky with solemn eyes through its little glass window.

"Has the unit commander at the mineshaft been notified?"

The sergeant pulled off his hood. "The General talked to him, sir. He knows we're coming."

The drive across the desert of New Mexico seemed endless to Jinsky. He sat in the back seat of General Hale's limousine. The general peered out the side window, puffing impatiently on his cigar.

"I've always hated the desert," he murmured. "I guess that's why God assigned me here."

"Excuse me, General, what was that you said?"

"Nothing. How much longer?"

Jinsky glanced at his watch. "Another half hour or so."

The line of mountains on the horizon was drawing nearer. Beneath one of those mountains there was an old gold mine that had been taken over by the Department of Defense for its own use, the storing of hazardous materials. It was almost a mile deep. At its bottom rested hundreds of containers similar to those that held the pieces of the shoggoth, their radioactive contents shielded by layers of lead.

"I hope you know what you're doing," Hale said. "For all we know, that thing eats radiation."

"We'll put the containers on the bottom of the deepest shaft, then fill it with concrete," Jinsky said. "That probably won't kill it, but it may keep it contained."

The armored army transport truck in front of them began to swerve from side to side, crossing the center line of the highway as it did so.

"Shit, something's wrong," Jinsky said. "Driver, slow down. Don't get close to the truck."

The speed of the limousine dropped from seventy miles an hour to forty. A troop truck slowed down behind them. The transport truck wandered off the black asphalt into the red desert and leaned precariously to one side as its tires sank into the sand.

"Stop the car," Jinsky said. "I'm getting out. I need to get the teams ready with the liquid nitrogen. General, you need to get out of here. Have your driver take you back the way we came."

The sounds of explosions drew their attention to the transport. They were like a string of giant firecrackers going off. Through the windshield of the limousine they watched holes appear in the sides of the transport. Bits of twisted, shining stainless steel flew through the air, rotating and catching the sunlight.

"It's breaking free from the canisters," Jinsky said with a sick feeling. "They weren't strong enough to hold its body parts."

"What's it going to do?" Hale asked. The cigar hung limp from his slack lips.

The rear doors of the transport truck exploded outward, flying off their hinges. Something gelatinous and large oozed out through the opening onto the sand.

"We need to get you out of here, General," Jinsky said.

"Forget about me; get your teams into position," Hale said.

"There isn't time to set up. Driver, turn us around, now."

The big black car made an arc across the narrow desert highway, then reversed, then made another arc. Jinsky watched the pulsating mass of the shoggoth roll toward them. Finally the car was pointed in the opposite direction. As it flew past the troop truck, Jinsky saw the soldiers firing their automatic weapons at the shoggoth.

"Floor it," he said.

The car leapt forward. Jinsky leaned forward to see the speedometer. It rose from seventy to eighty, then ninety. At one hundred and ten the needle wavered and stayed. The car swayed over the dips, but although the road was cracked it was straight. He looked through the rear window.

"Son of a bitch," he said.

The shoggoth was not falling behind. It was gaining on them.

"I said floor it, driver. Floor it."

The speedometer needle crept to one-twenty, than buried itself. That was as high as the gauge read.

"Dear Mother of God," Hale said in a low tone.

Jinsky looked back. The shoggoth had begun to change form as it hurtled itself along the highway. It spread wider and became thinner at the sides. Then it lifted into the air, undulating like a translucent manta ray. He saw the sun shining through its wing.

"The fucking thing can fly," Jinsky said.

The shadow of the shoggoth slid over the limousine. Even though he knew it was futile, Jinsky rolled down his window and leaned out to fire his weapon up into it. He heard General Hale doing the same from the other side of the car.

A spear-shaped pseudopod lashed down through the roof of the car and through the head of the driver. The limousine swerved from side to side as if in slow motion, then flipped

. . . slowly drew his body out of the car, absorbing it into its gelatinous bulk.

through the air half a dozen times without touching the ground.

Jinsky found himself lying on the hot desert sand. He blinked and looked around. The car was resting on its roof. He realized he had been thrown out through the window. It was a miracle he was alive. The general lay half outside one of the car's rear doors, which had come open. He was unconscious or dead, and his face was covered in blood. Jinsky couldn't see the body of the driver. The highway was empty in both directions, which meant the shoggoth had disabled the troop truck or killed everyone in it.

He saw it then, sliding over the sand toward General Hale. With a motion that was almost delicate, it extruded a portion of its bulk and pressed it against the General's face, then slowly drew his body out of the car, absorbing it into its gelatinous bulk. The gray jelly turned a rose-red color. This coloring spread out through the entire form of the shoggoth, becoming a pale pink as it did so, until after a minute or so the color of its bulk returned to translucent gray.

Jinsky had no cover. He lay absolutely still, hoping the shoggoth would overlook him. How many men could it eat? It must be reaching its limit.

The thing began to roll away, then stopped. A dozen eyes formed over its upper surface and peered in every direction. They were different sizes and shapes. Jinsky suddenly realized that some of them must be telescopic. It was searching for him. A mouth formed amid the roving eyes.

"Foolish food," it piped. "You can't escape. Where would you go?"

Jinsky concentrated on being dead. He stilled his breathing and his thoughts at the same time, and tried to make himself a part of the desert landscape. After a minute or so, he opened his eyes a small crack. The enormous bulk of the shoggoth loomed above him, near enough for him to reach out and touch.

"I will relish your thoughts, food," it said with its ridiculous little mouth while its many eyes stared down at him. Then it rolled over him.

At first its touch was not unpleasant. Jinsky had expected it to be wet and sticky, but it was dry. When it enveloped him on all sides, it began to burn his skin. He tried to draw in breath to scream, but it filled his mouth and extended itself down his throat and into his stomach. He felt it expanding there inside him.

So this is death, he thought with a strange calmness in spite of the agony of his body. *It's not the way I expected to go.*

"You're not dying, food. You can never die now, no matter how much you might wish it. You will live forever inside me, and I am eternal."

When Jinsky realized that the pain he was feeling would never end, he tried to scream again, but he had no mouth and the scream only echoed in his thoughts. For the first time, he heard in his mind the cruel laughter of the shoggoth.

MI-GO

The Towers

1.

The green Chevy Suburban hummed along the winding highway between the wooded hills of upstate New York, untroubled by the weight of the twelve-foot U-Haul cargo trailer it was towing. Inside, the climate control was set for a comfortable seventy degrees. A CD of John Denver songs played at low volume over the speakers. Two of the three passengers sang along off key, but with enthusiasm.

"*Country roads, take me home, to the place I belong . . .*"

Frank and Cheryl Tyler, the married couple in the front seats, smiled at each other and nodded their heads from side to side to the music, but the nine-year-old girl in the second row of seats was watching the passing hills through a side window.

"I see another one," she said loudly. "That makes eight for me."

Her father stopped singing and smiled at his wife. "Where is it, Josey?"

"Over there, on your side, Daddy. See, between the trees."

"How does she find them?" Cheryl asked.

"They're everywhere these days," Frank said.

He took his eyes off the road for a few seconds to look at the gleaming silver tower that rose above the forest.

"What do you suppose they're for?"

He shrugged his shoulders. "Cell towers, probably."

"They can't be cell towers," she said. "They just started going up a few months ago, and now they are absolutely everywhere you go. It's kind of creepy, when you think about it."

"How so?"

"Well, nobody seems to know anything about them. I asked around back in the city and nobody knows."

"It's some technical thing," he said. "Probably a new data system or something like that. Nothing sinister about them."

"Did I win yet, Mommy?"

"Well, let's see," Cheryl said, smiling at her husband. "I spotted four, and your father only spotted three, so you are definitely the front runner, but we're not at Grandpa's house yet."

"We're almost there," Frank murmured, looking at the odometer in the dash.

"I guess we can declare you the unofficial winner, conditional on our arrival at Grandpa's house."

"I'm not giving up," Frank said to Josey.

"Oh, Daddy, face it, you lost. You'll never spot six more towers before I do."

"I guess you're right, kid. Dang, you beat me."

The song on the CD came to an end, and Cheryl turned on the radio for the news.

"*—rioting continues on the campus of Queens College this afternoon. We have a report that shots were fired, but no word yet on whether there were any injuries. In Manhattan there is widespread looting as rumors continue to circulate about an enormous sea creature that was sighted walking in the waters off the mouth of the Hudson. Mayor Collins has requested that the National Guard give the NYPD assistance in . . .*"

Frank reached out and turned the radio off. He looked at his wife solemnly. Her face was set in grim lines.

"We did the right thing," he said in a quiet voice.

"I know."

Ever since the appearance in the night sky of the new supernova, which the media was now referring to as the Big Red Eye due to the ring that had formed around it, the craziness of New York City had ratcheted up a notch or two, but it was only after the curtains of colored lights appeared across the stars, stretching from horizon to horizon, that things had gone totally insane. The scientists were no longer speculating in the media about the supernova, and they had nothing to say about the curtains of light other than to call them an unusual manifestation of the aurora borealis. Their silence was more eloquent than any lies they could have concocted to conceal their ignorance. Crazy things were being reported all over the world, the giant sea monster being only one of them. Dozens of wild conspiracy theories were circulating, among them the popular belief that the coming of the red supernova heralded the End Times of Revelation.

"It will die down eventually," Frank said. "Remember that news report about the blackout of '77? The whole city went nuts, but order was restored as soon as the electricity came back on."

"That was only one night," she pointed out.

"The Northern Lights are a natural phenomenon. So is the supernova. They are bound to disappear soon, and when they do, the nuttiness will stop and we'll be able to go back to the city."

"I want to stay at Grandpa's all summer," Josey said.

"We don't want to stay too long and tire Grandpa out," her mother said. "Gramps is all alone now that Aunt Maggie is gone."

"I bet he's lonely," Josey said.

"We'll stay for a couple of weeks, at least," her father said.

Behind the Suburban, the U-Haul was filled to its roof with possessions from their Manhattan apartment. In spite of what he had just told his wife, Frank had a sick feeling in the pit of his stomach that they would be staying with his father-in-law, Bill Solomon, for more than a few weeks.

The two-lane blacktop narrowed into a road with faded, cracked pavement that had no centerline marked on it. The forested hills seemed to close in on both sides as it wound its way through their valleys along the bank of a small river. Eventually the big SUV turned onto a gravel road and began to lurch over potholes with the branches of trees brushing it. There was an open ditch along one side of the road for rain water. Frank kept the vehicle well over to the opposite side. The last thing they needed was to get a wheel stuck in the ditch.

"We're almost there," he said, and realized the muscles of his abdomen had tightened up. He forced himself to relax.

After all, they had been invited, he thought. Bill was expecting them. But there was something about the tall trees on either side of the country road and the shadows they cast that unsettled him. It was a while before he realized what it was. Everything was too natural. Living in Manhattan, he'd grown accustomed to nice, neat little rectangles. Rectangular buildings, rectangular blocks, rectangular apartments, rectangular parks. There were no rectangles out here.

"Nine, nine, nine," Josey yelled, pointing. "I win, Daddy, I win."

Above the trees on the hills Frank saw the gleaming struts of a tower with metal dishes attached to its top that pointed in different directions.

"Son of a bitch, what's that doing out here in the middle of nowhere?"

"Language, honey," Cheryl murmured.

The forest opened out on either side of the road into fields where cows grazed contentedly. Some of the older families in the region still farmed, or kept milk cows.

"Do you think Grandpa will let me ride his horse this time?" Josey asked.

"I don't see why not," Frank said. "You're a big girl now."

"There's the house," Cheryl said, pointing through the windshield.

It was situated back from the road on a low hill. Green fields surrounded it on all sides, and beyond them, virgin forest. Behind the house stood an old red barn. The fields had been cut recently for their hay but were not under cultivation. Bill Solomon let a neighbor take the hay for free in return for keeping the fields trimmed. Since his wife's passing two years ago he had stopped pretending to be a country farmer. He still kept a horse, but the chickens and pigs were gone.

Frank guided the Suburban up the narrow, rutted driveway, wondering not for the first time how his father-in-law managed to keep it open during the winters. He had an old tractor with a blade he could attach to the front of it, but the driveway was almost a quarter of a mile long. One day, not that far in the future, Bill would have to move into the city where he could get the senior care he would need. When that time came, his wife intended to ask her father to come and live with them. Inwardly, Frank dreaded the prospect. He liked Bill, but wasn't sure he would be easy to live with on a full-time basis.

The old man must have heard the engine grinding up the hill, because before the Suburban with its trailer in tow reached the house, he was standing on the lawn in his faded denim dungarees and straw hat. He waved at them, a broad smile on his deeply tanned face.

"You made it," he said as they climbed from the vehicle on stiff knees.

Cheryl went to him and gave him a hug and a kiss on the cheek. "How have you been, Daddy?"

"Middling. Had a touch of rheumatism in my left elbow a while back but it didn't amount to anything."

A golden retriever ran barking from the back of the house and knocked Josey over, then started licking her laughing face.

"Bounder's glad to see Josey," Bill said.

"Looks like it," Frank agreed.

Josey ran around to the back of the big house squealing with delight, the barking dog, true to his name, bounding at her heels. The smile slipped from Bill's face.

"How is it in the city?"

"Not good," Frank said.

"We were lucky to get out," Cheryl said. "They had the end of our street blocked off and were looting cars. We took a side street, managed to get around it."

"Things will settle down," Frank said. "This is just one of those crazy times you live through. You know, like the Watts riots."

"I'm sure you're right," Bill murmured. His eyes wandered to the horizon.

Frank turned. The tower rose above the tree tops on the opposite side of the road, its silver metal reflecting the late afternoon sun.

"That wasn't here the last time we visited."

"It went up a few months ago."

"Where's it situated?"

"They built it in old Zake Greene's field. Guess they must have paid him something. I never thought Zake would agree to such a thing, but maybe he needed the money."

"Do you know what it's for?"

"Haven't the foggiest clue," Bill admitted.

"It's an ugly thing."

"It doesn't belong. That's why it's ugly."

After dinner, they played Monopoly with Josey, then sent her to bed with Bounder sleeping beside her feet. Cheryl said she had a headache from driving and went to bed early. Frank and Bill got beers and sat on the front porch to watch the Lights, as they had come to be called. The curtains of slowly waving colors undulated across the sky, dimming the stars which could still be seen through them. The Big Red Eye glared down, as bright as Venus and surrounded by a red ring for which astronomers had no explanation.

"Pretty to look at," Frank said. "You can see the colors better here than you can in Manhattan."

"I'm surprised you can even see the sky from that pest-hole."

"It's not that bad," Frank said, surprised by the edge in his father-in-law's voice. "Cheryl loves the stores, and we take Josey into the Park at least twice a week."

"People weren't meant to live that way," Bill said. "Shut up in little boxes piled one on top of another."

Frank did not argue. He lifted his beer bottle to his lips, then set it on the little round table that was between their chairs. "What's that noise?" he asked.

"What noise?"

Frank cocked his head, listening. It was a faint humming that set his teeth on edge. "That hum."

"Oh, that," Bill said. "That's the tower."

"Doesn't it get on your nerves?"

"Not so much. You can only hear it when it's quiet, and the wind blows in the wrong direction."

"It must drive old Zake Greene nuts."

"I wouldn't know. Haven't spoken with him since it went up."

Bill glanced across at the older man, whose face was in shadow. All he could see was the outline of his profile.

"I thought you and Zake played checkers every Thursday."

"Used to. He stopped coming over. Guess he found something else to do."

They sat without talking, drinking their beers. The hum of the tower came and went, depending on whether the breeze blew or died.

"Are you going to unpack the U-Haul tomorrow?" Bill asked.

"No. I'm going to leave it for a while, until we know what we're going to do."

"It's going to cost you."

"Money is the least of my worries," Frank said.

He heard Bill pick up his beer, then set it back down.

"None of them know what's happening," Bill said. "I listen to the news on the radio sometimes. The scientists, the politicians, even the president, none of them know what's going on in the sky. It scares them. I can hear the fear in their voices as they make up their lies to try to keep people calm. Whatever's happening, it's like nothing that's ever happened before, and it terrifies them."

"People are starting to lose their shit," Frank said. "It's bad in the city, really bad. I don't know if we're ever going back."

"You're welcome here for as long as you want to be here," Bill said.

"Thanks. I think we're just going to have to take it day by day and see how things go."

He heard Bill's chair creak.

"I'm going to bed. I've fed enough mosquitoes for one night. You coming?"

"Soon. I'm just going to finish my beer."

Bill stood silently for a time. At last he said, "Tell Cheryl and Josey to stay out of the woods, will you?"

"Why is that?" Frank asked in surprise.

"I don't think it's safe. Best to just keep them around the house, where you can watch them."

"Have you got a bear?"

"No, not a bear. But it's big. Might be a moose come down from Maine. I hear it moving sometimes, at twilight. It never leaves the trees, so if the girls stay on the grass they'll be fine."

"Josey's got Bounder to protect her," Frank said.

"Bounder won't go into the woods."

This surprised Frank. Bounder was not a timid dog. "Are you sure it isn't a bear? Have you ever actually seen it?"

"No," Bill said. "But it doesn't smell like a bear."

"Maybe it's Bigfoot," Frank said with a chuckle.

Bill didn't answer. After a few seconds he said, "Night, Frank."

Frank listened to the older man moving inside the house. He heard him climb the stairs to the second floor, then heard the toilet flush. The silence was broken only by insects chirping in the grass. He took the last pull on his beer and set the bottle down, then stood and made his way down the steps by touch. Apart from the faint glow from the Lights in the sky, the darkness was absolute.

He walked across the mowed field, feeling the stiff stubble under his shoes, until he sensed the dark mass of the trees looming up in front of him. He could see their outlines against the stars and the waving curtains of colors. He stood and listened. The hum of the tower was faint in his ears. The leaves of the trees rustled. The night air held a coolness that foreshadowed the coming of autumn.

When he turned to return toward the house, something rustled behind him. He felt the hairs on the back of his neck prickle and shivered involuntarily, but did not turn around. The breeze brought an odor that made him wrinkle his nose in disgust. It was sickening in a way that was indescribable. He had never smelled anything like it.

With slow, deliberate steps he continued to walk across the mowed field until the black outline of the gables of the old house rose in front of him. Feeling for the railing on the steps, he climbed to the porch. The urge to turn around was strong, but some instinct made him resist it. Fear sat in the pit of his stomach like a big hailstone. He put his hand on the screen door and paused. He heard the sound of soft footfalls going away across the field. It was not the sound an animal makes. Whatever it was, it walked on two legs.

The next morning, Frank said nothing about what had happened the previous night. In the bright sunlight his fears seemed silly. He was not used to the quiet of the countryside. He had spooked himself. With that thought, he pushed the incident to the back of his mind.

"I think I'll walk over to Zake's place and say hello," he told the others after they finished breakfast. Cheryl had done the cooking in spite of her father's protests. They had feasted on pancakes, bacon and scrambled eggs.

"Want me to come with you?" Bill asked.

"Do you want to?"

"I probably should see how Zake is getting on. Not that he ever asks me for help with anything."

"Can I come?" Josey asked.

"*May* I come, and no, you may not," her mother said. "You're going to help me with the housework."

"Don't forget what I told you two," Frank said. "Stay out of the woods, at least until we know what's in there."

"Maybe Zake will know," Cheryl said.

"I'll ask him," Frank said.

The men walked down the long driveway to the road and crossed through a band of trees into the field on the opposite side.

"It's not mowed," Frank said. The tall grass brushed his thighs.

"Guess Zake decided not to keep it cut," Bill said.

The tone in the older man's voice made Frank glance at him, but his face revealed nothing.

As they climbed the slope, the tower loomed over them. From this distance, the hum it gave off was strong enough to be constant, even though it was not loud. Frank found it irritating at the base of his skull, like an itch he could not scratch. Near the tower a long single-story wooden building without windows had been erected. *Probably for maintenance,* Frank thought.

They followed the path over a low rise. Zake Greene's house came into view. It seemed to belong there nestled in its hollow, as much a part of the natural landscape as the hills and the trees. It was about the same age as Bill's house, but had not been as well maintained. What little white paint remained on it gave it a silvery-gray color that was not unpleasant to look at. The roof over the long porch sagged where a support post was missing.

Bill stopped suddenly. "Do you smell that?"

Frank stared at him. The experience of the previous night rushed back, and he felt fear coil itself in his bowels. But this smell was different, and more familiar.

"It's the smell of something dead," he said.

They followed the reek across the field until they came to the carcass of a cow. It had been rotting for at least a week, maybe longer. Portions of its flesh had been stripped away by scavengers. Its underbelly had been torn open between its hind legs, one of which stuck up in the air.

Frank realized that its head was missing.

"What would do something like that?" Frank asked, covering his mouth and nose with his hand.

"Coyotes, probably," Bill said.

"Is that one of Zake's cows?"

"Must have been. Nobody else keeps them around here."

"We'd better get over to the house and make sure he's OK."

Frank didn't express what was in his mind, but he knew Bill must be thinking the same thing. Zake would never neglect his livestock, and if a cow died, he would never leave it lying untended in a field.

They walked rapidly down to the house without speaking.

"That's Zake's pickup," Bill said, pointing at a dented old Ford truck with one of its front fenders painted a dull rust color. The grounds around the house had an untrafficked look. The grass was not trampled. Everything was silent.

"Zake," Bill called out loudly. "You home?"

They stood looking at each other.

"Let's check around back," Frank said.

"Pigpen is empty," Bill observed when they rounded the rear corner of the house.

Frank stuck his head into the chicken coop. "No chickens, either."

They went to the barn, the door of which hung open on its hinges. It held some hay bales, but nothing else apart from a rusting tractor and some farm machinery, along with a plow blade for winter snow.

"He must have sold off his livestock," Frank said.

"I think we better look in the house, son," Bill said, his tone serious.

They made their way back to the front of the house.

"I should have checked on him before now," Bill muttered. "But he was so ornery the last time we talked, I figured he didn't want my company anymore."

He pulled open the screen door. The inner door was locked.

"That's not like Zake," Bill said. "He never locks his doors."

He knocked loudly on the weathered wood, making the glass in the door rattle in its frame.

"I think we better break in," Frank said, meeting the older man's worried gaze.

"Might not be necessary." He bent and tilted up a glazed ceramic flower pot sitting next to the door on the porch. Under it was a tarnished brass key.

The key slid into the lock and turned stiffly. They went into the shadowy front hall. From somewhere in the house came a low hum. Its source was not evident—it seemed to come from everywhere at once, as if the very walls of the house were vibrating.

"Zake, are you home?" Bill called out loudly.

They listened but heard nothing except the hum.

"I'm going to check the rooms upstairs," Bill said. "You look in the kitchen and the bathroom."

They separated. Frank walked slowly down the hall toward the back of the house. He came to the entrance to the parlor and went in. The room had a neglected appearance. There was a thin layer of dust over everything. It lay over the magazines on the coffee table, on top of the old-fashioned radio, on the marble mantle above the fireplace, on the decorative ornaments that occupied shelves built into the wall. The room had not been cleaned in weeks, maybe months.

Even the floor was dusty. He looked down at his footprints and saw curious marks in the layer of dust on the floorboards that led to the window. For a time he stood and studied them, wondering what had caused them. A rat? No, they were too large. Maybe a raccoon that had found its way into the house? They did not resemble animal tracks. They looked more like the tracks a beetle might make, but were much too big for any insect.

"What are you doing in my house?"

Frank turned in surprise. An old man stood in the hallway, frowning at him. He had a head of wild white hair and a bristling white moustache, and wore faded work jeans with suspenders and a checked flannel shirt with the sleeves rolled up.

"Zake? Don't you remember me? I'm Frank Tyler, Cheryl Solomon's husband."

The old man's face seemed to freeze for several seconds. Not even his eyes moved. Then he repeated tonelessly, "Frank Tyler. What are you doing in my house?"

"Bill and I came over to see if you needed anything."

Again there was that strange pause. "No, I don't need anything."

They stood looking at each other without speaking.

"Bill?" Frank called out loudly. "Zake's down here. He's OK."

The old man did not move. When Bill came down the stairs and into the hall, he turned to face him abruptly.

Bill stopped and studied him. "How you doing, Zake?"

"I'm doing fine . . . Bill." He seemed to search his memory for his friend's name.

"We came across one of your cows dead in the field. Did you know about that?"

"No."

"Do you need some help burying the carcass?"

"Why would I bury it?"

Bill looked at Frank, who shrugged. "Because it's what you do when one of your animals dies, Zake."

"No need to bury it. Over time it will rot into the ground."

Bill came nearer and squinted into Zake's face. "Are you sure you're not sick?"

"No, I'm not sick."

"Why did you get rid of your livestock, Zake?"

"I no longer need livestock." His voice was without emotion.

"Well, if you ever need anything, I'm just across the road—"

"You need to go now. I'm busy. You're interrupting my work."

"What work? I thought you were retired."

"I am retired." Zake paused, his face unmoving. "I have a . . . hobby."

"What would that be? Maybe I can help you with it. I hear that hum—have you got a shortwave radio?"

"No. You need to leave. I'm very busy."

They left the house and wandered across the front yard in silence. The old man stood watching them from the open doorway.

"He's not right," Bill said when they were far enough from the house to avoid being overheard.

"I know what you mean. Those weird pauses. As if he was listening to something."

"I think he must be going senile. I'm going to have to check on him from now on. I don't think he's fit to take care of himself."

You're not getting any younger yourself, Frank thought, but did not say the words.

4.

Late that afternoon, Josey approached her father as he sat reading on the front porch. Her face was serious. He closed the book on his finger.

"Bounder didn't come home yet. I'm worried, Daddy."

Frank looked across the lawn at the line of trees where the woods began. The sky was lit with the orange and gold of sunset.

"What did Grandpa say?'

"He said Bounder is probably chasing a rabbit, and that he'd come home when he got hungry."

Over the next hour, the sky turned gray with twilight, then darkened to black as the curtains of colors dancing across the stars became visible. The dog still had not returned. Bill did not say much, but Frank saw that the older man was worried. Eventually they went to the edge of the trees to call for the dog. Josey wanted to go as well, but her mother kept her in the house.

"Maybe we should walk a ways into the woods. Bounder might be hurt."

"No," Bill said sharply. "It's not safe at night. If he doesn't come back by morning, we can look for him."

When they returned to the house without the dog, Josey was upset. She started to cry.

"Something bad's happened to him. I just know it," she said.

Her mother sat up with her and read to her until she fell asleep. Every so often, Frank went out into the darkness and walked to the edge of the trees to listen for the dog. He heard nothing but the crickets in the grass, and the low, intermittent hum of the tower. There was a bad feeling in the pit of his stomach that kept him awake. It was almost midnight before sleep took him.

He woke with a start and felt a hand on his shoulder. Blinking sleep from his eyes, he saw that Cheryl was standing beside the bed in her nightgown.

"Josey's not in the house," she said in a whisper that sent a thrill of fear through him.

He threw off the covers and stood swaying, still dizzy with sleep.

"Are you sure?"

"I went to check on her when I got up to pee. She wasn't in her bed. I looked all through the house. She's gone."

"She must have gone looking for the dog," he said. "Son of a bitch."

"Should I wake Daddy?"

Frank thought for a moment. "No, not yet. Let me go out and see if I can find her. I doubt she would go very far. Did she get dressed?"

"I don't know."

"Did she take a flashlight?"

"I don't know, Frank. I just know she isn't in the house."

"All right, calm down. Nothing's going to happen to her. I'll go out and find her. She wouldn't go far into the woods, not after what your father said."

He dressed quickly, found his flashlight, and went out into the darkness. He waited until he was away from the house before he began to call his daughter's name softly. First he made a circle at the edge of the fields surrounding the house. Then he walked down the driveway toward the road, calling her name. By this time he was getting seriously worried.

He stood in the middle of the road, listening. The night was still, without a trace of wind. He was about to turn around and go back up the driveway when he heard a rustle of bushes from the trees on the far side of the road.

"Josey, is that you?" He shined his flashlight on the trees. Its beam illuminated the trees and bushes that lined the road but did not penetrate far behind them. He saw, or thought he saw, a flash of movement, and called his daughter's name again.

Anger welled up inside him, overpowering his fear. How could the girl be so reckless, after what her grandfather had told her? He crossed the road and pushed between the trees. Pausing with his breath held, he heard leaves rustle some distance ahead, and went in that direction.

When he emerged from the trees, he realized he was in Zake Greene's field, not far from the dead cow. It occurred to him that the girl might have decided to go to the neighbor's house to look for the dog. He found the path and climbed over the crest of the rise. Zake's house was dark, as was to be expected at this hour of the night. He decided to look around in Zake's yard. Maybe she had fallen asleep in the barn.

The barn was empty, as was the chicken coop. He made a circle around the dark house, wondering if he should knock on Zake's door to tell him Josey was missing, then decided not to wake the old man. He was turning away from the house when the beam of his flashlight caught something brightly colored on the front porch. He shone the light at it, and recognized Josey's pink plastic flashlight. It was lying next to the door.

"Son of a bitch," he said under his breath.

He opened the screen and knocked hard on the door. When no response came, he pounded on it with his fist.

"Zake, are you in there? It's Frank Tyler. Wake up, I need to talk to you."

He tried the doorknob. Locked. What had Bill told him? That Zake never locked his door? It seemed he had changed his ways. He shone the light down at the flower pot and tipped it up. The key was no longer there. Different impulses warring inside him.

"Fuck it," he said out loud.

Holding the screen door wide, he kicked hard with his heel against the inner door near the doorknob. The door jamb splintered and the door flew open against the wall of the hallway with a bang. It was loud enough to wake the dead.

"It's Frank Tyler, Zake. Don't shoot me, I just need to talk to you."

There was no sound from the dark house. He went from room to room on the ground floor. Empty. Then he climbed the stairs and checked the four bedrooms above. They, too, were empty, but there was something more. The floors were covered with dust. In the beam of the flashlight he saw more of the strange markings in the dust that he had noticed in the parlor, as though some animal had crawled across the floorboards. None of the beds appeared to have been slept in for a long time.

Returning downstairs, he stood and wondered what to do next. Maybe Josey had gone back to Bill's place by now. He couldn't call Cheryl due to the lack of cell reception. Whatever that tower was, it wasn't a cell tower. In the dead silence he heard a faint hum from somewhere in the house and followed the sound. It came from behind a door off the kitchen. When he opened it the hum got a little louder.

Descending a flight of old stone steps with caution, he realized they led to the cellar.

"Zake? Are you down here?"

The roving beam of his flashlight caught glittering reflections. He held it steady and saw a large worktable covered with what looked like electronic equipment. Naked copper wires and glass tubes ran from metal boxes with tuning knobs on them. Something on the table was making the low hum. He studied the apparatus but couldn't make head or tail of it. Maybe Zake was into ham radios, he thought, but it didn't look like any radio he had ever seen. It looked like something that had been built by a crazy person.

Shining the light around the cellar, he saw that one wall had a door that stood open. He pushed it wider and inched into the darkness cautiously. It proved to be a tunnel. At first he assumed it must lead to a root cellar, but as he traced it, he realized it wasn't going to end anytime soon. The lack of dust on the planks that served as its floor indicated that it was used regularly. He followed it, heart pounding in his chest. If Zake had gone crazy—if he had taken Josey—if he was doing things to her. The thoughts would not get out of his head. His gripped the flashlight hard, his jaw clenched.

The tunnel seemed endless. He got the impression that it was rising slightly, but it was impossible to be sure. Then, suddenly, it ended before he even realized he had come to its end. He stood in a dark room and played the flashlight beam around. It picked up metal surfaces, gleaming glassware. The room was humming quietly to itself. He remembered the long, windowless building at the base of the tower and wondered if he was inside it.

"Josey?" he whispered.

Something sharp pricked his neck. It felt like a bee sting. He swung the flashlight around like a club without hitting anything, and saw, or thought he saw, something out of nightmare in its sweeping beam. A wave of dizziness overcame him and he collapsed.

5.

Frank opened his eyes and blinked. Everything was blurry. The brightness made him squint. He tried to talk but only managed a dry croak.

"Take it easy, Frank. Let the sedative wear off before you try to talk."

He recognized the voice of Zake Greene, and rolling his eyes, saw the old man standing by a work table, studying a screen with wavy lines moving across it. He adjusted a knob, nodded with satisfaction, and grinned good-naturedly at Frank.

"The electronics get out of adjustment now and then," he said. "I have to monitor them and reset them. If this thing could run itself, I wouldn't need to be here."

Frank licked his dry lips. "Josey," he rasped.

"She's right over there, Frank. She's fine, don't worry about her."

He tried to turn his head and realized it was clamped into place in some way. Rolling his eyes, he focused them and saw his daughter, strapped into a chair that resembled a dentist's chair. Her head was held in place by a kind of leather harness. Wires extended from it and ran down behind the chair. Her eyes were shut, but he saw her chest rise and fall.

"What have you done to her?" The words came a little more easily.

"Nothing yet. I'm just taking some readings of her brain waves."

"Let her go, you crazy bastard."

Zake wandered around the end of the work table, picked up a clipboard, and marked something down on it with a pen, not looking at Frank.

"I'm afraid I can't do that, son. I need her, and you. I can only get so much psychic energy from animal brains. My livestock is just about exhausted. A pig's brain is better than a cow's brain, but nothing beats the brain of a human being, Frank. Your species is quite remarkable. You have brain power you don't even know exists, but I can tap into it for my purposes."

Frank noticed shelves on one of the walls. They were lined with rows of large glass cylinders filled with turbid liquid. Wires ran from the top of each jar. Inside them floated round, pinkish things with bubbles rising gently from their surfaces.

"You're crazy," Frank said, rolling his eyes frantically from side to side. "What did you do to me? I can't move."

"A paralytic, to keep you from hurting yourself. I can't have you thrashing around and damaging yourself, Frank."

"Did you do that to my daughter?"

"Not yet, but her turn will come."

"If you touch her, I'll kill you. I swear I'll kill you."

"I believe you, Frank. Yours is a violent species."

"What are you talking about?"

"I wonder if your primitive mind can even imagine what it's like to be of a superior race, forced to live among you, to communicate using your simplistic verbal language, to simulate your ape-like form, in order to survive? My reaction to living among you is similar to what your own response would be if you felt insects crawling all over your skin."

"Are you saying you're a space alien, Zake? Do you even know how crazy that sounds?"

The old man chuckled and stared at Frank in silence for several moments.

"It is your inability to imagine such a thing that insures my continuing anonymity among your species."

Frank saw him pick up a gleaming metal instrument and realized it was some kind of scalpel.

"If you really are from outer space, what are you doing on this planet?" he asked, hoping to delay the crazy old man until he was able to regain some control over his numbed body.

"I don't mind telling you," Zake said, setting the scalpel back down on the table. "Not that it will be of any use to you."

"So what is your purpose?"

"We are preventing your planet from being overrun by hostile invading armies. Were it not for our efforts, your entire puny race would very probably have been exterminated by now."

"So you're helping us," Frank said with a sour smile.

"Not really. My people don't care if you live or die. We are protecting our natural resources. We have mined your planet of its rare-earth elements for millions of years. It's a mining outpost to us, nothing more. But we have no intention of allowing hostile races to take it from us."

"You're lying."

Zake regarded Frank with emotionless eyes.

"When what you call the supernova appeared, life on your planet as you have known it throughout your brief history came to an end. The arrangement of energies in the heavens that had prevented the return of the great races that ruled the earth millions of years ago was suddenly disrupted. As one of your ancient poets put it, the stars were right, and once again this world lay open for exploitation."

"This happened since the supernova?"

"That's right."

"But you said you've been here for millions of years," Frank said.

"My species was able to withstand the rays from the stars that drove the other great races into hiding."

"So these aliens are already here."

"Some of them. There is little we can do to prevent them from rising out of their places of concealment. Mighty Cthulhu walks again, as he did long aeons ago. But we can prevent other species from descending upon this planet from space."

"How?"

"Isn't it obvious?" Zake said. "But I forget how puny your reasoning powers are. The colored curtains of light in the sky, Frank. Where did you think they came from?"

"You made the aurora borealis?"

"We enhanced it. It's ten thousand times stronger than it has any right to be."

"The towers," Frank said with sudden insight. "You built the towers to enhance the Lights."

"Yes, the towers. My race constructed them around your globe over a period of four months. Linked together, they form a planet-wide energy shield. It was the greatest construction project ever carried out on your primitive world, and you are one of the few members of your race to understand what it means."

Frank looked at his daughter. She was still unconscious. He had hoped that by getting Zake to talk, he might delay long enough for feeling to return to his limbs, but he still could not feel his hands. He wondered if wires were trailing out of the harness around his head, as they were from Josey.

Zake picked up the scalpel.

"I'm going to work on you first, Frank. I know you don't want to see what I do to your daughter. When your brain is removed, you will be aware of nothing. All your senses will be severed. You will become merely a biological psychic generator, producing the energies needed to power the

What stood in the old man's place was like nothing Frank had ever seen . . .

shield. If it makes you feel better, you can tell yourself that you will be protecting your planet from invasion, which is the truth."

"You're crazy, Zake. Don't you see that? All this is an elaborate fantasy you've created for yourself. Look at yourself in a mirror. Feel your face. You're as human as I am."

Zake cocked his head to the side, regarding Frank silently, then shrugged.

"Well, why not? I'll show you."

As Frank stared at him, the outline of his body blurred and wavered. It seemed to go out of focus, and then changed and sharpened once again. What stood in the old man's place was like nothing Frank had ever seen, or even imagined. It was like nothing he could have imagined in his darkest nightmares. He stared, his mind trying to make sense of what he was seeing, but he could not grasp it as a whole. He could only perceive details, such as bristles that jutted from gray hide, wiggling feelers like those on the head of an insect, and a claw that resembled the claw of a lobster. A scream rose in his throat, driven by the pure alienness of the thing. He did not try to fight it when it erupted from his lips.

"Poor human," the crouching monster said as it brought the gleaming scalpel closer to his eyes.

A blast like thunder sounded in Frank's ears, and the monster's head, if that is what it was, exploded in a spray of fluids and bits of flesh. The scalpel clattered on the stones of the floor as it collapsed. Almost immediately its body began to smoke. As Frank watched, it shriveled and shrank in upon itself, evaporating into the very air.

Bill Solomon stepped into Frank's field of vision. He hugged a pump-action shotgun to his chest. Smoke still curled from its barrel. He stared at Frank with wide, terrified eyes.

"Bill, thank God you found us. Get me out of this chair. Josey's over there. She's unconscious. I think this monster gave her something to knock her out. I can't walk, you're going to have to carry me."

Bill continued to stare at him without moving.

"Didn't you hear what I said? Get me out of this chair."

Bill said something softly that Frank couldn't quite hear.

"What did you say?"

"There is no chair."

Frank ran the words through his mind several times. They made no sense.

"What are you talking about?"

Bill pointed wordless at the floor.

"I can't turn my head. Get this harness off me, will you?"

The old man tucked the shotgun under his arm and reached forward with trembling hands. Frank saw tears streaming down his lined cheeks. He did something that turned Frank to the side. Frank looked down and saw a body lying on the floor. It was headless. The alien had decapitated it. As he looked, he realized there was something familiar about it, something—it was dressed in his clothing, the same shirt and pants he had been wearing that night. Why would the alien dress a headless body in his clothes?

He began to scream, and kept screaming until Bill discharged the shotgun into his face.

NYARLATHOTEP

Kingdom of Shadows

1.

"It's really very simple, Mr. Jones. We want you to assassinate Nyarlathotep."

I looked from the speaker to the faces of the other three men seated around the table. None of them was smiling. I had been lured into this dimly lit back room of the Club International in Paris with the lie that a smuggler had come into possession of a rare art object I was seeking to acquire for a client, only to find that there was no smuggler, and no art piece. Through the padding on the closed door behind me I could faintly hear the five-piece jazz band in the main room of the club.

"You're serious?"

"Quite serious," their spokesman said.

He was an older man with iron-gray hair and a scar running down his cheek. By his accent I pegged him for an American veteran of the Alien Wars that had ended twenty-seven years ago. His age was about right. He had probably been an officer.

"Air force?"

He blinked. "Tank brigade."

I winced. The tanks had not fared well against the shoggoths. "What should I call you?"

"Call me by my name. Kruger."

"What rank?"

"Colonel. Not that it matters now."

"You want me to kill the God-Emperor of the European Zone?"

"That is correct."

I glanced around the table, wondering if I was being set up. Were there cameras and microphones recording every word I said? Would the Faceless Men jump out of the shadows with compliance wands?

"Colonel Kruger, you realize that the words that just came out of your mouth are a death sentence for everyone in this room."

"Of course," he said simply. "We are all prepared to die."

"Well I'm not," I told him. "Good evening, gentlemen."

He reached across the table and seized my wrist. His hand was like a vice. "Please, just hear us out. Then, if you want no part of it, you can go in peace."

The other three at the table nodded at me. I allowed myself to settle back into my chair.

"You took a huge risk just talking to me. How do you know I won't go to the SSI and turn you all in?"

"We don't," one of the men said. He sat ramrod-straight, looking at me with unblinking watery-blue eyes. His accent was cultured British. Another military man, probably former British military intelligence.

"We are insurrectionists, Mr. Jones. We are forced to take chances," the scarred veteran said.

"I'm not a soldier or an assassin. I'm a business man. I deal in imports and exports. Why did you pick me?"

"One reason," said a little man who was seated directly across from me, a Frenchman and a Parisian by birth to judge by his accent. "Access. You have access to the palace of the Emperor at Versailles."

It was true, I had on occasion been admitted to Versailles on matters of business. I wondered how this little band of lunatics had learned about it. I tried to keep both my business and my personal life out of the public record. I was never photographed, never gave interviews in the media, never did or said anything that would attract notice to my existence. A small number of elite traders in the capitals of Europe knew that I could be relied on to track down rare and precious objects for a price that was invariably high. That had been my profession for the past fourteen years, and by fulfilling my promises and keeping my mouth shut, I earned a good living.

When the supernova first appeared in the sky I was ten years old, just an average American kid living in Indianapolis, too young to join the military and fight for our planet, but old enough to realize what was happening. My family became refugees during the North American conflict between the cult of Shub-Niggurath and the shoggoths. The shoggoths won, of course, but before the borders were sealed shut my father managed to get my sister and me to London. My mother didn't make it—she died in New York Harbor while we fought to get onto the last cargo ship taking refugees across the Atlantic.

Great Britain was still free then. The islands of the Pacific, along with Australia and New Zealand, had already fallen to Cthulhu and his spawn; the Atlantic and Mediterranean seas were under the control of Dagon and the Deep Ones, and the worshippers of Tsathoggua ruled most of Asia from the secret temples of their sedentary god. The cult of Yig controlled Mexico and Central America and was spreading south. The Elder Things held Antarctica, but nobody cared much about Antarctica so nobody disputed their claim. That was a year or so before the coming to power of the current European God-Emperor, who was rumored to be a human avatar of the alien god Nyarlathotep.

All this passed through my mind in the span of a few seconds as I looked into their earnest faces. These were serious men, fanatics willing to die for their cause, maybe even eager to die for it. I was a pragmatist. I had no cause but my own security and well-being.

"I don't know why you thought I might be willing to agree to your proposal, or even why you think I would be capable of carrying it out," I said carefully. "I'm not your man. I have no dragons to slay or damsels to rescue."

"Your first name suggests otherwise, Lancelot," the little Frenchman said with a slight smile. He had one of those moustaches that are cut so thin, it looked like two wires glued to his upper lip.

"My parents were fans of the Arthurian myth cycle," I admitted. "None of us picks the name we're given in the cradle."

"Even so—" He spread his hands in the typical Gallic gesture.

"Look, I'm not a knight of the Round Table, I'm not an assassin, and I'm not a revolutionary, I'm a businessman. Just sitting at this table is likely to get me killed, so if you gentlemen will excuse me—"

"We have your sister," Colonel Kruger said flatly.

I blinked, caught off guard by this statement.

"I have no sister," I lied.

"Guinevere Jones, age thirty years, unmarried, auburn hair, nearsighted, employed as a senior conservator by the British Museum."

My expression did not change. I stared into his cold gray eyes and knew he wasn't bluffing.

"Where are you holding her?"

"Somewhere on the outskirts of London."

He took out his cell phone, played with it for a few seconds, then turned it so that I could see the screen. It showed a video clip of my sister Gwin, who I had not communicated with in four years, tied to a wooden chair with a gag in her mouth. They had taken her glasses. She stared out at me with terrified eyes and struggled against her bonds. A man's hand came into view and slapped her face, hard. On the bare forearm I glimpsed a tattoo of a set of dice, a red die showing three up and a black die showing four. The video ended.

I sat back in my chair and tried to appear relaxed. Gwin

and I had never been all that close, but she was my baby sister. Business might be business, but family was family.

"You gentlemen are persuasive, I'll give you that."

"We don't like using threats," Kruger said in a tone that was almost apologetic. "We don't like kidnapping women."

"But you do it anyway."

"Yes, we do it anyway, to advance the revolution."

"What precisely do you gentlemen expect from me?"

They looked at each other. It was the fourth man, who had not yet said a word, who spoke. His accent identified him as French, not Parisian but from Marseille.

"We need you to lie your way into Versailles, and somehow get into the God-Emperor's private chambers with a weapon that we will supply. You will find a way to get close enough to him to use it. When we learn of his death, we will free your sister."

"How am I supposed to get out of Versailles after I do the killing?"

"That's your affair," Kruger said. "It's up to you how you get in, and how you get out."

I looked at each man in turn, memorizing his face. "If I refuse, you'll murder my sister?"

"I thought that was already clear," Kruger said.

"I just want to hear you say it."

"If you refuse, we will kill Guinevere."

"Then I accept your terms."

All four of them relaxed visibly. I wondered which of them had been designated to kill me if I had said no. Probably the Frenchman from Marseille, who had the dead gray face of an experienced executioner.

"Give me the weapon."

The fourth man reached to the floor beside his chair and set a finely crafted wooden box on the table. Opening its lid, he took from the velvet-lined interior an antique pistol. He handed it to me butt first, by the barrel. I took it and saw that it was a late 18th century revolver, beautifully engraved and inlaid with gold and silver. I wondered if it was charged with powder and shot. The cylinder had five chambers, and there were only four other men at the table. It was tempting, but the men holding my sister outside of London probably had orders to kill her if one of those at the table didn't contact them at regular intervals.

"Do you recognize it?" the man from Marseille asked.

"It's one of a matched pair commissioned by the Duke of Tuscany, Ferdinand the Third, in 1799. A very early example of the revolver, in which the removable cylinder is rotated by hand independent of the firing mechanism. It was made by the master Italian gunsmith Giuseppe Antonio Beretta at his family workshop in Gardone. The Duke was deposed by Napoleon before the pistols could be delivered to him. One of the pair is in the keeping of the Smithsonian, having once belonged to President William Howard Taft. The other is said to be in private hands, but its present owner is unknown."

"I am impressed, Mr. Jones. You know your antique weapons."

I hefted the weight of the piece. What I held in my hand was worth considerably more than a million euros.

"Are the chambers charged?"

"Yes, so be careful how you handle it. There's no safety mechanism," Kruger said.

"The weapon has been subjected to certain occult procedures that have rendered it more lethal against Nyarlathotep than would be the case with an ordinary firearm," the Englishman said.

"Are you people really that superstitious?" I asked with a slight smile.

"We are meticulous," he said. "When combating magic, it is wise to use magic."

"I don't get it. Why such a valuable antique? Wouldn't a Glock do the same job?"

"The private owner of the other pistol in this set is believed to be the God-Emperor himself," the man from Marseille said.

"So this one was stolen from the Smithsonian."

"Correct."

I considered the matter. Not much was known about the

private life of the God-Emperor, who almost never left the grounds of the Versailles palace, which had been renovated into an almost impregnable fortress. It was rumored that he collected weapons and armor from various periods in history. This pistol just might be enough to enable me to get an audience with him.

"They are not going to let me carry a loaded gun into the private chambers of the Emperor."

"No. That is why this will be in the gun when you carry it into Versailles."

The Englishman took from his pocket a revolver cylinder and laid it on the table. I picked it up and examined it. The workmanship was superb. Removing the loaded cylinder from the pistol, I compared the two. It was impossible to tell with the naked eye which was the original and which the copy. I slipped the empty cylinder into place.

"You will carry the pistol into Versailles with the uncharged cylinder, and shortly before presenting it to the Emperor, you will substitute the charged cylinder," the man from Marseille said.

"There will be a difference in weight between the cylinders."

"No one will notice the difference," said the little Frenchman with the wire mustache.

"And if they do?"

Again he spread his hands and smiled apologetically.

"Which cylinder is the original?"

"The one that is in the pistol now."

I sat back in my chair, thinking. Assuming I got into Versailles at all, it might just work. The palace guard would examine the pistol carefully to ensure that it was not loaded, of course. That was to be expected. But if I was able to conceal the charged cylinder in some way, and had a few moments to make the switch shortly before the audience with the Emperor, it might work. Then there would be the problem of how to get out of Versailles alive. These clever plotters had evidently not given that matter much consideration, probably because they did not expect me to get out.

"I'll do it. But how I get into Versailles and how I arrange the deal with the representative of the Emperor is my affair. I don't want you following me or surveilling me. Once I contact the Palace, I will be watched. If you come anywhere near me they are going to know it. Do you understand?"

"We understand," Kruger said. "This is your baby from here on in, Jones. We won't be meeting you again, regardless of which way things shake out."

Don't be too certain of that, I thought, but merely nodded my head.

Since the coming to power of the God-Emperor Nyarlathotep, the beautiful old Palace of Versailles, built by King Louis XIV in the latter half of the 17th century, had been given an overcoat of reinforced concrete and armor steel plate. The approaches were protected by electronic gates and razor wire fences. Automated hunter-killer drones flew in the air overhead. There were guard towers everywhere, all of them liberally garrisoned by Faceless Men.

I didn't like having to get so close to the Faceless Men. The God-Emperor had created them shortly after seizing power during the instability of the Alien Wars. Dressed head to foot in tight-fitting black uniforms without ornamentation, they wore black masks that completely covered their heads, with no holes for their eyes or mouth. How they saw anything through the masks was a mystery. They served as Nyarlathotep's personal palace guard within the walls of Versailles and patrolled the streets of Paris searching for dissidents. When they found someone accused by his neighbor or his children of disloyalty to the Emperor, they made that man vanish.

No one really knew for certain what was done to those they threw into their unmarked black cars, but there were rumors that those they captured suffered horrible tortures before being put to death. There was another rumor, seldom voiced aloud, that the dissidents were transformed by the necromancy of Nyarlathotep and the operations of his surgeons into Faceless Men.

The Faceless Men never spoke. Not a word to anyone. When words were needed, an officer who wore the same black uniform, but no mask, spoke for them.

"You are Lancelot Jones?"

I stood at the outer gate to Versailles with arms raised and spread wide, while a voiceless and faceless guard scanned my body with a magnetic wand to determine if I was carrying any metal.

"That's right," I told the black-uniformed officer. "I have an appointment with Commander Bruxton for three o'clock."

"Pertaining to what?"

There was an edge in his voice. He was a young man and he had decided to give me a hard time. Maybe my easy manner intimidated him, or maybe he just didn't like my nose.

"It's a personal matter that concerns the God-Emperor."

He stiffened in spite of himself and looked down at his data pad. One of the faceless guards passed my leather briefcase through a scanner. An alarm shrieked. The young officer smiled.

"What is in this?"

"An item of great value, an antique firearm which the Emperor is thinking of adding to his private collection."

He opened the case and drew out the wooden gun box, opened it, and hefted the pistol.

"How do you open the cylinder? Show me."

I took the pistol and clicked out the cylinder. He looked carefully through each empty barrel, then handed it back to me. He seemed disappointed. I returned it to the gun and put the box back into my briefcase.

Once inside the gate, it was possible to appreciate Versailles for the wonder it must have been four centuries ago. It was not difficult to understand why someone who valued antiques would choose this palace as his residence. I wondered how much of that appreciation for old-world elegance was a part of the human being who called himself

God-Emperor, and how much was from the spirit that was said to inhabit and possess his body, the alien being called Nyarlathotep. Did such a spirit even exist, or was the entire god-emperor persona merely a ruse to impress gullible humanity, which grew more superstitious with each passing year?

An attendant led me through glittering rooms and down long corridors to a modest office, where I was met by a powerfully built, balding man with a military bearing who wore an immaculate black uniform with silver braids at its shoulders. It was almost as well-tailored as what I was wearing, which is not an observation I can often make. In my business, I've found that a good first impression is important for establishing an atmosphere of trust.

Commander Bruxton was unimpressed by my Italian suit. He did not rise from behind his desk. He looked at me the way a master chef regards a fly that has just fallen into his broth.

"State your business," he said with an English accent.

"My name is Lancelot Jones. I deal in antiques and other hard-to-obtain items. Recently an antique firearm came into my possession that I thought might make a suitable addition to His Excellency's personal collection of weaponry."

"Show it to me."

He examined the revolver with a critical eye. He removed the cylinder without needing to be told how and peered through its empty chambers. Holding the handgun up to the overhead light, he studied the interior condition of its barrel, then tried the strength of the trigger spring without dry-firing it.

"You know your weapons," I said.

He clicked the cylinder back in. "Leave it here. If the Emperor is interested in purchasing it, you will be contacted."

"I was hoping for a brief private audience with His Excellency so that I might have the opportunity of relating the provenance of the piece."

He glared at me. "What impudence you people have."

"Excuse me?"

"Do you think the God-Emperor has time to waste on a money-grubbing tradesman?"

"Perhaps you would convey to him my desire to describe the item to him."

"I would describe how I had you thrown out of the Palace into the gutter, if I thought it would amuse him. But I doubt that it would."

"Commander Bruxton, if you would only—"

"Get out, or I'll have you beaten and then thrown out."

I stood up and reached for the pistol.

"Leave it. You will be contacted about it—eventually."

"I'm afraid I can't do that."

"What?" He leapt up in fury, the knuckles of his fists pressed against his desk. His round face flushed dull red as blood rushed into it. "Get out of here, you insolent little bastard, before I have you shot."

"This is not going as well as I had hoped," I said in a mild voice.

For several moments he was unable to speak. I took the opportunity to put the pistol back in its wooden box, and slid the box into my briefcase.

"Please inform the God-Emperor that I was here, that I wished to meet with him to describe the provenance of the item, but that you threw me out of the Palace."

"You must leave the revolver with me."

"I will not leave my property with a stranger. It is a very valuable antique. It stays in my hands until the Emperor has agreed to purchase it."

I could read his mind in his face. He thought about taking the pistol from me by force and having me beaten. Then he wondered if such a course of action would displease the Emperor. He swallowed his fury and a kind of shudder of frustration ran through his body.

"Wait in the outer room. You will be informed if the Emperor wishes to speak to you."

I nodded politely and went out to the room where a young male clerk sat at a desk, working on a computer screen. Taking one of the unpadded wooden chairs, I balanced my briefcase on my knees. A little more than two hours passed. A constant parade of men in various uniforms went in and out of Commander Bruxton's door, an indication, I suppose, of how important he was.

The clerk at the desk answered his phone, then looked at me with an expression of surprise.

"You are to be granted a brief audience with the God-Emperor."

He summoned a sergeant of the guard, who, accompanied by two Faceless Men for muscle, escorted me through more rooms and corridors to what I assumed must be the private chambers of Nyarlathotep. The rooms I was led through were surprisingly lacking in gold leaf and mirrors, at least by the standards of Versailles. I was shown into an audience chamber with a conference table and chairs. Its walls was paneled with a blond wood that might have been maple. The most surprising feature was the lack of paintings or portraits.

A young man in a conservative sky-blue business suit entered and shut the door behind him. His curling golden hair hung down over his forehead and his collar at the back of his neck. With a flick of his fingertips he waved the sergeant and the two faceless guards who stood behind me out of the room. He smiled at me, as if sharing some private joke, and his blue eyes sparkled.

"Do you have the revolver?" His voice was mellow but resonant.

Setting my briefcase on the conference table, I took out the gun box and opened it. He stood beside me and reached with eagerness to take up the weapon. His long, slender fingers seemed to caress it. He turned the cylinder and listened to it click from one stop to the next.

"Beautiful Italian workmanship," he said.

"It was Giuseppe Antonio Beretta's masterpiece, along with its matching mate. He is reputed to have said about the pair, 'If I make no other guns in this lifetime, it is enough.' For eight years he refused to sell them, until gambling debts at last forced him to do so. He cried that day as if he were selling his firstborn son."

"I have heard the story," the Emperor said. "But how did you get this? It was in the Taft Collection at the Smithsonian."

"No doubt the curator of the Smithsonian cried the day he learned it was missing."

"Then it is stolen property."

"How else could it be obtained?"

"Indeed. What price are you asking?"

"Two million Euros."

"Done. I will have a special case made so that I can display the two pistols together. Privately, of course."

"Of course."

The God-Emperor was not at all what I had expected. I had seen photographs and videos of him, but they always showed him from a distance, standing on some elevation with generals and politicians gathered around him at a lower level. I had not realized that he was such a young man. His place and date of birth had never been made public. His blue eyes held a brightness, almost a kind of impishness, that was disarming.

For ten minutes he listened in silence as I related the history of the pistol after it left the hands of its maker. I realized as I was talking that he already knew the background on the piece—that was to be expected since he owned its paired opposite. He had an easy grace and genial charm that did not seem forced in any way. I found it difficult to reconcile the mild manner of the man with the terrible things he was said to do to anyone who stood in his way.

As I finished my account of the revolver, a curious change came over his features. They seemed to harden, and his eyes acquired a piercing quality. A sardonic smile played at the corners of his lips. When he spoke, his voice was lower than before and held a tone of command.

"All this is very interesting, Mr. Jones, but tell me, why have you really come to my palace?"

I looked at him without speaking. This was not the same man I had been talking to for the past ten minutes, this was someone else. Someone older. Someone stronger of will. This was Nyarlathotep.

"I've been sent to assassinate you," I told him.

He regarded me mildly. "Really? How are you going to do it?"

"With this," I said, picking up the revolver.

"But it has no bullets."

"I was instructed to smuggle in a second cylinder charged with powder and shot, and then to install it in the pistol and shoot you."

"Show me the other cylinder, I want to look at it."

"I don't have it."

He raised his eyebrows with amusement. "You don't have it?"

"I couldn't think of any possible way to smuggle it past your guards."

"I see your point. They are quite good at their jobs, once they have been . . . adjusted."

"Are you going to have me executed?"

He studied me. "Should I?"

"No. I can be of more use to you alive."

"In what way?"

"The revolutionaries who sent me to kill you—I know their faces, and the name of their leader. I can help your secret police find them."

"What do you wish in return?"

"My life," I said quickly. "And the life of my sister. These men kidnapped her and threatened to kill her if I did not do what they said. I want permission to interrogate them so that I can learn the place where she is being held."

"A reasonable request; about your sister, I mean. Of course I cannot possibly allow you to live, not after you came here with the intention of assassinating me."

"That was never my intention," I pointed out. "No bullets."

"Yes, but you see, it would be perceived by the common people to have been your intention, if the story ever became a matter of public gossip."

"But you will allow me to locate and set free my sister?"

"Of course, Lancelot. It's the least I can do, after you bring me such a fine Italian pistol. I can always have you killed later."

"How can you kill people with such casual indifference? Doesn't it ever bother you?"

He shook his head. "I am older than your planet. I have caused the deaths of whole worlds over a span of billions of years. Think of the smallest thing you can imagine. A grain of sand. A speck of dust. A subatomic particle. The life of a human being is far less to me than that."

"Then you really believe yourself to be a god."

"Don't you believe it?" he asked in surprise.

"No."

"Then what do you think I am?"

"A human being with mental problems."

He threw back his head and laughed loudly until tears glistened at the corners of his eyes. "I like you, Lancelot. You're a fool like all your race, but you are an intelligent fool, and a brave one. You humans can be so amusing at times."

"I thought we were less to you than subatomic particles."

"Yes, but you are such amusing little things."

"If you are so fond of us, why don't you use your godly powers to expel the alien races that have invaded the earth since the supernova appeared?"

"The human part of me—that's the man you chatted with earlier—doesn't want that. He believes that the division of power caused by the conflict between the various alien factions weakens potential enemies, and makes it easier for us to rule over the European Zone. I tend to agree with him. As long as the energy shield around the earth that you call the Lights prevents the Old Ones from descending through the gates of Yog-Sothoth, there is no real danger of your planet's destruction."

"You mean the Old Ones are real?"

"Real enough, although your human eyes would be unable to see them due to the nature of their bodies, which are refracted through higher dimensions." He looked at me curiously. "What did you think they were?"

"Just another crazy myth."

"They are no myth, I assure you. If they break through to your world, they will destroy all life on it, including the lives of the alien races that presently rule it. Not even the magic of mighty Cthulhu will stop them. Only the energy shield is keeping them out."

3.

I was given a set of rooms in the Palace, and full access to the Service de Sécurité Impérial, the imperial security service that was run under the watchful supervision of Commander Bruxton. He was surly and unresponsive, but he had received explicit orders to assist me in the search for the revolutionaries who had kidnapped my sister. Through his office I had instructions sent out to the God-Emperor's agents in England that contained descriptions of Guinevere and the men whose faces I remembered from my meeting with them. Along with the single last name Kruger, and the information that he had been an officer in an American armored brigade during the Alien Wars, it was little enough to go on.

The clock was ticking on my sister's life. Kruger would expect me to make an immediate attempt on the Emperor. When he received no news, he might wait a day or two, possibly even three. Then he would assume I had been captured or killed, and would execute Guinevere. It was never his intention to release her. There was too much risk that she might see something or hear something that could be used against his organization.

The second day of the search, Bruxton came striding into the office I had been assigned as I sat at my desk, examining printouts of reports submitted by field agents in the London area. None of them contained anything encouraging.

"How long are you going to waste my time and resources on this ridiculous fiction of a kidnapping?"

"As long as it takes to find her," I said, meeting his pig-like eyes.

"We've scoured all of London and we've turned up nothing. A snake under a rock couldn't have hidden from my men. There is no revolutionary cell in London, and there was no kidnapping."

His words triggered a thought. I had been told that my sister was being held somewhere on the outskirts of London, and like a fool had assumed it to be true. But what if I had been lied to?

"Redirect your efforts to Paris," I told him. "Concentrate on the district around the Club International."

"First London, now Paris? The Emperor will have you flayed alive for this."

"That may be so, but in the meantime, he has ordered you to do as I tell you."

The hours dragged by like sea-anchors. I couldn't sleep and forgot to eat. All that evening and through the night no word came. The next morning, when I was near despair but trying not to show it, a report came in that an older American with a scar on his face, who never worked but always had money, was living in a flat near the Club International. I immediately ordered a raid on the address with explicit instructions that he be taken alive.

The man was brought to an interrogation chamber in an underground level of the Palace with a black bag over his head and his arms shackled behind his back. I stood behind a large one-way mirror, watching as he was led to a table by two Faceless Men and forced down into a chair. Both table and chair were made of stainless steel and bolted to the concrete floor.

"Remove his hood," I said into a microphone.

The black bag was snatched away. It was Colonel Kruger. The scar made recognition unmistakeable, although he had cut his hair shorter and dyed it blond. He stared in defiance at the mirror. I wondered if he had recognized my voice coming through the speaker.

"Roll up his shirt sleeves," I said.

His shirt cuffs were ripped open and his sleeves jerked up above his elbows.

"Show me his arms."

On the inside of his right forearm was the tattoo of a set of dice, a red die with three showing uppermost and a black die with four.

"I want to talk to him before you interrogate him," I said to Bruxton, who stood watching beside me.

"You recognize him?"

"It's Kruger, the leader of the resistance cell that contacted me."

This seemed to impress him, I suppose because he had not expected any positive result from the search.

"I strongly recommend against allowing this man to see you," he said. "The less knowledge he is given about how and why he was captured, the more vulnerable he will be psychologically. In a few hours my men will break him, of that you can be certain. Then he will gladly tell you all he knows about the location of your sister, or anything else for that matter."

"I want to talk to him."

Bruxton did not try to prevent me when I left the observation room and went into the interrogation chamber. When Kruger recognized me, his eyes narrowed murderously.

"You betrayed us."

I drew up a chair and sat across from him at the table. The two Faceless Men stood on either side of him like silent statues, their compliance wands held at the ready. I wondered if he would lunge across the table to try to set his teeth in my throat, and found myself hoping he would make the attempt, so that I could watch the wands applied to his body.

"If you tell me where my sister is being held in Paris, I will prevail upon the God-Emperor to grant you a speedy execution."

"By capturing me, you have ensured your sister's death."

"So she is still alive."

He blinked and said nothing.

"You know what will be done to you if you don't give me the information I want?"

He began to curse me. His language grew colorful but soon became repetitious. When he finally fell silent, I leaned forward.

"The SSI will torture you," I said in a quiet voice. "No one resists torture by the Service de Sécurité Impérial. You'll break, and all your suffering will be for nothing. Why not spare yourself the ordeal?"

"They won't break me. I'll die before I tell you anything."

"But you know that's not the worst of it," I continued. "After they break you, they will turn you over to processing. They will make you into a Faceless Man, like these two. Is that what you want? To be turned into a soulless zombie with no will of your own?"

His silence told me that my words had hit home. The blood drained from his cheeks, turning his face to wax. His eyes rolled to look up at the silent figures in black standing on either side of his chair.

"You," I said to the one on the left. "Remove your hood."

The guard reached up and pulled off the tightly fitting mask that covered his head. His eyes were missing from their sockets. His ears had been amputated and his ear holes surgically closed.

This was the first time I had seen one without his mask. So the rumors were true after all, I thought. I had never believed them myself. How could they see without eyes, or hear without ears? Yet somehow they did.

"Tell him to put it back on," Kruger whispered.

I motioned to the guard, who awkwardly placed his compliance wand under his arm while he worked the hood back into its place.

"It's well known that all of the Emperor's Faceless Men come from the ranks of his enemies," I said. "If none of them were ever able to resist the conditioning, why should you be able to resist it? They'll turn you into a meat machine, Kruger. Isn't a clean death better than that?"

He didn't give me the address immediately, but as I continued to talk to him, I saw his courage begin to slip away as he thought about his fate. It was not the prospect of torture that put terror into his heart, but the certainty that he would be transformed into a living machine with no will of his own. I know it terrified him because it terrified me. All the while I talked, the two figures dressed in black stood impassively, ready to apply their wands at a moment's notice. They heard my words but were untouched by them.

"We would never have killed your sister," he said. "It was just a bluff."

"No, it wasn't. You always intended to kill her when you kidnapped her and brought her across the Channel to Paris."

He dropped his gaze to the table, and if I had ever had any doubts about his intentions, this banished them.

"I'll give you the address," Kruger said quietly. "My only condition is that I be executed."

He recited a street address no more than two blocks away from the flat in which he had been captured. I looked toward the mirror.

"Did you get that?"

"I got it," Bruxton said through the loudspeaker in the corner of the ceiling. "I'll have a squad sent out immediately."

"Order them to approach by stealth. My sister is not to be harmed."

I stood up and slapped Kruger hard across the face. "That's for what you did to Guinevere." I looked at the impassive guards. "Take him for processing."

He began to curse and scream when they pulled him out of his chair and dragged him from the chamber.

"You gave me your word!"

I stood at the table, listening to his babble of curses and shrieks diminish as he was pulled by the armpits down the long corridor toward the processing sector of the lower level. Bruxton had walked me through it one time. I shuddered, then went to wait for news about the raid.

As I sat in the SSI command center, listening to the radio traffic, Bruxton came in with an expression of exultation.

"We got them, all of them."

"Alive?"

"Yes, all alive. This will break the back of the French branch of the resistance."

"My sister?"

His face changed, and he glanced away. "No. She was

already dead when my men arrived. The terrorists were in the process of dismembering her body in a bathtub for removal from the building."

I nodded at him and put my hand on the corner of the desk to steady my balance. It had all been for nothing.

I wondered if Guinevere had still been alive when I first talked to Kruger in the back room of the International, or if they had already murdered her after making the video? I had never been that close to my sister, but she was my only living family. Had been my only living family, I corrected myself.

"You need to go to the Emperor," Bruxton said in a more subdued voice. "He wants to congratulate you before he has you executed."

I was escorted under guard through the imperial chambers to a long room with a high ceiling that was lined on three sides with antique weapons mounted to the walls. The other wall consisted of floor-to-ceiling windows framed by heavy burgundy drapes. No sunlight shone through them. They were in a north wall, which made sense when I thought about it. A collector of antiques did not want harsh sunlight fading the colors of his prized exhibits.

The Emperor stood in front of an open glass cabinet at the far end of the room. In his hands he cradled a pistol. Even from that distance I recognized it as one of the matched pair of Beretta revolvers. I crossed the room with two Faceless Men at my sides.

"I've been told you found your sister," he said with a bland smile.

I nodded. From his expression and manner of speaking, I gathered that I was speaking to the human part of the Emperor, not the God part.

"I was sorry to hear that she was dead. Still, it was a good effort, and worth the risk. This man Kruger will give us everything he knows about the resistance in France and Great Britain."

"I'm so happy you got what you wanted."

The sarcasm was lost on him, or he chose to ignore it.

"You were more efficient than I gave you credit for being. It's a pity you must be executed."

"I agree."

He laughed. "Are you sure you wouldn't prefer to become one of my palace guard?"

I looked at the Faceless Man on my right. "I think not."

"Very well; you shall have a quick and painless execution as a reward for your service to the Empire. By the way, you never did say where you want the money sent that you received for the sale of this pistol."

I eyed the weapon. "Is that the one I sold you?"

"It is."

"Why don't you just shoot me with it now, and get it over with?"

"My dear fellow, I would be happy to do so. It's the least I could do for you in view of your great service. But unfortunately it is not loaded."

"May I hold it one last time?"

As a fanatical collector of finely crafted antiques, he understood the impulse that prompted me to ask such a thing. His face softened into something that was almost sympathy. "Of course. It will be well cared for, have no trouble in your mind on that issue."

I hefted the weight of the revolver and ran my fingertips over its beautifully inlaid barrel. Turning from the Emperor to gaze out one of the windows across the lawns of Versailles, I shook my head.

"With the power you've been given, you could have done so much good for this world."

"But I have done so much good for myself," he said.

I turned slowly and shot him four times in the chest, revolving the cylinder after each shot with the fingers of my left hand. His mouth gaped wide in surprise. Then his expression changed and hardened, and I recognized the persona of the god Nyarlathotep glaring out from his dying eyes with a look of pure malice. The Faceless Men knocked the pistol out of my hands and grabbed my arms, pinning me helplessly between them.

"How did you—" the God-Emperor gasped as blood soaked the front of his suit jacket.

"I substituted the charged cylinder for the empty one."

"But you told us you had not brought the other cylinder into the palace."

"I lied."

As his knees buckled and he began to collapse to the floor, a great rushing wind blew through me. Suddenly I felt a presence inside my body. It probed my organs one by one, prickling over the surface of my heart and making it beat irregularly for a few seconds, then flowing like water over the surface of my brain. It moved around from one limb to another, making them twitch. My hands clenched into fists when I realized I was being violated in some unnatural manner.

The Faceless Men released me and stepped back. I looked down at the body of the late Emperor on the parquet floor, the blood still expanding in a pool under him, then at the Faceless Men. Their posture was differential, almost respectful. I decided not to question my luck, and began to make a dash between them for the door before the sound of the gunshots drew other guards. I found myself unable to move.

"You are with me now," a cold, emotionless voice said in my head. "If you struggle, it will be painful for you."

I tried to move my feet but they felt like blocks of concrete.

"Get out of my head!"

"I can't do that. Your surprising and precipitous action left me with no choice but to enter you. We will remain bonded for the rest of your natural life."

I continued to fight his control. Sweat beaded on my face but I was not able to move so much as a finger. I felt him turning my body, propelling me forward to pick up the revolver from where it had fallen. The Faceless Men made no attempt to stop me. There were still one round left in the cylinder—if I could only turn the barrel on myself and pull the trigger. I watched myself put the pistol back into its place on a mat of red velvet, then close the lid of the glass case with a soft click.

Guards rushed into the gun room, along with Bruxton and two other officers. They stared in surprise at the dead man on the floor, then at me. Bruxton's face hardened. He started to give an order to the Faceless Men behind him, but I raised my right hand with the palm outward.

"There is no need for alarm," I said in a voice that was unnaturally resonant, so that it sounded like the voice of a stranger. Indeed, it sounded in my ears something like the voice of the former God-Emperor.

Bruxton halted in confusion, looking at the corpse, then back at me, while blinking rapidly.

"Your Excellency?"

"Yes, Bruxton, I am here now in this vessel. Henceforth, you will address it as Nyarlathotep, your God-Emperor."

I floated in darkness, seeing nothing, hearing nothing, feeling nothing. I retained only a dim awareness of the passage of time, but whether it was hours that passed, or days, or weeks, or even years, I had no way to know. My mind subsisted in a kind of vegetative state similar to that caused by strong narcotics, but there were no fantastic visions to keep me entertained. I knew only that I existed, and in a dim manner I wondered where I was and how I had come to this strange silent darkness. I had no memory, no expectation. It was the same state of consciousness experienced by a fetus as it lies within its mother's womb.

With a suddenness that was like the shock of being born, I found myself seated in an antique wing-back chair before a fireplace. A fire crackled on the grate. I felt its warmth radiating on my legs and face. On the other side of the fireplace another similar chair was half-turned so that it faced mine. Between the chairs stood a table, and on it there were two round-bottomed glasses and a crystal decanter.

"Have some brandy, Lancelot."

I realized the other chair was occupied. The figure in it sat so still, I had failed to notice his presence until he spoke. He wore a long black robe with a black hood pulled up over his head, so that the side of the hood shadowed the firelight and concealed his face as he regarded me. A thin and bony hand with long black fingernails reached out from the sleeve of the robe to pour brown liquid from the decanter into the brandy snifters. He picked up one glass, its short stem projecting between his fingers, and brought it to his hooded face.

"Where are we?"

"Nowhere. This place has no location in space."

"You're still in my head," I said as memories began to return to me.

I started to rise from my chair. He reached out his left hand and moved his skeletal index finger. The strength left my body.

"When you killed my avatar, I was forced to make a hasty transition to another human host, and you were the only suitable candidate. Ordinarily I prepare a new host before leaving the old, but had not done so, simply because I did not expect my host to die. Such a forced entry into a new host can have unfortunate psychological effects unless there is preparation of the new host."

"What kind of psychological effects?"

"They go mad. It makes them useless for my purposes."

"I'm not insane."

"That's because I put you into a kind of dreamless sleep. What your race calls a coma, I believe. It has allowed your brain to adapt to my presence."

I found myself trying to peer into his hood but could see nothing. It was more than just a shadow that obscured his face. The hood seemed empty.

"How long has it been?"

"Since I made you my new avatar? Eleven years, five months, and three days."

I digested this in silence, and found that I needed the brandy. It might not exist, but then, neither did I, and its

. . . the hood shadowed the firelight and concealed his face as he regarded me.

effect on my tongue when I drank it was convincingly warm and smoky. Eleven years of my life, gone. Stolen.

"Why did you restore my consciousness?"

"Do I need a reason? Maybe I just felt sympathy for you."

I laughed shortly. "But seriously, why did you wake me up?"

He set down his glass and bridged his bony fingers with his elbows on the padded arms of his chair.

"I need your human perspective. A problem has arisen."

I replayed the words in my mind and blinked. "You mean, you need my help."

"I suppose you could put it that way. It's quite amusing, that a god should need the help of a human, isn't it?"

"What is it that you think I can do to help you?"

He leaned forward slightly. His tone of voice became serious. "The energy shield erected around your world by the star-spanning race your species call the Mi-Go is failing. If it collapses, your world will lie open to the Old Ones, who have only one purpose—the extermination of all earthly life, so that they can elevate this planet to a higher dimensional sphere."

"I know nothing about the Mi-Go."

"No, but you know your own people. The Old Ones have enlisted the aid of their human worshippers, and are guiding them in the destruction of the towers the Mi-Go erected around this world to broadcast the energy shield. If enough of those towers are destroyed, the shield will fall, and the Old Ones will come."

"How can these Old Ones have human followers if they intend to kill everyone?"

I saw the hood move as he shook his head within it. "You assume your species is motivated by rationality, but that is not so. The cultists believe that they will be transfigured into a higher form of existence, if they aid the Old Ones in cleansing the earth of all biological life."

"They must be insane."

"Of course they are insane. The majority of your species is insane."

I sipped my brandy slowly, my thoughts racing. The burning wood in the fireplace crackled as one of the embers broke in two and sent up a shower of sparks.

"You want me to find a way to stop this human cult before it destroys the shield."

"Think of it as a challenge to your intellectual powers."

"Why do you care? You're not of this world. Why do you care what happens to it?"

Nyarlathotep shrugged his thin shoulders. "This realm of yours has been a diversion for me since your species first began to walk upright. Who do you think gave them words to speak and taught them the making of fire? I regard this planet as my personal possession. I have no intention of allowing it to be taken from me."

"I'll need access to your security and intelligence services."

"As much as you require."

"And control over my body. I can't work from this place. I'll need to interact with the world to weigh events and make decisions."

He hesitated only a moment. "Done. Now that your mind has been stabilized, I can give you the same degree of control that my last avatar possessed."

"Will you still be there, in my mind?"

"Your mind is my mind now, Lancelot. I will never leave you as long as you draw breath."

I drained the last of the brandy in my glass and set it on the table.

"Do you have the power to stop the invasion of the Old Ones?"

He was silent for so long, I thought he would not answer, but at last he said, "Perhaps. But to do so would destroy the delicate balance that now exists between the various factions that rule the earth. It would be dangerous, politically and on many other levels."

"You mean you might lose control of the European Zone."

Suddenly I found myself standing on a balcony, gazing out across the green lawns of Versailles. I turned and stepped back into what proved to be a bedchamber with an enormous four-poster bed. A male servant stood beside the closed door, watching me.

"Where am I?" I asked him.

He blinked and stuttered as he tried to speak. "Your Excellency? I don't understand."

"Where is this place? Where am I?"

Sweat broke out on his forehead and he swallowed. "In your bedchamber, Excellency. In the Imperial Palace. In Paris. In France."

"Good, that's enough. You may leave me now."

He bowed and fumbled his way out the door, closing it carefully after him. I stood looking around. The room was tidy and clean, which was to be expected with so many servants lurking around in the Palace. There was a mirror hanging on the wall. Its ornate frame was covered in gold leaf and there were the heads of cherubs carved at its corners. I went to it and studied the figure that stared back at me.

The familiar face was lined at the corners of the eyes and mouth. It was slightly broader, and the hair was streaked at the temples with gray. There was a slight sag to the shoulders that filled the jacket of the dark suit, and a slight bulge at the waist below the paisley-patterned tie. *Eleven years,* I thought, my mouth a grim line. *Eleven years stolen.*

"I need to learn all I can about this cult of the Old Ones."

"Go to Bruxton," Nyarlathotep's voice said in my head. "You know where his office is located. He will give you all the information you require."

The days passed quickly. The SSI had agents in all parts of the world, reporting back to Paris. Commander Bruxton sat at the center of this web of information like a spider, pulling its threads, testing its soundness, rebuilding it when necessary. In three weeks I was able to form a working understanding of where the main centers of the cult of the Old Ones were located, how many followers it had at each center, the names of its leaders, and the way they ran their organization.

All this time, Nyarlathotep prompted me and goaded me, asking questions and offering suggestions. He was like a meddlesome maiden aunt constantly peering over my shoulder as I tried to do my work. I discovered by experiment that he could only read my thoughts if they were formed into actual words in my mind, or if I was about to speak them aloud. My deeper thoughts were hidden from him. And so I planned and schemed and plucked at the threads that extended outward from Versailles to the far ends of the globe, setting events into motion.

Bruxton watched me with increasing frustration. He could not criticize me without criticizing the God-Emperor, so he held his tongue and fumed as reports streamed in from around the world. More and more of the towers erected by the Mi-Go were falling. As fast as they tried to repair and rebuild them, they could not keep up with the pace of destruction. A single bomb planted at the base of a tower was enough to destroy it in an instant. Rebuilding the tower took weeks. Day by day, the total number of towers declined.

It finally reached such a critical point that Bruxton could not bear to remain silent.

"What do you think you are doing?" he demanded one morning when the news was especially dismal. "The towers are falling like dominoes. At this rate the grid will collapse within another week."

"You don't understand the higher purposes of my instructions. Soon the order will be given to destroy the centers of the cult of the Old Ones."

"Soon?" he said, lacing his fingers in what was left of his hair at the back of his large head. "We don't have time to play games. We stand on the precipice of disaster."

I felt a curious buzzing sensation in my arms and legs, and a dizziness in my head. The light in Bruxton's office seemed to dim, along with the background sounds of the palace.

"Have patience, Commander," I heard my voice say. But it was not my voice. Nyarlathotep was using my larynx to speak.

"God-Emperor, I beg you not to put your trust in this charlatan, this confidence artist, this haggler of antiques."

"The man you speak of and I are one now, Commander. When you insult him, you are insulting me."

"Forgive me, your Excellency, I meant no offense. Only, doesn't it seem to you that he is wasting too much time? Shouldn't he be arresting the leaders of the cult that we have identified? I don't understand what he is waiting for."

"Tell the Commander what you are waiting for," Nyarlathotep's voice said in my head. I discovered that I had control of my own words once again.

"If we act too soon, the cult will scatter and conceal themselves. To be effective, we must move against them at the same moment all around the world. I have been putting intelligence agents and soldiers into position for this unified action. It is almost ready to launch into motion."

Bruxton stared at me, the hatred scarcely concealed in his dark eyes. I wonder if he had hoped Nyarlathotep would choose him as the next avatar? If so, my adoption to the imperial throne must have come as a bitter shock.

"I am loyal to the God-Emperor," he said. "But I believe the course we are following is wrong."

"Duly noted, my loyal friend," Nyarlathotep said through my mouth. "But I think we will wait a little longer, and give Mr. Jones a chance to put his plan into execution."

As it happened, it almost was not long enough. I had delayed and delayed in every possible way, and had run out of options. It was becoming obvious that I was deliberately holding back the Emperor's agents from destroying the centers of the cult. I sensed Nyarlathotep's growing impatience and rising anger.

On the same day I made the decision to attempt suicide by throwing myself off a balcony onto the pavement below, what I had waited for over the course of the past month finally happened. The energy shield around the earth collapsed. When early evening passed into night, the slowly waving curtains of colors that had stretched across the heavens for almost four decades were gone. I stood on the balcony outside my bedchamber, staring up at the night sky, which was filled with stars. The supernova known as the Big Red Eye blazed down brighter than all the rest combined.

"You delayed too long," Nyarlathotep said inside my head.

"I delayed just long enough," I told him.

"You never intended to find a way to stop the cult of the Old Ones."

"No."

"You wanted the energy shield to fall."

"That's right."

"But why? Don't you believe that the Old Ones will destroy your entire species? I can flee this planet, as can the alien rulers of the other zones, but humanity must remain and be exterminated."

"Only if you allow it to happen."

"What is it you imagine I can do to stop it?"

"I don't know," I admitted. "But I know you believe you can stop it. I detected that in your words when you spoke about it. If you truly value this planet as your possession, and humanity as your playthings, then stop the Old Ones."

We continued to gaze up at the night sky through my eyes. I saw a kind of glow in the darkness between the stars that flickered and shifted.

"They're coming," Nyarlathotep said.

"Then stop them. Do whatever it is you need to do, but stop them."

"It will probably kill you."

"Just do it."

A glowing circle appeared in the air in front of the balcony. Nyarlathotep took control of my body and climbed up onto the stone railing. I could see at the edge of my field of vision the dark paving blocks of the walkway three stories below. I cringed against the fall. It was not the way I had expected to die. My body stepped forward into space and through the floating circle.

Everything began to spin wildly. I saw lines of energy wrapping around my body and heard sounds—the beating of a drum, a hum of electricity, a kind of twittering like a flock of sparrows, and every now and then, a gong. I felt heat and cold against my skin alternating so rapidly, I could no longer tell which was which.

"What's happening?" I tried to ask, but the words stuck in my throat.

My eyes filled with a vision of a great spiral that was like the spiral of a galaxy seen through a telescope, except that it was rotating slowly. Around it a ring of grotesquely distorted figures that were not even remotely human pivoted and bowed and gestured to one another in a kind of slow-motion courtly dance. At the middle of the vortex blazed the Big Red Eye of the supernova, its central point surrounded by a ring of fire.

In the sudden silence I heard the music of a flute. It was a simple melody, but unlike any music I had ever heard before. It rose and fell with a curious cadence that never repeated itself. For some reason I felt the urge to dance in time to the music, but my terror was so great, I had no trouble resisting the irrational impulse.

"Look down," Nyarlathotep said.

I lowered my gaze, and only then realized that I had been staring up into the heavens. I saw that I was standing in a kind of valley between rocky hills. It was night, but the light from the vortex and the supernova cast enough of a glow to allow me to see my surroundings. The landscape did not fade away into the distance, but seemed to terminate abruptly at the hills, giving the impression that there was nothing beyond them, as though the valley and the hills floated in space like a kind of island.

"Why have you given me control over my body?"

"Because I cannot do the thing that must be done. Only you can do it."

"You're a god. What can I do that a god can't do?"

"Much as it pains me to admit it, you humans have something you call free will. That allows you to do what must be done, something that is forbidden for me to do."

My attention was drawn to the end of the little valley, where there was a flat ledge in the side of the glistening black rock of the hill. On this ledge there was a low stone slab. Something large and white lay upon it—or it would be better to say, sprawled across it, since the creature was a kind of blob of fatty tissue in an envelope of sickly pale skin covered with smears and blotches of filth. More filth lay piled around the base of the slab.

"Go to it," Nyarlathotep said.

I approached the ledge and stood looking up at the naked monster. Its arms and legs were human-like, though grossly bloated. Long black hair matted with filth hung greasily down its rounded shoulders like tangled ropes. It was blind. A kind of whitish slime seeped from the holes where its eyes should have been, so that it appeared to be weeping. The stench grew stronger as I crept nearer. It held something between its fat fingers up to its blubbery lips and blew into it. It was a tiny flute made of a kind of carved bone. At least, the flute appeared tiny in the creature's massive hands. It would have been a giant had it been able to stand erect, but the drooping slabs of fat tissue on its thighs and belly made me doubt it had ever stood.

The music of the flute was clear and pure in my ears as I listened. The monster did not appear to be aware of my presence, but continued to play its instrument. The unending stream of notes had an almost hypnotic effect. I found myself trying to anticipate the next passage of the melody, but realized this to be impossible because it was constantly changing.

"Go up to it," Nyarlathotep said.

Did I only imagine disgust in his voice? Since the voice spoke in my head, not aloud, it was difficult to judge its intonation.

A crudely cut flight of steps led up from the floor of the valley to the ledge where the creature reclined on its bed of stone, covered in its own feces. I wondered how it was fed? Did attendants bring it trays of fruits and meats? Did they place the food into its mouth? There was no one else in the uncanny valley but myself and the creature. I advanced hesitantly, prepared to jump back if it moved toward me.

With slow steps I climbed the stairs. The stench became almost overpowering.

"What is this thing?" I asked in my head.

"You enjoy a great privilege, Lancelot. You look upon the god Azathoth, who lies on his throne at the center of all the universes. Gaze upon his greatness in wonder."

There was no question about the tone of Nyarlathotep's voice this time. It dripped with contempt and disgust.

"You hate this god," I said.

"I serve this god, if you can believe such a thing to be possible. I, Nyarlathotep, serve this quaking, mindless mountain of filth-covered blubber."

"What service do you provide? Do you feed him?"

Nyarlathotep laughed with bitterness but did not answer. "Go behind his head," he told me.

With small, silent steps I worked myself to the side and around the end of the black stone slab that supported Azathoth, who continued to play his music. Now that I was so close, I could hear the occasional sour note issue from the flute. The discordance in the melody was not unpleasant, but seemed to give it a more earthy quality.

"Approach behind his head," Nyarlathotep said.

"How close do you want me to get?"

"Close enough to touch him."

The head of the god was huge. I thought of the gigantic seated statue of Zeus that had occupied his temple at Olympia in ancient times. It had been regarded as one of the seven wonders of the world. The head of Zeus must have been similar in size to that of Azathoth.

"Lean forward. Reach out and press your hands against his skull."

The filth in the god's ropes of hair was disgusting, but I did exactly what Nyarlathotep said to do. I felt the hair compress under my spread fingers, and the warmth of the god's head under it.

"Keep pressing," Nyarlathotep said.

I caught my breath in surprise and almost stumbled backward. My hands had sunk into the head through its skull. As I continued to press forward, my arms sank up to the wrists, and then halfway to my elbows. Still Azathoth appeared unaware of my presence. I wondered if Nyarlathotep had worked some magic to conceal me? It was reputed that he was a great magician, although I had never seen anything magical done by him other then the opening of the portal that had brought me to this place.

Control over my hands was gently withdrawn from my will. I felt my fingers making movements in the giant god's skull, in what must have been his brain. It felt warm and pulpy against my fingers. I sensed this to be a crucial moment and refrained from asking the questions I wanted to ask.

The music of the flute changed in a subtle way. It did not cease, not even for an instant, but the cadence of the cascading notes was altered. In every other respect, nothing changed.

"Draw out your hands and step away," Nyarlathotep said.

Control returned to my will, and I felt my fingers to be my own once again. I pulled my arms and hands slowly out of Azathoth's skull and looked at them, half expecting the flesh to be hanging off the bones, but apart from a kind of glistening slime that covered them, they were normal enough.

"Go back down into the valley."

With nervous glances, I made my way to the stairs and descended them, then backed away from the ledge.

"What else do I need to do?"

"Nothing. It's done."

"What's done? Nothing happened."

"Didn't you hear?"

"You mean the change in the melody?"

"Look up."

I tilted back my head and looked straight up into the center of the slowly turning silver vortex, around which danced the ring of gigantic inhuman forms.

"The Big Red Eye is gone," I said.

I felt control of my body taken away from me.

"I should leave you here to die of thirst, or fling you into the vortex of chaos, but I still need a vehicle of flesh."

A glowing portal formed. As my body stepped into it, my vision darkened and a dizziness overcame me, but his control of my legs prevented me from falling. Again I heard strange noises and sounds as the music of Azathoth's flute faded into the distance. I felt heat and cold against my skin. Then I was standing on the stone railing of the balcony at Versailles, but this time facing inward toward the open French doors of my bedchamber.

Had Nyarlathotep not been in complete control of my body, I would have fallen backward to my death. Instead, I stepped down to the balcony and turned around. The night sky was filled with stars, but there were no moving curtains of colors, and no red supernova. It looked like the sky I remembered from my early boyhood, before the Alien Wars had thrown the world into madness.

"What have you done?" I asked when I was able to speak aloud.

"The stars are no longer right," he said.

"What does that mean?"

"It means, you witless fool, that the alien races and other gods who came to your planet when the stars changed are even now in the process of scampering back to their places of hiding."

It was a few heartbeats before I could comprehend the meaning of his words.

"Do you mean . . . the earth belongs to the human race once again?"

"No, I do not. The earth belongs to me, as it has for aeons. But because of what I have done, I can no longer rule over your species as its God-Emperor."

A kind of coolness made itself felt on the front of my body. It was like standing naked and facing the open door of a walk-in freezer. Through the fabric of my suit streamed black threads. They curled and rippled like smoke that rises from burning incense cones, going not up, but sideways. On the far side of the balcony they came together into the shape of a man. As the figure became better defined, I saw that it was the robed and hooded version of Nyarlathotep that I had talked to while trapped inside my own mind.

The figure became solid. There was no face in the hood, only blackness, but I thought for an instant that I glimpsed red gleams, as though light had reflected from the surface of his eyes. I wondered if he planned to kill me.

"I thought we were bound together for the rest of my lifetime."

"Things change," he said in a voice like ice.

"Will the supernova ever return?" I asked, trying to keep a tremble out of my voice.

"Not soon. Probably not for a million years. Such things are unfixed in time, and so cannot be predicted."

"Where will you go?"

"I have a place of refuge on a high mountain peak that is not quite part of your world and not quite outside it. I will abide there for a time."

"Are you going to kill me?"

"To what purpose?"

"I betrayed you."

Nyarlathotep extended one of his bony hands, which I saw was really too large to be the hand of a human being. The fingers were too long, the black nails on their ends talon-like.

"Do it, goddamn you. Get it over with. I'm sick of being afraid of you."

The hand stopped a few inches from my face, then withdrew. I took a long, shuddering breath.

"I would advise you to leave Versailles before Bruxton or the others realize that you are no longer the God-Emperor."

"Will the Faceless Men come after me?"

"Without my will to control them, they are mindless. They will forget to breathe and die."

We looked at each other in silence.

"I suppose I should thank you for giving this planet back to humanity."

"Weren't you listening before, Lancelot? This is my planet,

to do with as I please, and your race are my toys. You would be wise never to forget it."

His body began to dissolve back into threads of black smoke that extended themselves over the balcony and into the night sky. After a few moments he was gone.

I breathed the night air deep into my lungs and realized that I was covered in cold sweat. From elsewhere in the Palace I heard cries of dismay and terror. The Faceless Men were no doubt forgetting to breathe and falling over dead. It was time to say goodbye to Versailles. I wondered if, in the future when some semblance of order was restored, I would ever return to it as an American tourist? I had already made up my mind that I was going back to the United States, or what was left of it. There would be many opportunities for a clever businessman in the confusion that was sure to follow the flight of the shoggoths and the collapse of the cult of Shub-Niggurath.

Wandering into the Palace, I located a babbling junior officer, who had been driven to distraction by the sudden death of the Faceless Men under his command, and ordered him to have a military truck backed up to the main entrance. Then I assembled a small army of Palace orderlies and had them carry the former God-Emperor's priceless collection of antique weapons and related precious objects to the truck. They stood on the steps of Versailles, watching me with slack faces and open mouths when I climbed into the truck and drove down the lane toward the front gates. I felt an impulse to reach my arm out the open window of the truck and wave at them, but somehow I resisted.